PRAISE FOR *THE LOBOTOMIST'S WIFE*

"Based on extraordinary real-life events, *The Lobotomist's Wife* is a riveting and impressive debut that had me in its grasp from the very first page. Samantha Greene Woodruff has crafted a suspenseful tale of good intentions gone awry that features an indomitable heroine who finds her strength and voice in the midst of harrowing circumstances. I simply could not put it down."

—Paulette Kennedy, author of *Parting the Veil*

"In her stunning debut, Samantha Greene Woodruff explores the fascinating world of midcentury mental health treatments with deft attention to rich historical detail and memorable characters who carry the story with heart and heft. Woodruff has skillfully crafted a novel with an artfully structured second story line, a propulsive ending, and an underlying theme so relevant to the struggles of the modern day. I absolutely loved this novel and can't wait to see what she does next!"

—Susie Orman Schnall, author of *We Came Here to Shine*

T0001887

THE
LOBOTOMIST'S
WIFE

THE
LOBOTOMIST'S
WIFE

A NOVEL

SAMANTHA GREENE WOODRUFF

LAKE UNION
PUBLISHING

This is a work of fiction. Names, characters, organizations, places, events, and incidents are either products of the author's imagination or are used fictitiously.

Text copyright © 2022 by Samantha Greene Woodruff
All rights reserved.

No part of this book may be reproduced, or stored in a retrieval system, or transmitted in any form or by any means, electronic, mechanical, photocopying, recording, or otherwise, without express written permission of the publisher.

Published by Lake Union Publishing, Seattle

www.apub.com

Amazon, the Amazon logo, and Lake Union Publishing are trademarks of Amazon.com, Inc., or its affiliates.

ISBN-13: 9781542036214
ISBN-10: 1542036216

Cover design by Faceout Studio, Tim Green

Printed in the United States of America

To my husband, who has been saying "I just want you to be happy" for as long as we've been together

and

my mom, who has always believed that I could do anything (and never stopped hoping that someday that "anything" would be a writer)

No man chooses evil because it's evil. He only mistakes it for happiness, the good he seeks.

—*Mary Wollstonecraft*

Prologue

Margaret looked around at the gaggle of friends and neighbors occupying her living room. This was quite a good turnout for her first presentation, and she knew she should be elated. But she wasn't. All she could think about, as she tried to chat with Mrs. Millhouse, was how the skin around her stomach created bulges in the nipped waist of her favorite dress. She could barely breathe. Maybe she should have listened to her mother and worn the more forgiving canary-yellow shift that Frank had bought her. Damn Frank. She knew he was trying to be kind, to make her feel good, happy, beautiful again. Instead, she felt like he had given up on her. Did he now think of her, at only twenty-seven years old, as one of those women who needed a wardrobe designed to hide the flaws in her figure?

She looked jealously at Carolyn Carterson, her tiny waist accentuated by that pink belt. Eight weeks ago, they had both delivered babies. Yet, there Carolyn was, back in her prepregnancy clothes, her rich auburn hair curled just so. Margaret, on the other hand, had required the assistance of her mother to zip her dress. And her hair, once a lovely golden blond and soft as the silk tassels on her curtain pulls, was now dull and unable to hold a proper curl. She had pinned on a small Miriam Lewis hat to cover the mess, which she also hoped distracted from the dullness of her face. She hated to look in the mirror these days—she couldn't escape the fact that the bright blue of her eyes, one of her best features before pregnancy (and typically made even brighter by the robin's-egg hue of the dress she was wearing today), had transformed into a washed-out gray. The rosy complexion that used to make her look as though she had just come in from an afternoon of ice skating had gone sallow; even with the bright red lipstick she had chosen for today, she looked ghostlike. Not Carolyn, who sparkled from head to toe as she stood by the coffee service, laughing easily. Margaret felt like a cloud of fog, darkening everything in her path.

She felt her nose begin to tingle and the tears start to form in the corners of her eyes. Not now. Oh, please, not now. She made fists and dug her sharp nails—she had barely forced herself to clip them, let alone paint them with the red polish she had purchased for the occasion—deep into her palms to distract herself from the sadness, all while smiling bigger at Mrs. Millhouse. This was not a time for melancholy. The baby was with Margaret's mother. The older children were at school. This was her time. The beginning of the next chapter in her life, where she could be more than Frank's wife or John, Maisy, and William's mother again.

Lucy crossed the room and grabbed Margaret's arm, an ear-to-ear smile plastered on her pink lips. "Mrs. Millhouse, so sorry, but I need to borrow our hostess for a moment." Thank heaven for Lucy. She steered Margaret toward the sideboard, which was covered with a store-bought spread of sweets. Carolyn surely wouldn't have had to buy her nibbles from a store. In the past, Margaret wouldn't have either; she had been a wonderful baker. But that had gone along with her figure.

She shuddered as she thought about yesterday's attempt to make a simple shortbread.

The flour everywhere. The butter that wouldn't cream, and then, when she had finally gotten her mediocre batter in the oven, that smell, the smoke as her mother shook her awake.

"Maggie, hon, I think you need to get started!" Her best friend, Lucy, broke her from her momentary daze, and Margaret looked at the clock on the mantel. The children would be home soon. How had so much time slipped away? She wasn't sure she could do her presentation. Why would anyone even want to listen to her?

As if sensing her hesitation, Lucy announced, "Ladies, our hostess would love your attention," as she steered Margaret to the makeshift table in front of the fireplace. Margaret had covered it with the company-provided white tablecloth to showcase the rainbow of pastel colors and variety of sizes and uses for the different pieces. When she signed up to become a dealer, she really had been impressed with these revolutionary new products, but more, she relished the promise that hosting these parties would enable her to contribute something to her household and community.

Today, standing in front of a room of women who all seemed so at ease, so happy, she couldn't believe that she had ever thought this was a good idea. She wasn't one of them anymore. No longer the neighbor who watched her friend's children or hosted weekly cards and tea for the girls; Margaret was now the odd one, the one who had suddenly lost her looks and nearly set the kitchen on fire when she tried to make cookies. *Maybe burning down the house would have been better.* No. That was wrong. She knew that was wrong.

Gathering herself, she looked at Carolyn, who returned her gaze with a perfect cheerleader smile. Margaret wanted to strangle her. Instead, she broke through the din of chatter with a tentative "Ladies, thank you all so much for being here today." *You can do this. You must do this.* "I believe some of you are already very familiar with this miraculous product: Tupperware." She smiled a broad, hard, fake smile as she turned her right palm upward and moved it along the base of the table. "I know we all need to watch our pennies and, I promise, I am not here to sell you a thing. Instead, I want to share some of the wonderful ways that Tupperware has made me a better wife and mother." *Lies.* "With Tupperware, a single meal lasts longer. Tonight's roast becomes tomorrow's sandwich and the following evening's stew. Cook once and eat three times! All that wasted food can now be neatly packed, stacked, and stored to save you time, money, and space in your refrigerator."

Margaret looked out at the warm smiles on the faces of her friends and neighbors and began to feel stronger. She continued with her demonstration, showing how the remains of an entire turkey dinner could be stored for days. She asked some of her friends who also used Tupperware, including Carolyn, to share their stories. Margaret just had to present one last item and then she could start writing up orders. And she was sure she was going to get a lot of orders.

Margaret smiled broadly at the group. "Finally, I couldn't help but share this wonderful innovation with all of you. One of the latest products in the line and one that even you regular users may have never seen." She crossed her living room into the kitchen and returned carrying a plastic container shaped like a Bundt pan with a lid that looked like a plate. "Who doesn't love a Jell-O mold?

"Jell-O makes such a wonderful presentation, but you have to have the right-sized plate to release the mold into. And then, suppose you have some left over, how can you get it to keep its shape? Tupperware has solved both problems for you with this perfect piece. Simply turn the mold upside down, and the Jell-O drops right into place on the lid, which becomes a plate pretty enough to sit alongside your finest china!" Margaret demonstrated the mold gleefully. As she held aloft the masterpiece of red-, orange-, and yellow-striped Jell-O, studded with specks of white marshmallow and bright red maraschino cherries, for all to see, applause filled the room.

4

"And then, when it's time to clean up, all you need to do is pop the mold back on the plate!" She grabbed the base and attempted to snap it, but it was too unwieldy. She needed a table; unfortunately, Tupperware covered the one behind her. She lifted her knee to prop the lid and demonstrate the all-important "burp" seal, but instead of a burp, she heard a tear. Her jerky motion had ripped open her too-tight dress, and her flesh poured out the side of the torn seam above her girdle. Desperate, she reached to cover herself, inadvertently throwing the Jell-O into her chest, where it splattered before sliding to the floor below.

Margaret heard a collective gasp and then silence. She fell to her knees and began scraping the cheerfully colored mess off the brown carpet with her hands. *Look at the homecoming queen—she can't take care of her children, she can't properly fit into clothing, she can't even demonstrate how to use a stupid plastic container.* Margaret curled herself tightly into a ball, covering her face, her ears, as best as she could. Then, quietly, she began to sob.

Somewhere in her mind she realized Lucy was gathering the guests and shooing them out the door. She smelled her mother's perfume and felt several pairs of strong hands carrying her upstairs to her bed. She heard the sound of her children begging to get in, to see Mommy, and she prayed that no one would let them. Prayed that she could hide under the blankets forever. Because she couldn't face any of these people ever again.

PART 1
RUTH: 1933–36

Chapter One

Ruth approached the large brick edifice and swung open the ornate wrought-iron gate. It was difficult to ignore her family's name carved into the strip of black iron that sat at eye level, but she did her best. As far as she was concerned, she was simply an employee of this hospital.

Inside the gates, the exterior courtyard was filled with trees, their leaves just beginning to show signs of vibrant reds, purples, and golds. In the next few weeks, this space would transform from a summer garden into a colorful autumnal sanctuary for new patients and their families. Emeraldine Hospital might be a public institution right in the middle of New York City, but from its inception, her family made sure that it wouldn't feel like those cold, dark public asylums with their peeling paint, dim lighting, and stacked beds. They had created something new: a public hospital for the insane with the care and amenities of a private country retreat, a direct relationship to a medical school, and a first-class research facility.

It was something of a miracle that her father, Bernard Emeraldine, son of the great industrialist Thomas Emeraldine, was as passionate about this new hospital as Ruth was. Really, it was the one cause they were aligned on, even though her interest in science and medicine did come from him. It was his idea, after all, to create a hospital that would treat people of all classes with first-rate care. That was why he chose to give a million-dollar endowment to the New York Hospital for the Insane (now renamed Emeraldine), instead of the luxurious Payne Whitney Psychiatric Clinic, where her brother, Harry, had been a patient after the Great War.

Back then, Ruth was so devoted to her brother's care that she hadn't paid much attention to her father's hospital project. She hadn't paid much attention to anything, really, having stepped aside from her work with the suffragists, to her father's delight. She had even failed to turn up for her former fiancé, Lawrence, so frequently that he had ultimately given up on her, marrying one of her more available classmates from Mount Holyoke instead.

Only when they lost Harry did this hospital become her mission. While Bernard and her mother, Helen, appropriately mourned the loss of their son, receiving visitors and taking a pause from their day-to-day life, Ruth made herself busier than ever. She channeled her grief into ensuring that her family's unprecedented endowment went toward the creation of a premier research and care facility. To hopefully spare other families the pain of unnecessarily losing one of their own.

Looking back, Ruth was surprised her father had permitted her to step in and work directly with Charles Hayden, the new superintendent. Though she suspected that her father thought the subordinate position would keep her occupied until her next beau came along, Ruth had immediately made herself indispensable. Now, more than a decade later, as assistant superintendent, she spent her time overseeing the day-to-day details of the hospital's operations, helping to keep track of the patients' progress, and even assisting in hiring decisions. Emeraldine Hospital had become her life's work. Or, more accurately, it had become her life.

With Harry gone, the hospital was all Ruth had. Even now, with the hindsight that her dedication couldn't have saved Harry from himself, Ruth still would have devoted herself fully to the hospital. Yes, she was thirty-four years old and undoubtedly on her way to becoming a spinster. But she had her hospital. Her patients. And every day, as she made her way up First Avenue, she felt a quiet hope that she was destined for something bigger. To change outcomes for all sorts of families. To find a better way to care for, and possibly even cure, the insane.

As she walked inside, past the redbrick entrance with its high ceilings and large arched windows, down the long hallway, carpeted with bright oriental rugs and illuminated with crystal chandeliers, she felt proud that she had helped make this a place where all patients received the highest standard of care. With its warm wood floors, open courtyards, and even a proper ballroom for dancing, Emeraldine Hospital felt like a home instead of an institution, a place where real healing could occur.

Ruth entered her office and placed her brown crocodile handbag next to the chaise by the window, then removed her feathered hat and hung it on the brass rack in the corner. She smoothed her dark hair, tucking a few loose strands back into her tight chignon, and took a quick glance in the looking glass. While given an uncomfortable amount of attention in college for inheriting her mother's striking good looks, she hated to fuss with her appearance; still, she was in many ways an ambassador for the hospital and expected to look the part. Thankfully her mother's dressmaker always sent her what she needed to stay abreast of fashion.

She had arrived early, as usual, so she would have time to make her tour of the wards before her day officially began. Without consulting her calendar or looking at the pile of files on her desk, she set off to do the part of her job that she cherished most. She typically started at the farthest ward, in continuous care. This ward housed men and women assumed to be "lifers" at the hospital, the truly hopeless cases in the eyes of most doctors and even the patients' own families. Ruth didn't think of them that way, though. With the exception of the criminally insane, who occupied a locked ward at a prison hospital on Blackwell's Island, adjacent to the old Octagon (made infamous by Nellie Bly's damning exposé), Ruth held out hope that all the men and women could be cured, at least enough to safely return home again. This required the most comprehensive treatment program: cutting-edge medicine combined with compassionate care for all.

As much as she wished empathy and fresh air could be enough, she had seen firsthand that patients needed more to cure their suffering. Harry had enjoyed all the fresh air he desired at the pastoral Payne Whitney. He had seemed to find respite in the woodshop, making birdhouses. And, because Ruth spent a portion of nearly every day by his side and consulting with his doctors, she knew that they were as compassionate as possible. Still, none of that had stopped him from fashioning a noose out of his bedsheets. No, Ruth knew that there had to be more to treatment. And she spent every day trying to ferret out the methods that might work best.

She walked speedily and arrived at the continuous care quadrangle in less than two minutes—a feat, as it was several buildings away. She went first to the indigent dormitories. Emeraldine was one of the few hospitals large enough to accommodate every level of need. For those with means, they of course offered private rooms, but Ruth took great pride that even the quarters for the poorest patients held only a maximum of sixteen people, unlike most other public hospitals that were lined wall-to-wall with beds.

Still, as she entered the dorm, she could hardly hear herself think over the screaming, singing, and babbling of its inhabitants; she wondered how deafening the noise must be in those other hospitals. It alone would be enough to drive a person mad.

"Miss Emeraldine—you met my pet parrot?" An older woman rushed toward her, smiling broadly as she pointed to the pillowcase tied on her shoulder.

"Why, no, Miss Nellie. What is his name?" Ruth obliged kindly, bringing her face closer to inspect the imaginary bird.

"He?" Nellie cackled. "He! This is a women's ward. You a moron or somethin'?" Nellie suddenly looked enraged as she tried to scratch at Ruth's face with her long fingernails.

Ruth ducked Nellie's swing as a nurse and two orderlies came to her rescue. "I'm fine," she said firmly, while grabbing Nellie's hands and holding them tightly in her own. "Nellie and I will just go sit on her bed and wait for you to get the straitjacket so she can calm down a bit."

"Not the straitjacket! It will kill my parrot! You bitch! Ruth, you bitch!" Nellie shrieked and flailed as Ruth held her hands even tighter, and the other women in the room began to laugh and cheer.

Ruth had long ago convinced Mr. Hayden to eliminate the use of cage-like "cribs" and leather-belted chairs with hoods to constrain violent psychotics. At Emeraldine, when cases required restraints, they used the gentler straitjacket form.

"Nellie," Ruth said in a loud and firm tone. She tightened her grip on the woman's writhing arms. "We will put your pet on your bed, right next to you. If you can get yourself under control before they return with the jacket, perhaps you won't have to put it on. But, right now, you clearly need some help to calm down. Ladies"—she looked around sternly at the other women in the room—"you all have moments when you need help controlling yourselves, so I suggest you mind your manners and give Miss Nellie a moment to collect herself."

Fifteen minutes later, with Nellie significantly calmer and safely in the straitjacket, Ruth stood and assured Nellie they would release her from her restraints soon, then turned on the heel of her white-and-brown lace-up oxfords to move on with her rounds. She looked at her watch and was disappointed to find that it was nearly nine o'clock already—she wouldn't have time to visit the colored dormitories or the women in the private rooms if she wanted to check in on the new patient admitted the evening before. This woman had been brought in from the Bowery, her body covered in bruises, her face bleeding, her left eye swollen shut. She would have been taken to the medical wing had she not been ranting and raving.

"I'll kill him before I let him touch me again," she had screamed over and over in a shrill wail as the orderlies brought her in. Ruth shuddered as she thought of what might have happened to the poor woman.

She walked directly to the hydrotherapy room, where she assumed the doctor would have placed her. The warm, continuous-flow bath was hardly cutting-edge, but Ruth still believed it was one of the best tools in their arsenal for calming agitation.

The room was lined with eight metal tubs, each containing what appeared at first glance to be floating heads. From the neck down, the women's bodies lay beneath a hinged lid that ran the length of the tub, designed to ensure they remained submerged and unable to flail in the water, which could be made extremely hot or intensely cold to either shock or soothe their systems. Ruth found the woman from the previous evening reclining calmly as a nurse fed her some broth.

"And how is our new patient today?" Ruth asked the nurse while offering a welcoming smile to the woman in the tub.

"She has calmed down, but now she is refusing to speak." The nurse raised her eyebrows in exasperation.

"Welcome to Emeraldine Hospital." Ruth pulled a chair over next to the woman's tub. The woman looked away. "I'm sure you are scared, but you're safe here, I can promise you that. We only want to help you. Can you look at me?" The woman turned her head slightly in Ruth's direction, and Ruth struggled to hide her shock. Up close Ruth realized that this was not a woman at all, just a girl, likely no more than twelve years old. "Sweetheart, I'm Ruth Emeraldine, the assistant superintendent for this hospital. That means I'm not a doctor here, just a person who will make sure that the doctors and nurses do everything in their power to help you. Can you tell me your name?"

"Mary," the girl replied, almost whispering.

"Well, Miss Mary, do you know why you are here?"

Mary nodded.

"Can you tell me?"

"'Cause this time I tried to kill him." Her response was deep and guttural. Ruth could hear the anguish in her voice.

"Who did you try to kill?" Ruth asked calmly, knowing that if this girl had actually attempted murder, she would be having a very different conversation with a very different kind of warden over on the island, not here with Mary in a warm bath. "Someone seems to have hurt you pretty badly. Can you tell me who hurt you?"

"Is he dead? I can only tell you if he's dead."

"Honey, I don't know who you are speaking about, so I'm afraid I cannot tell you with certainty whether anyone you might know is dead or alive."

Ruth watched Mary's face grow gray with fear, and the girl's eyes started darting wildly around the room. "He's gonna find me. He's gonna come get me. He said if I told anyone, he'd kill me. Kill me and do it to my dead body. Even though I scratched at him, kicked him, told him it's ungodly, but he doesn't care. Keeps holding that knife at me and . . ." She looked away, clearly embarrassed.

"It's all right, you haven't done anything wrong. You can talk to me. I promise." Ruth reached out to stroke the girl's head.

"Well, this time when he tried, I was gonna show him. I got his knife, hid it in my mattress. When he came home smelling all sour and pawing at me, I tried to scare him off." She paused and started to scream and wail as she had the night before.

"Mary." Ruth remained unflappable as she waited for Mary to come to the other side of her fit. Unfortunately, this painful story was one she had heard too many times from too many of the female patients at Emeraldine. After a moment, the hydrotherapy calmed the girl, and Ruth continued gently, "We can send police around to scare some sense into him. Is it your father?"

"My father?" Mary looked confused. "He's dead."

"Then who do you live with, dear?"

"My ma—and my brother."

"Ah." Taking another breath, Ruth continued to stroke Mary's head. "What has happened to you isn't your fault, do you hear me?" She took Mary's face in her hands gently, turning it so Ruth could look her squarely in the eyes. "I know you're scared, but you have done nothing wrong. We will help you to get better, and I promise that I will keep you safe. Your brother cannot get to you in my hospital. You can start fresh from here."

Mary looked at her with doubt in her eyes as she began to cry and nod her head. "Thank you," she said in barely a whisper.

"Mary, do you like flowers?" The girl looked at her quizzically. "We have many beautiful gardens here. If you can stay calm for me while I'm gone, perhaps later we can go and look at some of the flowers. Right now, I'm due at a meeting, but the nurses will take good care of you. They will make sure you are safe. Can you let them do that until I return later?" Mary nodded hesitantly as Ruth stood. She wished she could stay longer, but she was afraid that the superintendent might have already arrived. Ruth took pride in being well on top of the day's schedule by the time they had their morning meeting. So, she gave the nurse instructions to ensure that Mary received no visitors and to notify her immediately if someone did come looking for her, and then made her way hurriedly back to the administrative wing.

As she sat down at her desk, she noticed a stack of new files next to the stained-glass lamp her mother had insisted on—its undulating pattern of lilacs rendered in light greens and soft purples to add a more feminine touch to the dark wood-paneled room. A note from Superintendent Hayden sat atop the pile: *Interview today at 10:00 a.m.* She stood quickly and headed down the hall.

"Charles!" Ruth popped her head into her boss's office. "If I'd known you would be here early, I would have made my rounds later in the day."

"Ah, Ruth! Don't be silly, I had an early meeting. In fact, that is what the file on your desk is about. I am sorry to foist this upon you at the last minute, but this doctor is only in town for the day. The provost of the university and I met with him last night, and they are very interested in him as a chair for their Neurology Department. Interesting fellow. He is both a neurologist *and* a practicing psychiatrist, and his passion is research. Exactly what you have been telling me we need. I would have had you meet him first, but the school set up the dinner at the last minute. So, since you have been spearheading this search, I wanted to be sure you had the opportunity to see him today."

"Of course. And thank you." She kept her voice even and professional when she really wanted to embrace him with gratitude for the faith he always put in her. Never mind her family name, she knew how fortunate she was to be a woman in this position, and how rare it was to find a man willing to treat her with the respect of a colleague.

"Have a look at his curriculum vitae. He comes highly recommended from the folks at Yale. He has also been working with some very innovative medical researchers in Europe. The university is quite impressed with him."

"Well, they were impressed with the last three, and they were less progressive than the doctors who worked with my brother thirteen years ago." Ruth twisted the slim timepiece on her wrist.

"You are a tough critic, Miss Emeraldine. But that is exactly why you're the perfect person for this job. Stay tough with your interviews. We need a new point of view around here. Find the innovators and instigate change. We owe it to our patients!" Mr. Hayden slammed his fist on his imposing wooden desk and smiled, his salt-and-pepper mustache turning up slightly and the corners of his eyes crinkling. Ruth really couldn't believe her good fortune in having this man as her employer.

"Will do, sir."

Ruth made her way back to her desk and began to read over the candidate's résumé. If this doctor was nearly as competent and cutting-edge in person as he was on paper, he might be just what Emeraldine needed. But her hope deflated as soon as he walked through the door.

Everything about his appearance was designed to impress, from his impeccably tailored suit to his ridiculous goatee. He was dressed like yet another striver who wanted to appear more successful than he was and who, she suspected, would ultimately follow the path of so many of the field's most promising doctors: The initial enthusiasm worn down by an inability to break through. The fine suits replaced by stained shirtsleeves. Why bother dressing for work when your patients were often covered in the food they refused to eat, or worse, the excrement they smeared on themselves in some fit of fury?

Ruth pictured the spark in this man's eyes dulled by reality until he, too, inevitably resorted to those old practices of padded cells and chains. That was not what Emeraldine aimed for. They were going to do better. To do more.

But then this man, this Dr. Robert Apter, began to talk. "Miss Emeraldine, I want to speak with you immediately about the protocol in this hospital. Madam, you could be doing so much more for your patients."

Ruth cocked her head. "First off, I'm not a madam, and second, we have yet to even make introductions and you are already criticizing our hospital? We've designed every aspect to be current with the latest treatments and to give our patients the utmost dignity. As you know, these are the sickest of individuals; many have become dangers to themselves and others. I struggle every day to find ways to make our inmates more comfortable, to help them live lives that have some shred of humanity, while soldiering forward with protocols that will bring them the most relief." Ruth felt the hairs on the back of her neck prickling in irritation. What a presumptuous, impertinent man. She looked out the window to collect herself. By the time she turned back, Dr. Apter had crossed the room and now stood directly at her side. He lifted Ruth's hand and took it in his own. What was he doing?

"I am sorry, Miss Emeraldine. I am Dr. Robert Apter. So very pleased to make your acquaintance." Was he mocking her? In her own office? "Now, may we get to the task at hand?" His rich brown eyes looked directly into her own and he winked. Winked! In the first moments of an interview at an insane asylum. Who was this man? "Miss Emeraldine, I know the reputation of this hospital, and of its forward-thinking administrative team. This is the reason I am being so forthright with you. Because I believe you are a rare person of like mind."

"I s-see," Ruth stammered, stepping away from him to regain her composure. "Because you believe, after just a few hours here, you now know enough about our hospital to comment on our hard work and that of our doctors?"

"I do not intend to offend. Simply to suggest that you expand your thinking."

"Expand my thinking? Sir, I read every relevant medical journal on the treatment of insanity and associated mental disorders, some that even our doctors don't read. And there is no one more devoted to employing the most progressive and promising treatments for my patients than I. So, please, do get to the point." Although her tone was sharp, she had the smallest shine in her eye. Someone who knew her well would know she was more interested than she let on.

"Ah, but if I get right to the point, where will the suspense be?" he answered playfully. "You need to hear the overture before you experience the crescendo!"

"While I greatly appreciate the symphony, its place is not inside my office." As irritated as she was by this theatrical display, she found herself struggling to suppress a smile. "Please, Doctor, tell me why it is that you might be interested in this job, and how you would intend to do your work here, so that I may get back to mine."

"All right, I'll tell you plainly if you insist." He settled his compact body into the leather chair opposite her desk. She sat as well, although more formally, back straight at attention in the wooden seat of her desk chair. "I understand that you were one of the first hospitals to use convulsive therapy to treat your patients, is that correct?" he asked.

"It is. We are very excited about the promise of metrazol-induced convulsions as a behavioral modification technique. Our early trials on several of the men in the continuous care wing have been promising."

"Yes, yes." He cut her off. "I'm quite aware of the benefits of this kind of therapy, having been one of its pioneers. What I appreciate about your use of it is that it indicates that you understand insanity cannot be cured by psychoanalysis."

My, this man was brusque. And arrogant. And yet, somehow, she wanted the conversation to continue. "I do have mixed feelings about the theories of Dr. Freud. I assume that's what you're referring to? Certainly, there are factors in a patient's early life that can impact their illness, but I've seen too many sick people to believe that just talking about one's past is enough." *It certainly wasn't enough for my brother*, she thought woefully.

"Yes! Exactly. What we should be doing in mental hospitals is curing the diseases of the mind, not revisiting past injustices." He paused, and even though Ruth could see it was entirely for dramatic effect, she couldn't help but feel on the edge of her seat, waiting for him to continue. "Miss Emeraldine, in your reading, have you come across any work at all that discusses the mechanics of the brain?"

"The mechanics . . . I'm not sure I know what you mean?"

"Ah, not surprising. It is rather a radical idea, hasn't yet been embraced by the American psychiatric community, in spite of the well-documented connections between neurologic and psychological conditions."

She noticed him looking at her and was shocked to feel her pulse quicken. "Dr. Apter, as you seem to be aware, here at Emeraldine, we are not averse to radical ideas, as long as they can help ease the suffering of our patients and their families. In fact, we urge our doctors to bring us new approaches."

"Ease suffering. Miss Emeraldine, that, right there, is the problem."

"I beg your pardon?" Ruth leaned across her desk, searching for his eyes to meet hers again.

"While I am sure your intentions are worthy, you hospital administrators are spending too much time doling out sympathy and trying to manage symptoms, when what these patients need is extreme action!" He leapt up from the chair, lifting his arm in the air dramatically.

"Extreme action?"

"Here, finally, is my point: I have come to believe that there is something about the brains of the insane, physically, that causes their maladies, at least in the most extreme cases. And I am certain that, with enough study, we can find these abnormalities and address them to improve patients' lives and get them out of hospitals and back into society. Permanently." He looked at her again, and this time she was so entranced by his passion, his sudden earnestness, that she couldn't look away. He smiled and went on. "I plan to be relentless in my quest, Miss Emeraldine. Because I know that this is what I was put on this earth to do."

Ruth contemplated this man. He wasn't traditionally handsome. His nose was a little too big for his face, his jawline was more elongated than it was square (which was exacerbated further by his goatee), and he wasn't particularly tall. Still, somehow, it all came together in an arresting way. Moreover, something about Dr. Robert Apter made her want to help him accomplish anything and everything that he set his mind to. Her heart pounded in her chest. She composed herself and, as she snapped out of his thrall, began to contemplate what he was suggesting. "Dr. Apter, your theory is fascinating. But, I wonder, how would you propose studying these brains?"

"Well, as I assume you know, if you read up before my arrival, I have been working at a research facility in Europe for the past several years. The way I see it, Emeraldine Hospital, with its academic relationship to the New York School of Medicine, is the ideal place for me to set up a new research lab. Here I will have access to both live patients for behavioral study and cadavers for the real work."

"Cadavers?"

"Yes, of course," he said matter-of-factly, looking at Ruth like she had asked whether the forecast called for rain. "I must study the brains of dead patients, or should I say, former patients. With the school's and your hospital's reputations, we will easily be able to procure all the specimens we need. And, Miss Emeraldine, I am certain that once I study enough of them, I will find that difference." He walked toward her and stopped dead in front of her desk, staring her down. "Quite frankly, I am not going to stop until I do."

Ruth realized she had been holding her breath. Standing to collect herself, she crossed from behind her desk to square off with this man, this stranger. As she realized she was taller than him, she quickly leaned against the edge to meet his gaze.

"Dr. Apter—"

"Please, call me Robert."

"Dr. Apter," she said with more conviction, "if there is a possibility that what you're saying is true, it could revolutionize the care of the insane."

"Yes, Miss Emeraldine, I'm well aware of the potential magnitude of this work. My question to you is: Do you want this hospital to be the place that makes it possible? We could make history."

Ruth felt herself blush. In spite of her family's pedigree, or perhaps because of it, Ruth was a very private person. Having been raised not to make waves, or seek attention, she preferred to keep her life and her work quiet and hidden away from the public world. Yes, she desperately wanted to revolutionize treatment for the insane. Yes, she wanted to do anything and everything she could to make that happen. But the idea that she would deliberately seek the spotlight for the hospital was abhorrent. Fame was not her goal. She strove for progress, better treatments, a cure. Dr. Apter couldn't have known how badly Ruth wanted these things. Still, somehow, he seemed to intuit them.

Ruth had interviewed many candidates in the past, but never had she hired one on the spot. She didn't really even have the authority to do so. Still, there was something about this man. His arrogance might become infuriating, but his passion was inspiring. "Dr. Apter, please, tell me more about the specifics of what you think you'll need for your research. Because I would like to offer you a position here, effective immediately."

After she spent years hoping for it, someone had finally walked through the door who just might help them find a cure, and she simply couldn't risk losing him.

Chapter Two

Before she met Dr. Robert Apter, Ruth was quite certain that the "swept off your feet" feeling so often portrayed in the cinema was just that: a theatrical conceit. She wasn't oblivious to the charms of the opposite sex, but the men who crossed Ruth's path had never made a lasting impression. Ruth saw dating as a chore, particularly after Harry's death, so when she did entertain suitors, they were generally selected by her mother and resembled her ex-fiancé, Lawrence—perfectly bred and not the slightest bit exciting. A few of them managed to hold her interest in the bedroom, but anywhere else, she found that they had about as much dimension as a sheet of paper.

For a time in the late '20s, Ruth had an uncharacteristically active social life, courtesy of her dearest friend, Susie Davenport. Although they belonged to the same sorority at Mount Holyoke, they hadn't met until 1917, when they were awkwardly paired to hold opposite sides of the banner MR. PRESIDENT, WHAT WILL YOU DO FOR WOMEN'S SUFFRAGE? at a demonstration in Washington, DC.

"Figures they would stick the chipmunk with the giraffe," Susie said teasingly. "Can you at least bend your knees? You know, so we don't look lopsided?"

Ruth laughed. Rarely did anyone at school dare to poke fun at her. She looked around the street and found a garbage pail, which she turned upside down for Susie to stand on.

"I get it now." Susie smiled as Ruth helped her climb on top of the makeshift riser. "It's not that you hold your head high because you think you're better than the rest of us, it's just that you're so damn tall you literally have your head in the clouds."

"You believe that *I* think I'm better than you?" Ruth was surprised. She was quiet in school, but that was because she took her studies seriously. If her parents wouldn't let her go to the front to volunteer as a medical assistant with her brother, she would make the most of her education.

"Well, *I* don't think that. Everyone knows the Emeraldines are nothing compared to the Boston Davenports. My mother can show you our lineage all the way back to the *Mayflower*." Susie rolled her eyes and giggled. "As if that will do a damn for anyone in the world, right, Raffey?"

"Raffey?" Ruth looked at Susie askance. "I'm . . . Ruth?" While these young women had not previously met, they lived in the same sorority house. Was Ruth so invisible that Susie didn't even know her name?

"Geez, you're dense." Susie grinned as she casually threw her arm around Ruth's waist. "Your name may be Ruth, but you tower over me like a giraffe. So, if it's all the same to you, I'll call you Raffey."

"Raffey it is then, I suppose." Ruth smiled back. She clearly had no choice in the matter. But that suited her fine. Other than Harry, she'd never been close enough with anyone to warrant a nickname. It seemed she'd finally found her first real friend.

After college, Susie rejected her family's plans for her to marry a fellow Brahmin and, instead, moved to Greenwich Village, where she lived a "liberated" life with Meg, a female photographer who had won her heart. Ruth envied Susie's bravery. While women never held a romantic interest for her, Ruth would have loved to live among the like-minded radical thinkers in the Village, but she valued her work at the hospital too much to risk marring the family's name with such a blatant disregard for society's rules. A Village bohemian could not be the assistant superintendent of Emeraldine Hospital. So, when she moved from her family's Gramercy Park mansion into her own townhome, she relocated to Madison Square Park, a tony and "appropriate" neighborhood slightly north from her parents.

In those early days, Susie often reminded her that just because Ruth didn't live downtown, that didn't mean she couldn't enjoy it, and she was often Susie and Meg's third wheel at the jazz clubs and salons they frequented. Susie's downtown friends were fascinated by the enigma of the stunningly beautiful heiress who seemed to care about neither her looks nor her breeding. Hart Crane invited her to his poetry readings, Cole Porter solicited her opinion on his latest songs for the *Greenwich Village Follies*, and for a time, the doorman at the Cotton Club up in Harlem knew her by name. Well, he knew her as "Raffey," but that was Susie's fault. In those years, her nights out with Meg, Susie, and the men in their circles were a salve for the open wound of life without Harry, but eventually, the hospital began to fill that void entirely.

By the time she hired Dr. Apter, Ruth had accepted that her greatest passion was her patients, and when she wasn't working, she was more than content to stroll around the city on her own or curl up with a book by the parlor fire of her townhouse. She relished her solitary life and had little concern about finding a man.

It stood to reason, therefore, that in the first few weeks Dr. Apter was at the hospital, Ruth attributed the unusual, fluttery sensation in the pit of her stomach to professional excitement. He seemed more committed to finding a cure for insanity than even Ruth herself. Yet, six months into his tenure, Ruth found that she yearned to be in his presence more every day. She knew when he took his lunch and made a point of venturing to the staff dining room at that hour. She tried to justify it as professional interest, but she knew the truth: she desired him, romantically. It was humiliating, unprofessional, and entirely unexpected. But she couldn't stay away. She had never been drawn to any man in the way she was to him, and the more she tried to hide her longing, the more she seemed to let it show.

In fact, Ruth believed that Dr. Apter used her unrequited crush to his advantage. In their one-on-one meetings, he always managed to graze her knee or place his hands on her shoulders to look over a file on her desk. He must have noticed how she blushed when they were alone together, seen the sweat form on her brow. She couldn't believe how little control she had over herself when it came to him. She had never had this problem before in her life. Normally, this kind of attention in the workplace would have insulted her. But when it came from Dr. Apter, she found herself quietly hoping for more.

At night, she fantasized about him, dissecting each of his glances, his casual touches, in the hopes that they might reveal he felt about her the same way she did about him. In the morning, she vowed she would never act on her feelings.

Ruth had always worked late, but now, she often made a point of staying until she knew she could go straight home and collapse, avoiding torturous hours tossing and turning like a teenager. And then, one night, as she read through the stack of files on her desk, Robert interrupted.

"Lady Emeraldine, burning the midnight oil again?"

Ruth smiled. He was the only person in the world who could poke fun at her pedigree without inflaming her. "As I'm sure you know, Dr. Apter, the volume of paperwork associated with our patients is overwhelming. This is the quietest time to get it done. Once they're all asleep." She felt her cheeks warming already. *Please let the light be dim enough to hide my flush.*

"Of course. I agree completely. But it is also important to take a break, you know. Helps clear the mind to make space for the new ideas to emerge."

"I take a break when I sleep."

"And when you eat, I hope? Although I'd say, from the looks of it, you don't eat often enough! Food feeds the brain. How about you join me for some dinner?"

Ruth felt her insides flip. Was it really happening? Could he possibly be asking her on a date? Or did he just think it was a smart practice to stay on her good side?

"Where were you planning to go?" The venue might give her a better indication of whether he intended business or pleasure.

"Are you saying yes? If so, might I suggest we make an evening of it and head to the El Morocco?"

"The El Morocco. Why, I'm not really dressed for it." *It is a date.*

"Nonsense, you look lovely, as always."

"I do have an awful lot to do tomorrow." She looked at her desk; she couldn't let him know how eager she was to accompany him.

"How about if I promise to deliver you home by ten o'clock?"

"Nine thirty." Ruth tried to hide her grin as the fleet of butterflies grew in her stomach.

"Wonderful." He smiled broadly. "Now where is your coat? I sense the need to get you out of here before you change your mind."

Ruth collected her things quickly and made a brief stop in the ladies' room. She looked at herself as she carefully reapplied her lipstick. Here she was, a thirty-four-year-old woman, giddy to be heading out to dinner, on a date with a man who, she was growing to believe more every day, was her mission's greatest hope. She didn't recognize the person looking back at her in the mirror, but she was so happy that she didn't care.

When they arrived at one of the city's most talked-about new supper clubs, Ruth was surprised to see that Dr. Apter was apparently something of a regular. She had, of course, heard about this place, but since nights out like this had long ago become a thing of her past, she had never been. As the host escorted them to what was clearly a prime table, in direct sight of the band, Ruth felt particularly drab compared with the zebra upholstery of the banquettes that lined the room and covered the bar, and the glitz of the patrons. Ruth wasn't easily impressed by celebrity or family name, but surrounded by so many all at once—Errol Flynn, Clark Gable, multiple generations of Vanderbilts—she felt a bit humbled.

Before they even looked at the menu, the waiter brought them a bottle of champagne. Ruth rarely drank, but being here with Dr. Apter made her want to celebrate. She took a big sip, and as the Moët tingled her tongue, both sweet and biting, she was transported back to childhood summers at the family's shoreside cottage and the lavish parties her mother threw on the lawn, with lobsters and clams and so much champagne.

She had her first taste at fifteen when Harry, already seventeen and more experienced with alcohol, stole a bottle from one of the ice buckets for her to try. Ruth smiled, thinking of the two of them giggling as they hid behind their favorite rock on the beach, the light and fizzy feeling the drink gave her in her whole body. She was a different Ruth back then, with her big brother to lighten her, cheer her, understand her. He appreciated her strength, her difference. She had locked away her need for someone to do that. Until now.

Ruth looked across the table at Dr. Apter, noting his magnetism. Women's heads had turned when they walked into the restaurant, flirtatious eyes darted at him now, and she was embarrassed to suddenly realize that he could easily have any girl. This wasn't a date. This was just a dinner.

"Do you know what you'd like to eat?" Dr. Apter raised his eyebrows at Ruth. "I'd suggest we start with an assortment of seafood—they fly it in fresh from Florida. That is, if you would be all right to share . . ." The corners of his mustache lifted, and his lips thinned enough to reveal his straight white teeth. Ruth thought, in that moment, that she would say yes to anything in the world that this man asked of her.

"That would be just fine. Thank you, Doctor."

"Wonderful. And please, if we are to be sharing shrimp and oysters, I think it is well overdue for you to call me Robert."

"All right, if you insist." She caught his eyes and said it slowly, the champagne making her unusually playful. "Rah . . . bert." She liked the way the name felt in her mouth. "So, any news from your dissections?" She was getting too comfortable. Time to bring things back to reality.

"Why, Ruth." He paused, lingering on her first name as if awaiting permission. "You would be the first person I would tell if there were. Unfortunately, no. I just know there is something I am missing. Or, I should say, that I haven't found yet."

"I really admire your determination. Although I do wonder about it sometimes. How do you not lose hope?"

"I can't afford to. This is what I am meant to do, what I must do. You've heard of my grandfather, Dr. George Hogart?"

"I'm afraid I haven't. Is he in our field?"

"He was in every field, I'd say." Robert smiled wistfully. "A surgeon, a physician—to presidents, no less—a pioneer. He held over a dozen patents."

"Well, now I'm embarrassed, as it seems I should know of him!"

"Nonsense, his world doesn't cross with yours. But to me . . . he was my world. My father was a physician too, you see. I think, when my mother married him, she thought he would be like her father. She couldn't have been more mistaken. My father was nothing like my grandfather. No, my father hated medicine, resented every day that he had to work. For him, it was a trade that he had to pursue to keep my mother living the life she had been promised. Servants and silks and a manor on Rittenhouse Square. You wouldn't know anything about that, I imagine." Robert gave her a wink. He did love to tease her about her wealth. Most men were intimidated by her family name, or desperate to get their hands on her legacy. Robert, though, seemed to simply find it amusing. "Yes, whereas my father was bitter, transactional, and distant, my grandfather was optimistic, innovative, and encouraging. He was the reason I went to medical school—in spite of my father's strong protest. Grandfather George helped get me my first job, my fellowship in Europe, and he encouraged my work in the lab. Any and all medicine was good medicine as long as it meant progress. That was his view of the world."

"He sounds like a truly special man." Ruth looked into Robert's eyes. She saw pain and, with it, a vulnerability that he hadn't expressed before. "What is it?"

"He was the only person in my family who understood me at all. Was quite a loss when he died. And I never got to show him what I was truly capable of. So, when I become discouraged, I know I must soldier on. For him." Robert looked down at his plate, and Ruth felt overwhelmed by the softness deep inside this man. They were so much alike, she and he. Both earnestly and doggedly pursuing something bigger, for their families. For the world.

"Robert." Ruth put down her small seafood fork and brazenly touched his hand. "From what I have seen, I have no doubt you will accomplish all that you set out to. And more."

"Well, I might have to suggest that I am nothing compared to you." He released his hand from hers to refill their glasses with champagne and lifted his in the gesture of a toast. "I had, of course, heard about the feisty female heiress at Emeraldine Hospital, but I had no idea how miraculous you would be. To you, a miracle."

Ruth hesitated to meet his glass, unused to such admiration. "You must stop. I am hardly a miracle. But I have come to feel that this work is . . . well, that I was destined to do it." She emptied her glass.

"Destined?"

Ruth looked away. Many at the hospital, of course, knew her family's history, but for as long as she had worked there, she made a point not to talk about her own experience. It might, she feared, make those who were looking for a reason question her judgment. But tonight, her inhibitions were gone. "My brother, Harry," Ruth said with fondness. "He wanted to change the world. When he went off to war in '17, proudly, all bluster and bravery with such a sense of purpose"—Ruth smiled remembering it—"I was furious with my father for forcing me to finish my studies at Mount Holyoke instead of letting me join my brother on the front.

"He came back from France a year later, broken. We didn't realize it at first. He was good at hiding it. He resumed normal life, even reenrolled at Harvard, claiming he wanted to get all the education he could before he took his place in Father's world."

She brazenly refilled her own glass and gulped down the champagne before continuing.

"The first time he tried to take his own life, Mother and Father attributed it to school. They encouraged him to spend a few weeks at Magnolia Bluff, our cottage, but he refused. He said he had had a bad few days, too many exams, and he was fine. I knew it was something more. We were less than two years apart in age, but I always felt we were more like twins. Not that we were similar—on the contrary—he was charming, social, and easy, where I was shy and awkward. He was an inch shorter than me too." She laughed. "Very handsome, but not so tall. Anyway, we understood one another in a way that was unspoken. He could sense when I needed him to save me from Mother's attentions or Father's . . . inattention." She was being too bold, and she pushed her coupe away. "But I knew the moment I saw him step off that ship in New York Harbor that something inside of him was lost. I just didn't realize that it would never again be found."

"So many men were irreparably damaged. I worked at a veterans' hospital and I saw that look in those poor soldiers' eyes. I don't think any of us can truly understand what war can do to a man. I hope you don't blame yourself."

Ruth smiled softly. "Of course, I know what you are saying is true. But Harry seemed like he was getting better. Like he could be saved. As soon as my parents accepted that he was suffering from shell shock, they sent him to Payne Whitney, which, as you know, is lauded as one of the best facilities in the country. His doctors claimed he was improving. But in one of the many moments when they weren't paying attention, he managed to end his life. And that was it." She paused thoughtfully. "I had already devoted my life to caring for Harry. With him gone, helping others like him was just the logical next step. Father channeled his despair into creating a better facility. But he had no interest in, or time for, day-to-day operations. I did. I was determined to change things. And when I really want something I, too, can be relentless. So, I suppose, here we are." Ruth felt more exposed than she had ever been in her lifetime. She looked hard at her plate, terrified to gaze at Robert and risk humiliation. But she couldn't avoid him for long.

Robert slid his chair next to hers and gently lifted her chin so she had no choice but to look directly into his kind chestnut eyes. "Is it really possible that you have no idea how incredible you are? You are the most beautiful woman I have ever laid eyes on, yet you wear your appearance like an afterthought. You are so smart, frighteningly smart, yet you seem to feel the need to apologize for your role and dismiss your brilliance. I watch you daily with awe and wonder, so capable, so caring. If my grandfather were alive to meet you, he would tell me to grab tight to you and never let go. How is it possible that no one has taken you as their own?"

Ruth blushed, turning away from Robert's glance to break the tension. "I have, generally, not been available to be taken."

"Of course. You need a partner in life, not a master."

"Why, yes." Ruth was taken aback. Could it be that Robert not only understood her, he appreciated her for who she was, as she was? "Well, yes and no. I am really fine on my own."

"Of course you are. Just look at you and all you have accomplished." Robert slid back to his plate, picked up his knife and fork, and stabbed at his iceberg wedge nervously. Ruth was shocked to see the always perfectly collected Dr. Apter so exposed. His vulnerability surprised her, but also endeared him to her all the more. She had not misjudged this man or this moment. She had shared her most personal secrets, and he still sat here with her. Smiling at her. Robert leaned in and asked her quietly, "Ruth, I was wondering, well, hoping really, would you be open to the idea of sharing just a little sliver of your life with someone else? Someone like me, perhaps?"

Ruth's whole body suddenly felt as warm as the rhythm of the band; the high-pitched horns and low rattle of the drums matched the beating of her heart. "Yes, Robert, I think I would."

He smiled wider, raised his glass to hers, and looked her in the eye. "Ruth Emeraldine, I think this might be the beginning of a great adventure."

Even then, she believed him completely.

Chapter Three

Ruth awoke with a start and angled the clock on her marble-topped nightstand to catch the streetlight. Rubbing her eyes, still blurry from sleep, she switched on the lamp so she could get a better look at the man who had, in a matter of months, become inextricably interwoven into every corner of her being. "Robert, it's two o'clock in the morning. Are you just getting home?"

"Sorry to wake you, my love. I was deep into the cranium of a violent psychotic and thought I might be observing a meaningful idiosyncrasy in the thalamus. I couldn't leave the hospital until I compared it to my photos of several other specimens."

"And?" Ruth suddenly felt quite awake and leaned toward Robert enthusiastically, ever hopeful that his research would yield something miraculous.

"Unfortunately, it wasn't what I was looking for." He sat on the wingback in the corner opposite the bed and unlaced his shoes as he sighed. "But it has given me some new ideas for investigation." He stood up again and unbuttoned his shirtsleeves, then removed his trousers and replaced them with a nightshirt. After he climbed onto the bed, he stroked Ruth's hand, drew it to his mouth, and ever so delicately kissed it. "Don't worry, my darling, I will figure this out." He pulled Ruth toward him and began kissing her gently, first on the lips and then slowly, carefully down her neck and toward the space between her small breasts. "I have never been more determined, more inspired, or more certain of anything in my life."

Ruth had never before experienced the sort of physical yearning she felt for Robert. Robert wasn't the first man she had invited into her bed, but he was the only one whom she consistently wanted to return. In the bedroom, as elsewhere, they had an innate and all-encompassing connection. Each time they made love, she felt that everything simply fit, the curves of her body and his, the delicacy of his lips with her mouth. Even her hand rested in his grip so effortlessly that she felt they had been holding hands for decades. Though they knew enough to be covert about their living arrangements, when they were together at home, they were as one. They had no secrets, which was why Ruth was startled as Robert rolled away from her and reclined on his side, looking at her with an odd distance and awkward nervousness.

"Robert, why are you looking at me that way?" Ruth swatted his face like a kitten batting a ball of yarn. "Are you all right?"

"All right. All right?" He smiled and stroked her hand lovingly. "Such an interesting concept, this idea of 'all right.' I think, to that question, I will have to answer in the negative."

"The negative?" Ruth felt the room start to swim, and she bit her lower lip to steady her emotions.

"I am not all right. I am gobsmacked. Giddy, like a schoolboy, although I was never very giddy as an actual child." He chuckled. "Ruth Emeraldine, from the moment I walked into your office to be chastised by the most beautiful, brilliant, and astonishing woman ever to cross my path, I have harbored a tiny hope that you were my one. My wonderful Ruth, will you do me the honor of becoming my wife?"

Robert leapt from the bed, ran around to her side, and knelt there, theatrically bowing toward her hand. From the outside looking in, Ruth recognized that the moment was pure farce, utterly absurd in nearly every way—the timing, the dramatic gesture, the fact of her age. Yet, her cheeks were wet with tears. She took a deep breath, battling her disbelief and attempting to collect herself, but found she could not. The feelings overpowered her. Suddenly, she was laughing, crying, and bursting with a joy that she had long ago assumed she would never feel.

"Ruth? Are you upset? I know I don't have a ring. I hadn't been planning to do this today, but I just couldn't help myself—"

"Oh, Robert." Ruth patted her face dry. "I don't care about a ring. I care about you. I love you. Yes. Yes. I'll be your wife."

He jumped up, grabbing her in his arms, and even though she was an inch taller, lifted her from the floor to spin her around the bedroom. "You've made me the happiest man in the world!"

"And I'm the happiest woman." She kissed him and felt a charge of electricity course through her body. And then a sobering thought struck. "There's just one thing." She dropped her feet to the ground and looked him in the eye, so he would understand the gravity of what she was about to say. "I think before we make anything utterly official, it's time for you to meet my parents."

Chapter Four

Ruth's father, Bernard Emeraldine, was well-known in the world of industry for his fierce negotiating skills and standoffish demeanor. He had few hobbies, other than reading medical journals, and therefore had a reputation in society as someone you didn't want to sit next to at a dinner party. For the rare person who did find common ground with him, Bernard was engaging and loyal to a fault, but he had few true friends. He would say he preferred it that way.

Ruth believed she took after her father, uninterested in the formalities of society life, fascinated by learning and sharpening her intellect. Yet, even though Ruth's role at the hospital gave her more common ground with Bernard than she had in her childhood, she never stopped feeling judged by him for not being a boy, just as she felt judged by her mother for not acting like more of a lady. Being with her parents set Ruth on edge, so the idea of introducing them to the man she planned to marry was almost too much for her to bear.

Her parents knew they would meet Robert tonight. Ruth hadn't told them about the engagement but did indicate that he was a suitor. Helen insisted on a formal dinner, which meant Ruth needed to dress properly. Tonight, she wanted things to go as smoothly as possible, so she chose her grandmother's pearls and the peacock brooch that Helen had given her for her twenty-first birthday. Still, she worried. How could she expect her parents to welcome this unknown man into their family as her husband, when they hardly accepted her as their daughter?

A nearly crippling anxiety overtook Ruth as she and Robert strolled through Gramercy Park. If only she could turn back and hide with Robert in the bed of her townhouse. No, she couldn't do that. Instead, she walked as slowly as she could manage, pretending to admire the wreaths and trees in the windows of the ornate mansions in celebration of the upcoming holiday season.

"Darling, you look pale as a ghost. Are you nervous? Don't be. I can charm even the most skeptical benefactors. And I can't imagine your father could be anything but easy compared to my own. The simple fact that he attends the balls that your mother hosts makes him exponentially more affable than mine ever was."

"I know you'll be delightful. It is just that my father has never approved of any decision I have made in my life." Also, Ruth thought to herself, as chairman of the hospital's board and its primary benefactor, he could control more of Robert's fate than just his personal life. Ruth had, of course, told her father all about the interesting new doctor—a psychologist *and* a neurologist!—when they had first hired Robert, but she had been extremely careful to hide the details of their evolving personal relationship. Still, if she was to marry Robert, she owed it to both of her parents to give them a chance to get to know him.

"Well, here we are." The opulence of their city mansion embarrassed Ruth more than ever these days. She knew that her father and his before him had worked hard for their fortune, but nevertheless she had difficulty reconciling their grand life when so many in the city around them still stood in breadlines, struggled to put food on the table, and shivered in cold rooms they couldn't afford to heat. "Welcome to my home." She looked shyly at her feet.

"I have to say, I thought the place would be larger." Robert smiled as they walked up the stairway toward the intricate iron-framed entrance. Ruth gave him a playful slap on the arm with her glove, grateful for his good humor and complete acceptance of her. As they stepped through the heavy red-painted door onto the tuxedo marble floor of the double-height foyer, she greeted the butler with a warm and familiar embrace.

"Arnold, you're looking well! Does that mean Mother isn't working you quite so hard this holiday season?"

"Miss Ruth, you know Mrs. Emeraldine never asks for anything more than it is my duty to provide. She is quite generous with me and my family."

"You don't have to lie to me, Arnold. I lived with her for twenty-five years, I know the truth." She lifted her eyebrow mischievously and smiled as he took their coats. "How's that new grandbaby of yours? Serena, right?"

"Just wonderful, Miss Ruth. A perfect angel. Thank you for asking." He proudly produced a photograph from his inside coat pocket for her to admire.

"She's beautiful. Congratulations," Ruth said. "My manners! I haven't introduced you yet to Dr. Robert Apter. I have a feeling you'll be getting to know him fairly well."

"Is that so? Well, I am pleased to meet you, Doctor. Miss Ruth is very special. I expect you to take good care of her." He shook Robert's hand and gave him the kind of admonishing look that would typically come from a concerned father.

"You can count on me." Robert chuckled.

"Well, much as I would prefer to spend the evening chatting with you, Arnold, I'm sure Mother is already irritated that we're late." Ruth gave Arnold a loving squeeze and then grabbed hold of Robert's arm, steering him to the right of the grand central staircase and into the living room.

"Ready?" She opened her large eyes even wider as she looked at Robert, silently offering him one last chance to escape.

"Utterly."

Ruth cared about interior design about as much as she did fashion, and after Harry's death, she had resented that her mother was trying to reinvent their home, to chase the memories of her brother from the corners where they hung like cobwebs. Now she appreciated the contemporary touches that mingled elegantly with the history of the place. Like the electric lights woven into the old chandeliers, Helen had managed to transform the Gramercy mansion into something fresh, while still retaining the sense of familiarity that made it feel like home. Her mother was careful to retain the original details that had been a hallmark of taste at the turn of the century—the leaded windows, the gilded balustrades on the imposing staircase, the intricately carved stone fireplaces that flanked each end of the great room, so large that Harry used to tease Ruth they would come alive and swallow her. But, wherever she could, Helen incorporated the fabrics, furniture, and colors that dominated the current world of international art and design. She had papered the walls in sumptuous teals and peacock blues and draped the windows in purple velvet and gold moiré. She had brought in some of the newer styles from Europe and New York—a pair of wooden chairs carved with the sinuous lines of art nouveau, a modern "fainting couch" upholstered in emerald green, a photograph by Alfred Stieglitz, and even a few bold abstract paintings from Picasso. From the look of the redone formal rooms, one might think that Helen Emeraldine had a modern view of the world. Unfortunately for Ruth, her mother's open-mindedness did not extend beyond fashion and design. Helen never failed to point out what a disappointment Ruth was to the family as a spinster. Never mind that she was second-in-command at a major hospital.

Well, tonight, perhaps, Ruth could make her mother and her father just a little bit proud. Or maybe she was hoping for too much. As they rounded the double archway and entered the vast room, Ruth saw that Bernard and Helen were seated at the farthest seating area, near the rear fireplace, sipping cocktails in silence. The canapés sat on the table untouched.

"Ruth, darling, fashionably late as usual, I see." Helen smiled as she turned to greet her daughter.

"Mother, Father, I'd like you to meet Dr. Robert Apter. Robert, my parents, Mr. and Mrs. Bernard Emeraldine."

"Dr. Apter." Helen Emeraldine reached for Robert's hand and shook it limply.

"Such a pleasure to meet you, madam." Robert made a little theatrical bow as he kissed Helen's hand, and Ruth saw a small smile escape her mother's lips. "You have a breathtaking home, thank you so much for welcoming me here this evening. And, Mr. Emeraldine," Robert addressed Bernard directly as he crossed the room to stand in front of his chair, "I have been looking forward to meeting you for quite some time."

"Doctor." Bernard did not stand and hardly even put out his hand to meet Robert's vigorous shake. He quickly broke the contact and turned to his daughter. "Ruth"—he paused, eyeing her up and down—"you look nice this evening."

"Hello, Father, thank you," Ruth responded softly, wishing what she looked like didn't matter so much, and then walked to her father's side to give him a forced kiss on the cheek.

"Well, I'm hungry, let's head into the dining room."

"Bernard, give them a moment to settle in, have a drink. They haven't even lost the chill from their clothes! I'll just go let Chef know that we will be ready shortly, but you three settle in for a cocktail."

Ruth saw her father shoot her mother a frustrated glance before he stood up and headed to the bar cart. "Dr. Apter, how do you take your martini?"

Ruth never stopped being surprised at the power her mother seemed to have over her otherwise domineering father. Helen and Harry were the only two people in Bernard's life who could soften him that way. Ruth wished she had the same skill.

"Dry with two olives, if you have them," Robert replied confidently. Ruth warmed inside, proud to see that her father couldn't easily intimidate her husband-to-be. "Mr. Emeraldine, I am anxious to know your thoughts on the direction we are moving in the hospital. Are you pleased with the development of the research lab?"

"I find it interesting," Bernard answered in a flat and dismissive tone as he walked back to the seating area with two cocktails. Ruth could see him working to remain indifferent and began to worry about the path the evening might take.

"Well, it is interesting! We Americans have become so fixated on analysis over the past few decades that we have lost track of the fact that mental health is part of the medical field. We need the discipline of deconstructive research. Dissection, imaging, biological exploration. Talking isn't going to move inmates out of asylums and into society again. We need medical action."

Bernard sat quietly, his lips tight, his eyes seemingly unblinking as he stared at Robert, almost daring him to continue. A clammy sweat began to form on Ruth's lower back, and she worried that her father would launch into one of his infamous tirades. She had never seen Robert challenged, and she feared he might be a fiery and defensive adversary.

Instead, her father said, "I couldn't agree with you more." Ruth was so stunned she nearly choked on her cocktail. "While I think

Dr. Freud's little theories are lovely for people with minor malaise, we are running a hospital. We need to think more medically. That's why I was so pleased when Ruth told me they had hired you." Ruth began to fume—if her father was happy about Robert's hire, he certainly hadn't said a word to her. In fact, she could hardly remember him registering the conversation, let alone having a positive opinion about it. "You might not be aware, but while I myself have no formal training in medicine, I have made an examination of the trade my second career. Would you like to see my study, Dr. Apter?" Bernard rose and Robert followed.

"Robert, you will enjoy this," Ruth said as brightly as she could, knowing that she should be glad that her father took an interest in Robert instead of hurt that, as usual, he excluded her. "Father has the largest medical library of any private home in the country."

"Larger than some universities," Bernard added as he ushered Robert out of the living room and down the hall. A painful sense of déjà vu overtook Ruth as she watched her fiancé and her father head toward the wood-paneled hallway. She felt as though she had spent her entire childhood on one side of the double doors while, on the other, Harry and Bernard had discussed everything she found truly interesting: contagion, virology, surgical innovations, and treatment trials.

Ruth and her mother sat for nearly an hour, Helen growing agitated about dinner and Ruth suffering through tales of the tribulations of this season's party schedule. "It is widely known that the Rockefellers host the first party of the holiday season. But this year, that Woolworth girl—you know, Barbara Hutton—stole the season right out from under them." Ruth looked at her mother, perplexed. "Oh, for heaven's sake, Ruth! Do you pay no attention? I am certain I told you about the event after you refused to attend with us—at the grand, new Ritz-Carlton? The eucalyptus and silver birch trees imported all the way from California? Four orchestras? It was a bit garish, but it was the absolute talk of the town. A party unlike any other. Of course, now Abby Rockefeller is simply beside herself because her Christmas ball will seem so pedestrian in comparison."

"Such a shame," Ruth said without intonation as she stared at the archway, waiting anxiously for Robert and her father to return.

"Why, yes, it is! And now Madeleine Astor Dick is talking about hosting an additional ball here in New York—she says it is all the rage to have more spontaneous parties. Honestly, I am not sure we will ever get to Palm Beach."

How could Helen possibly think that Ruth cared about any of this? What did it matter who hosted which parties and where, when people struggled every day just to stay warm? She knew the answer, of course, but somehow it never failed to hurt a little. Much like Bernard, Helen didn't see the woman who was actually sitting in front of her; instead, when forced to spend time with her daughter, Helen simply pretended Ruth was the person Helen wanted her to be. Just at the point when Ruth felt she might actually explode, the men returned. They had a relaxed energy between them, and an undercurrent of excitement that Ruth rarely saw in her father.

"Bernard, the entrée is likely to be entirely dried out at this point. Honestly!"

"Sorry, dear, but I have a feeling you won't care in a moment." Bernard stood behind Ruth and she almost jumped as he placed his hand on her shoulder. "Some good news! Our Ruth is finally getting married."

"Married?" Helen looked as if she was trying to mask her shock and contain her relief. Ruth knew she had long ago given up hope that her daughter would actually find a suitable mate.

"It is true. This fine doctor desires to make Ruth his wife." Ruth tried not to notice the slight sound of disbelief in Bernard's tone.

"Mrs. Emeraldine, I think your daughter is a magnificent woman, inside and out. I have found, in her, an unexpected partner. And, with your permission, I would like nothing more than to share my life with her as husband and wife."

"Oh my, yes!" Helen leapt up, clapping. "Yes! Yes! Yes!"

Chapter Five

Ruth had little time for or interest in frivolous friendships. She was collegial with the staff at Emeraldine, and she occasionally attended informal reunions with her classmates from college, but after Harry died, there was only one person in the world whom she considered a true friend: Susie Davenport. Besides the fact that she shared Ruth's desire to help the less fortunate—working as a social worker and an advocate for the poor in Manhattan—she understood Ruth implicitly, never pushing her to feel or be anything other than what she was. Ruth cherished Susie like a sister. Hers was the only opinion that Ruth trusted. So, when Susie insisted that it was time to bring Robert to Magnolia Bluff, Ruth knew she was right. Still, she hesitated. Before Robert, the happiest days of Ruth's life had been at Magnolia Bluff with Harry. She needed Robert to love it as much as she did, and she wasn't sure that he would in the off-season, when the estate was largely closed up, cold, and unstaffed.

"I don't know, Susie," Ruth said into the phone. "It isn't all that comfortable in winter. He works so hard all week and I know he likes to get some rest on the weekends. It is one thing to go there with you and Meg, but—"

"Excuse me? Am I speaking to Ruth Emeraldine? The same woman who told her former fiancé, the boy who every girl in our sorority house was dying to marry, that he needed to accept the limited time she had to spend with him, or find someone else?"

Ruth laughed. It was true. Ruth had never worried about taking care of the needs of a man (other than Harry). As she sat on the phone with her best friend, she suddenly felt like she had become her mother. "You make a compelling argument." Ruth smiled. "Still, I want Robert to love Magnolia Bluff as much as I do. Maybe I should wait until spring to bring him there."

"Nonsense. You love it there in winter. Meg and I love it in winter because of how much joy it brings you to be there. If the man you are marrying can't appreciate that, then he isn't worth your time. Anyway, if Robert passed the Bernard and Helen test, a cold weekend at the beach will be a piece of cake."

Ruth laughed. "All right, well, I still wish you could join us."

"We have a rally this weekend that we can't miss. But I will expect another invitation soon. Much as I adore living like a bohemian, I would never say no to the splendor of your family's summer estate. Especially in the coldest months of the year!"

"And that, Susie Davenport, is why I will love you forever."

Magnolia Bluff was one of the original estates on the Westchester waterfront. Built by Ruth's grandfather, Thomas Emeraldine, after he acquired the Western Railroad, the Tudor mansion was the toast of the summer season. Adorned with striking pitched copper roofs, the elegant main house was ornamented with sturdy but sophisticated herringbone-patterned brick, complemented by accents of wood on the stucco lower walls. It sat on an enviable land outcropping with the sea on three sides, and the property's expansive lawns and gardens were designed to take full advantage of the cool ocean breeze. In spite of its seeming formality, Magnolia Bluff held the majority of Ruth's most treasured childhood memories. It was the only place where she and

Harry could just be for weeks on end, happily swimming in the sound, sunning on their small stretch of sand, and riding bikes to the confectionery for Mary Janes and Hershey's bars.

The first few summers after Harry died, Ruth felt that her once joyful retreat had become more of a haunted house. The smell of fresh-cut grass mingling with the mild tang of the sea, the peaceful embrace of the canopy of trees that lined the long drive, the craggy rock stairs leading down to the water, all of it just reminded her of how alone she felt without her brother. How he would have marveled at the transformation of their once-quiet village. With the new D. W. Griffith studio on Mr. Flagler's old estate, her mother's parties were now often frequented by Douglas Fairbanks and Mary Pickford, and the yacht club had moved, expanding membership to include many insufferable young men that Harry would have loved to dissect and teasingly suggest to Ruth as suitable mates. But without Harry, all the joy of the seaside home was gone.

By the time Robert entered her life, Ruth avoided Magnolia Bluff in summer altogether, preferring to go when the house stood empty. Her parents thought she was mad, but she found it comforting, perhaps because the gloominess of a beach town in winter better matched her mood. The damp, dark rooms and covered furniture, the cold, windy beach and empty streets—she found it peaceful somehow.

Now that she was officially engaged, she knew it was time to clean out the ghosts of Harry and reclaim it as her own.

"Isn't there anyone at Magnolia Bluff to feed us?" Robert asked, amused when he found Ruth packing a picnic basket of provisions for their first weekend there.

Ruth smiled. "I'm afraid this isn't like the summers in Newport with your Yalies. Mr. Gilbert will open the house for us and keep the fires going in the bedroom and study, but he is the only staff in the off-season. We will really be on our own." She looked at him nervously, worried that he might be displeased and unsure how she would handle it if he were. "Is that all right?"

"Wonderful! Like camping. As long as I have my reading and my fiancée, I need nothing more." Ruth welled up with joy. There weren't many men who would be willing to set aside the comforts of a staffed townhouse for a weekend of roughing it by the blustery shore. Just another sign that they were truly perfect partners.

By the time they pulled up to the house, the sun was muted and low in the sky. The bare trees bent in the strong wind and the peaked roofs cast long shadows, obscuring the ornate details of the house's facade. Ruth worried that Robert would be put off by the coldness of it all. "Should we hunker down in front of the fire for the evening? We can walk outside tomorrow, when the sun is out and the air's a bit warmer?"

"What would you do if you were here alone, my darling?"

"Well." Ruth paused. "I'd go to the beach." Ruth connected the beach with her brother. She knew it was silly but, somehow, she felt that when she was there, at the edge of the shore, he was still with her.

"Well then, to the beach we will go."

Ruth rang the bell. Mr. Gilbert opened the door and quickly came outside to carry their things into the dark foyer. Robert, meanwhile, offered Ruth his arm, and she led him down the stone path, past the gardens and dormant trees to the craggy rock-lined shore. "Why, look at that, an island perfect for exploring. Do people swim out there in summer?"

"Of course! The island is actually part of the estate. Harry and I used to race there all the time when we were children."

Ruth smiled at the memory, as her mind drifted to being thirteen. She had had another fight with her mother. Helen simply couldn't understand Ruth's *peculiar interests*: climbing trees, ruining her hair in the ocean, and trying to study those "gruesome" medical books that filled her father's library, when she could have been trying on dresses and attending parties. "You really should have been born a boy, then I wouldn't have to worry about finding a husband for you."

Ruth was so distraught by the time she found Harry playing tennis with Marie, a girl who lived farther down the shore, that she demanded he put down his racket and come swimming. When he told her to get lost, Ruth stormed off. This summer he only had eyes for Marie.

It felt heavy and hot like August, even though it was only late May, and the swimming wouldn't really be tolerable until at least the Fourth of July. Still, the water beckoned, and Ruth wanted to answer its call. Harry be damned.

Ruth always waded in slowly, savoring the torture of the cold creeping up her body. This day the water was so icy that when it reached her waist, she forced herself all the way under to get the shock over with. She felt so alive as the enveloping chill took away all other thoughts for just a moment. She immediately broke into a vigorous crawl to warm herself.

Ruth was an excellent swimmer, stronger even than Harry. Her mind went blank as she got lost in the rhythm of her stroke—the reach of her long arms toward the island, the rapid kick of her legs away from the shore, and the steady turn and lift of her head for air.

Kick, kick, kick, kick. Stroke, stroke, breathe.

Kick, kick, kick, kick. Stroke, stroke, breathe.

She paused for a moment to see if she was nearing the island's shore. She still had quite a distance to go and she was beginning to feel fatigued. Maybe the water was too cold. Not wanting to risk anything, she decided she should turn back and accelerated her kick to bring her to shore faster. Suddenly a sharp pain overcame her. The back of her leg felt like a rubber band that had been pulled so taut it would snap. Instinct took over and she reached to grab her leg, which made it worse. Now she was afraid to move, afraid she would tear something. But she knew if she didn't move, she would drown.

She fixed her gaze on the shore, hoping to see movement, someone to help her. There was no one. She tried to stay calm and began to wave her arms, kicking her other leg as best she could. She screamed for help as she began to sink, flailing more aggressively, her awkward twists and turns driving her under the surface. "Help!" she coughed, splashing with all her might. She thought she could see a figure darting across the lawn toward the water's edge but feared she might be imagining it. And then she sank under completely, the water engulfing her. It felt as if time had slowed dramatically. Ruth tried to get to the surface, but her body felt so heavy. It was so cold. She didn't want this to be the end, but there was something eerily calming about slowly sinking to the bottom, so peaceful she thought maybe she should just let go, let go, let . . . but then he was there—*Harry!* Grabbing her around the waist and pulling her to the surface. He seemed so strong, treading water while he turned her on her back so she could breathe and float, and then swimming her to the safety of the rocky shore.

"What the hell were you thinking?" Harry screamed, not even trying to hold back the tears as he fought to catch his breath.

"I got a cramp." Ruth was dizzy, not entirely comprehending what had just happened. "I tried to call for you, but . . ."

"What do you expect swimming in the ocean when it is so cold? I told you it was too early to come out here! And then you went anyway. Alone?"

"You said 'no thanks.' What you always say about spending time with me lately. I—" She coughed, and some spit and salt came out with her breath. "I thought I ought to get used to being by myself since you hate me now."

"Hate you?" Harry's dimple appeared on the middle of his left cheek, the dimple he detested because it made it impossible for him to hide when he was really happy. He hugged Ruth as tightly as he could. "Ruthie, you are my best friend. My best family. There is no one in the world more important to me than you." He looked at her seriously and she saw in his eyes how very wrong she had been. He might fancy Marie, but his deepest bond was to her, as was hers to him. "Ruthie." He took her pinkie with his own. "I swear to you, no matter what happens, no matter where we are, it is you and me against the world. Always."

"Always." She returned the pinkie promise with a nudge on the shoulder and a wide smile.

Chapter Six

After that first trip, Ruth and Robert spent most weekends at Magnolia Bluff. They adored the endless hours in the wood-paneled library, curled on leather club chairs with snifters of brandy in front of the roaring fire. Robert loved that the peace of the shore allowed him to focus on his work beyond the hospital. He planned to present his latest project, a new method to photograph activity in the brain, at the Neurological Congress in London the following summer. Ruth and Robert agreed that this would be an ideal honeymoon, so in spite of how many months away it was, they decided to plan the wedding around the trip. Given their age (and the fact that they were already cohabitating, unbeknownst to her parents), Ruth would have preferred to get married as soon as possible, but she did love the idea of a "working" honeymoon. And this would give her mother ample time to plan the event.

With Helen Emeraldine at the helm of the planning, Ruth's wedding, in June of 1935, was the event of the summer season. Ruth took control of the few things that mattered to her. She insisted that she and Robert take their vows in front of the setting sun, with the "aisle" a lane in the crab apple grove, and the "altar" a clearing with views of Oyster Bay across the sound. She also opted to wear a simple white suit by Coco Chanel instead of the sumptuous draped satin gown from Vionnet that Helen advocated for. But, beyond these details, she let her mother have free rein.

The lavish affair showcased Magnolia Bluff in all its glory. After the simple ceremony, the guests moved to the great lawn, where waiters served the increasingly scarce beluga caviar by the pounds, along with buttery baked oysters Rockefeller on silver trays; champagne was served in clean-cut art deco coupes made especially for the occasion by Baccarat, and the string section of the New York Philharmonic played in the background. The cocktail hour was followed by a dinner of Waldorf salad and curried lamb—Robert's favorite—and dancing in the adjacent ballroom. Helen had secured Louis Armstrong's orchestra, the one extravagance that Ruth truly appreciated, since the joyful sound of a big band would forever remind her of the moment at the El Morocco when she realized Robert was her destiny.

There were many moments of her wedding that were truly special: seeing Bernard gaze at her with an expression that, almost, looked like pride as she made her way down the aisle on his arm; dancing gleefully with Robert to the swinging sounds of the orchestra until her feet were too sore to stand; and then the toast by Susie. Robert didn't have many close friends and didn't speak to his brothers, so they hadn't had a traditional wedding party. They were each other's best man and maid of honor and hadn't anticipated anyone speaking on their behalf. Still, Ruth shouldn't have been surprised when the petite, spunky redhead stood and began to tap her knife against her wineglass to silence the crowd. This was Susie Davenport, after all.

"I won't take up too much of your time, pinkie promise." She waved her pinkie in the air dramatically. "But I couldn't possibly let this momentous event pass without saying at least *a few* words. First, I must raise a glass to Mr. and Mrs. Emeraldine, our generous hosts this evening. I've been to one or two shindigs in my lifetime and I can say with confidence that this one takes the cake. Helen Emeraldine—you throw one hell of a party!" At this point in the evening, cocktails had been freely flowing for hours, and even the most proper guests laughed and nodded along. Susie just had a way of endearing herself to all, even as she sat at the table with Meg as her date beside her. "And then, on to the main event—the gorgeous giraffe in the white getup and her brilliant new husband. Raffey, you are one of a kind. A woman with the biggest heart, smartest mind, and longest legs of anyone I have ever met. The world is a better place with you in it and, Robert, you make this spectacular gal even more special. Thank you for showing her what love can be. To the most dynamic woman I know and the first man to keep up with her. May you together be forever unstoppable!"

Everyone in the room, even Bernard and Helen, smiled and lifted their glasses a second time, and while Ruth did not typically appreciate the spotlight, she couldn't help but enjoy being celebrated in this way, especially by her parents. To be the reason for their joy for the first time. Given all that her family had been through, they deserved this joyful moment. But even though it was absolutely perfect, they never forgot even for a moment how much better it would have been if Harry had been there too.

Chapter Seven

On July 17, 1935, the newly wedded Dr. and Mrs. Robert Apter boarded the SS *Manhattan*, the official steamer of the Second International Neurological Congress, to make their way to London for the main event. Robert had signed them up for the complete tour—with several stops in England on the way to London, and an extension in Brussels and Paris after the congress. While many newlyweds would look at three weeks of travel with a host of American neurologists—punctuated in the middle by a multiday meeting in a large university hall—as a downright rotten way to spend their honeymoon, for Ruth, it was a dream come true. She might have protested the extension, as it would add an additional week away from her patients, but she supposed it would be romantic to have a moonlit stroll with Robert in Paris, perhaps even a kiss in front of the Eiffel Tower. It would certainly be a much better visit than past trips when her mother dragged her to the family's pied-à-terre for endless days at the ateliers of every major couturier.

As an added benefit, the travel to the Continent and the days of touring with other US delegates offered an unprecedented opportunity for her to connect with some of the greatest minds in the field. Ruth didn't expect to attend the congress itself, so she seized the opportunity to meet and speak to the men during her days on the ship.

She felt fortunate that Robert treated her as a colleague even in this setting. During their elaborate dinners on the ship, he always included her in his conversations with the other neurologists. Instead of relegating her to insufferable discussions about cabin and dining room décor or the merits of the ship's chef with the other wives who were taking advantage of the European holiday this conference offered them, Robert welcomed Ruth into debates about the role of early childhood trauma in the developing brain, and explanations of the study of cerebral spinal fluid in disease diagnosis.

The most interesting dinner companion during their pre-congress travels was by far John Fulton. Ruth learned that he was transporting several chimpanzees in the ship's cargo hold for a presentation about the prefrontal lobe. She marveled at the idea of bringing monkeys on a transcontinental voyage, but more than that, she had learned from Robert that the brain's prefrontal lobe might be important in developing new approaches in the treatment of insanity. She made a note to encourage Robert to attend Dr. Fulton's presentation at the congress. She would have loved to observe it herself, but that was too much to hope for.

When the first morning of the Second International Neurological Congress finally arrived, Robert roused her with the rising sun. "Wake up, wake up! We need to eat so we can get our exhibition properly installed before the day begins."

Ruth looked at Robert quizzically. "*Our* exhibition?"

"Why, yes, we need to set up all my photos and research properly so they can be seen by as many attendees as possible!"

"You want me to come with you?" She hadn't dared to consider that Robert would invite her to join him at the actual congress. In fact, at her mother's insistence, she had even arranged a dreaded day of shopping with Mona von Bismarck, and that dull socialite only had two topics of conversation: the latest fashions and the wealthy older gentlemen she always seemed to be dating. Having an excuse to skip that was enough to make Ruth gleeful in its own right, but if she was to be at the congress . . . why, it was just too exciting to imagine.

"Of course, my darling. I expect you to be by my side for the entirety of the program. I know how much this interests you. Besides, there are *so* many demonstrations that we'll undoubtedly need two sets of eyes just to take it all in!"

Ruth scrambled out of bed and went immediately to the closet. She would likely be the only woman at the convention and needed to dress as professionally as possible. She selected a brown jacket and simple pleated skirt in a dusty rose, with a modest hat to top off the ensemble. As she laced up her oxfords, she laughed to herself, thinking her mother would be appalled by her choice of shoes without a heel, but she would be on her feet all day and didn't want her mind distracted by discomfort.

Robert explained the basic format of the next several days while they ate a small breakfast of eggs and toast, and then taxied to Gower Street to the University College. As they walked through the columned portico of the imposing institution, the sight of what she estimated to be over two hundred men setting up small demonstrations stunned her. She held tight to the map, worried that she might get lost without it. Robert, on the other hand, strolled casually, smiling and nodding at colleagues and seeming entirely at ease. Having attended the first congress in Bern several years prior, Robert knew many of the European delegates busily preparing to tout their latest research on the floor of the Great Hall.

Ruth was buzzing. Being able to listen, learn, and mingle with this breadth of great thinkers eclipsed every slight from her childhood, every moment she had been locked out of Bernard's study, every time she had been deemed a "foolish girl."

"Oh, this is excellent, I think they have put us next to Dr. Egas Moniz!" Robert waved in the direction of an older man who looked quite unwell. "Dr. Moniz?" Striding ahead of Ruth, Robert reached for the bulbous, swollen hand of the man occupying the stall next to theirs. "Dr. Robert Apter. I am honored to meet you, sir. I saw your presentation on cerebral angiography and was quite impressed. I, too, have developed a technique for capturing images of the brain. It is what I will be demonstrating here this week!"

"Well, there will surely only be one method adopted." Ruth had a hard time discerning Dr. Moniz's response through his heavy accent, but she had no problem hearing his sharp and cutting tone. How rude. They were colleagues. All research would lead to progress—wasn't that the point of sharing in a forum such as this?

"Ah, Dr. Moniz, I am sure you are right, but I would love to show you my technique, just to see what you think." Robert smiled, whistling as he pulled papers and images from his valise. Ruth was proud of Robert for maintaining a friendly demeanor toward this nasty man. As she watched him show some of his photographs to Dr. Moniz, who began to nod more encouragingly, Ruth was impressed, yet again, by her husband's seemingly limitless confidence.

The four-day congress sped by in a blur. By the time they reached their suite at the Metropole on the final evening, Ruth's body felt like it was moving through the ocean in an opposing current. It took every bit of energy to amble over to the settee and move aside the pile of the papers she collected during the presentations; once there, she flopped down like a rag doll. Robert, on the other hand, was more energized than ever. He paced the room excitedly, talking without pause.

"I think it is quite clear that the epilepsies are not one single disease but a collection of diseases within the brain."

"I agree." Ruth tried to engage in conversation in spite of her deep fatigue. "And I thought it was a fascinating and clever use of electroencephalography to better understand the epileptic seizures. We need to do more of that cross-purposing of equipment at the hospital. It would help justify the expense of some of these machines."

"Good thinking, I will keep that in mind if I bring you any requisition proposals." He nodded encouragingly as he filled a glass with water and continued to talk through the highlights of the days. "What about that paper by Otto Sitting? Proposing that Hughlings Jackson's view of the unconscious anticipated that of Freud's? Ha!"

"I thought you might have enjoyed that." She smiled, knowing that Robert reviled the popularity of Freud's analytic approaches to disorders Robert thought were neurological, and welcomed any research that discredited the originality of the renowned psychologist's ideas. "And what did you think of the doctors from Yale?"

"Fantastic! You were right to make note of Dr. Fulton when we were on the ship. He and Dr. Jacobsen are doing some terrific work in his primate research lab. Their presentation was the jewel of the congress!"

"I thought so too. In fact, I was considering inviting them down for a guest lecture when we return to the States. What do you think?"

"Excellent idea. I'm sure we could arrange for it. And I'd love to have some more time with them. I think their research on the frontal lobe is potentially groundbreaking. I am quite sure that there is something there that will help treat lunacy. I still haven't pulled it all together in my head, but I cannot wait to begin to pursue this avenue of thinking."

As she and Robert continued discussing the many presentations, Ruth was surprised that he made no mention of his own exhibition—his work on cerebral imaging. To Ruth, it seemed clear by the close of the congress that Egas Moniz's cerebral angiography would likely eclipse Robert's method for photographing the brain. Moniz had, after all, been given his own slot to present his work, unlike Robert, who was relegated to the general exhibition hall. Ruth thought the promotion of Robert's idea had been the impetus for their trip; yet, Robert seemed on top of the world.

Never one to be delicate, Ruth asked directly, "Robert, what did you think about Dr. Moniz's presentation? You know I initially found the man to be quite pompous and rude, but hearing him speak, I realized that he has a very impressive mind."

"I told you as much. I was quite inspired by him at the first congress."

"What did you make of his cerebral angiography this time?"

"Oh, that?" Robert shrugged her question off with a dismissive turn of his head, and she was suddenly worried she had wounded him. "Dr. Moniz has clearly figured this out already. His method will win the favor of the medical community. There are simply fewer risks. And I am not one to fight for an inferior idea if a better one has been found."

"You are remarkable, Robert." Ruth grabbed his hand tenderly as he paced past her. "A lesser man would be threatened."

"On the contrary, I am invigorated by the work of the Portuguese doctor. And I consider it my great fortune to have had this time to get to know him better. I am actually hoping that I will be able to correspond with him now that we have spent several days together. Did you notice that Dr. Moniz was feverishly taking notes during Fulton and Jacobsen's presentation? I wonder what he is contemplating."

"What do you suspect?"

"Well, you remember what Fulton and Jacobsen did, right?" Robert paused before taking on a professorial tone, deliberate in his movements and language as if to ensure that she understood what he was saying. If Ruth weren't so enamored with her new husband, she might have found the affect off-putting. Of course she remembered what they did. They had just been discussing it. Still, she was entranced by Robert's enthusiasm. "They removed some of the chimp's white brain matter, the attachments in the prefrontal lobe. Becky and Lucy, our primate cruising companions"—he winked—"who had been prone to violent outbursts before surgery, lost all their aggressive tendencies. Even after making the same mistakes that had sent them into a rage before. Essentially the same triggers no longer elicited the same violent response."

"So, you think that because these chimpanzees were made calm by altering their frontal lobes that . . ."

"That my hypothesis may be right? Yes! It is quite possible that there is a relationship between aggressive and unpredictable behavior and the neurological conditions in the frontal lobe. Imagine if we could find these connections and sever the bad ones? We could eliminate negative behaviors. I am not sure of the mechanics of it all, but I am almost certain Dr. Moniz was thinking about the same thing. This could be the beginning of a whole new approach to mental health treatment! Something much bigger than my minor cerebral imaging. I don't know exactly how or when, but I have a feeling that we are on the precipice of something huge." Robert crossed back to Ruth, grabbing her hand and lifting her to stand. "I know you are tired, but I simply can't let this evening go to waste. Please, let's go out and celebrate!"

Ruth wasn't sure she could keep her eyes open, let alone stand atop her two feet, but for Robert, she would try her very best. If he wanted to celebrate, she surely wouldn't be the one to stop him.

Chapter Eight

Ruth had a spring in her step as she walked down the corridor. The shining sun reflected in the thresholds of the open doors, beckoning her inside each room. While she had enjoyed every moment of her honeymoon, she was overjoyed to be back to work. The stacks of papers that had accrued on her desk would take her days to organize and, she reasoned, if they had waited this long, they could wait a few more hours. Her most important order of the day was visiting her patients.

The low-level din of chatter, laughter, and even moans of discomfort sounded like music to her ears today. She had decided to reverse her usual order and started in the private wing, where the morning painting class was underway. This way she could see all her wealthy "ladies" at once before moving to the state-sponsored patients in the hospital's other wings. As she entered the painting studio, she stood with cheerful enthusiasm, watching two women sketching with charcoals and waiting patiently for them to notice her. But the women were too focused on their canvases, so she approached them gently. "Good morning, ladies, what are you drawing today?"

"Miss Emeraldine!" An older woman leapt from her chair so quickly that the tall feather on her blue hat almost fell off. "You're here!"

"Mrs. Leighton! Why, you look awfully festive today." Ruth took in the woman, her face heavily made up, pink lipstick covering several of her front teeth. In addition to her elaborate hat, she had on a floor-length gown and several layers of necklaces and bracelets. "Your gown and hat, and those jewels . . . did you know I was coming?"

"These are paste," the woman said with disdain. "I wouldn't trust Louise here to get near my real diamonds." Mrs. Leighton turned her head snidely away from the woman next to her. "Those are in the safe deposit at my bank. Won't tell you which one. Don't want you to try to steal them either."

"I wouldn't dare." Ruth smiled, happy to be back in the midst of this particular kind of crazy. Evelyn Leighton had been a well-known Broadway actress, until a rumored affair with one of her leading men had apparently brought on an incurable psychosis. Her husband brought her to Emeraldine claiming he could no longer manage her hysteria himself—plagued as he was by the shame of having been made into a cuckold—but Ruth knew he never stopped loving her. He still paid handsomely for Evelyn to have her own private quarters, moved in a good portion of her wardrobe, and even arranged for her to go on supervised outings to private stagings on occasion.

"See, Louise, I told you she would be back"—she twirled triumphantly—"and here she is!"

"Evelyn, you old hag, stop acting like a child." Louise kept her gaze fixed on her paper, and Ruth felt she was refusing to look at her.

"Mrs. Dillington, were you worried I wasn't coming back?" Ruth walked around to Louise's chair. The woman wore a smart tweed suit, although her bobbed blond hair hung greasily on her head. When was the last time she had a bath? Ruth wondered as she took hold of Louise Dillington's charcoal-blackened hands and bent down to try to make eye contact. "I was away for an awfully long time, wasn't I?"

"I got two years older while you were gone!" Louise pulled her hands from Ruth's and kept her gaze fixed on her pad.

"Darling, I was only gone for a few weeks. And I know for a fact that you will turn thirty in October. Remember, we discussed a special strawberry shortcake to celebrate the occasion?" Louise's face melted into recognition and she managed a nod. "Oh my, look at that. What a terrific study of a pigeon. Have you been taking extra art lessons while I've been gone?"

"No. Just our usual schedule," Louise answered flatly. She seemed depressed, refusing to be even the slightest bit playful with Ruth. When she was in one of her better moods, she was the first to engage in friendly banter. Ruth was always especially pleased when these happier stretches included the weekend, so that Louise could enjoy the visits from her husband, who came to see her, diligently, every Saturday. But Ruth could see that she was in no mood for light conversation today.

"Mrs. Dillington, you know that I was away because I recently got married, right? It was my honeymoon." Louise nodded again but remained cold. "Well, I can promise you that I won't be going anywhere again for the foreseeable future. I hope we will be able to resume our afternoon walks. My waterside boardwalk project is nearly complete, and I would love to show you our progress. Now, ladies, since it is my very first day back at the hospital after my trip, I am afraid I am only here for a brief hello. I'll be back for a longer visit later this week, I promise, and I will look forward to seeing your progress on your drawings!"

Louise gave a small nod of acknowledgment as Ruth exited the room. Evelyn waved. "Welcome home."

Home. Ruth hadn't realized how much she missed this until now. As she walked purposefully down the hallway, she made a mental note to check in with Louise Dillington's doctor. It seemed she might need an ice bath or a course of convulsions to break her current depressive state.

As much as she would have loved to visit with everyone, there was one girl in particular whom she was most anxious to see. Penelope Connor had been a patient at the hospital for several years now. The poor woman had had an awful bout of bad luck, having lost her parents to influenza as a child. She then married a schemer who left her as soon as he discovered that her money was locked up in a trust administered by her aunt. When Penelope moved back into her aunt's home, she began harming herself regularly in an effort to "stay clean," and devolved into periodic fits of fury. Penelope's aunt had the money in the trust to set Penelope up quite comfortably at Emeraldine, and over the years, she never failed to pay a bill on time. Ever since she dropped Penelope and her trunks at the hospital several years prior, however, her aunt had not visited once. Ruth felt for Penelope and believed that, with the proper support, the woman could surely be cured.

Penelope hadn't been in art class as Ruth had expected. Now, her room was empty and looked as if it had been for several days. Ruth felt her heart pounding faster. Was the young woman ill? "Nurse Riley?" she called down the hall to a figure bustling with a small white hat atop her head. "Is that you?"

"Miss Emeraldine. Welcome back!"

"It is Mrs. Apter now." Ruth smiled as the nurse approached her. "Where is Penelope Connor? I was hoping to see her this morning."

"Ah, congratulations on the wedding, Mrs. Apter!" Nurse Riley shook Ruth's hand, smiling before her expression turned sour. "Penelope, I am afraid, has been transferred to the security wing."

"What? That can't be right! What happened?"

"I told them you would be upset when they transferred her, Miss . . . Mrs. Apter. But when you were away, Penelope started up again. Picking at herself and washing so much her fingers were bleeding, and she started to get scabs on her face so bad I worried about infection. I tried to get her into the continuous-flow bath, and she started throwing things, almost took my eye out with the edge of a book! I told the doctor I was okay, but he insisted she needed to be restrained and, well, it's not my place to tell him otherwise. I'm just a regular old nurse—not like you." She smiled earnestly at Ruth.

"Oh my." Ruth shook her head as she started walking quickly toward the exit of the ward. "Thank you for trying, Nurse Riley," she called over her shoulder. "And keep up the excellent work."

Ruth hurried through several buildings, across one of the hospital's inner courtyards, and down a set of stairs to the secure lower level. While a ten-foot iron fence fortified the perimeter of the entire hospital to ensure the inmates didn't wander out onto the streets of Manhattan, they were relatively free to move about their own wards. The secure wings, on the other hand, featured a series of bars and doors, much like a jail. A secure area was necessary for the safety of the patients and the staff, but Ruth still shuddered as she unlocked the gates with her master key. She couldn't imagine why Penelope, who had always been so gentle, would be placed in here.

When she finally arrived at Penelope's room, Ruth's sunny greeting of "Hello, Penny!" turned into a distressed gasp as she took in the scene in front of her. "Why is she in restraints like that?" Ruth welled with rage. Penelope was a slight woman, no more than ninety-five pounds, and not only had they removed her from the comfort of her room in the ladies' wing, they had placed her here among the most violent and difficult of all of Emeraldine's patients and immobilized her in a tight straitjacket.

"Doctor's orders, Miss. You'll have to ask him."

"Oh, I intend to, but in the meantime, I insist that you remove them. Penelope is as gentle as a lamb. There is no need for her to be restrained in this way. Penny, dear, are you all right?" Penelope nodded, but as Ruth looked at her face, she saw it was covered with scratches and scabs, her eyes rimmed red from crying and ringed with the black circles of sleeplessness. "Oh dear, you've been scrubbing and picking again?" Ruth tried to catch her gaze, but Penelope dropped her head, looking at the floor.

"I'm sorry."

"It's all right." Ruth encircled Penelope in a gentle embrace. Turning again to the orderly, she said with quiet emphasis, "Please, remove these restraints at once. This woman does not need to be bound this way." She watched him hesitate. "Sir, do you know who I am?" He stared at her like a stunned deer. "I am the assistant superintendent of this hospital. I can assure you that if Dr. Chisolm knew I was giving this order, he would oblige. And, I can also promise that I plan to take up these inappropriate actions with him straight away."

While the man hesitantly followed her directive, she went to the hallway sink to warm a washcloth and returned to Penelope's bedside, where she began gently stroking her head. As soon as the orderly left, Penelope burst into tears.

"I thought you were gone. That you had left me! I'm so sorry. I was so nervous. And I was just trying to stay clean. To stay healthy. But they told me to stop washing my hands. And wouldn't let me clean my face. But I had to get clean!"

"It is all right, Penelope. Remember that I told you I was going to get married and then be away for a bit on my honeymoon?"

"But Mother and Father were supposed to only be in the sanitarium for a short while and they never came back."

"Darling, I know you miss them. That awful influenza took many lives. But"—she lifted Penelope's chin to look her in the eyes—"remember what we talked about? It did not take yours! You are strong. You survived. And these preoccupations you developed can be fixed. We are going to get you better."

"I want that, I really do. But sometimes these feelings just overwhelm me, and I can't stop them."

"Well, the first thing we need to do is get you out of this ward. We need to get back to our chess matches and maybe even a little dancing in the social hall." Ruth looked at her with a reassuring smile and watched Penelope's face begin to brighten. "It will take me a bit of time to get the transfer back to the private wing in order. In the meantime, let's at least get you to the hydrotherapy room for a nice warm bath."

"Oh no, not the bath!" Penelope began to writhe.

"Why not? You love the warm baths, remember?"

"When you were gone, they tricked me and it was freezing. I couldn't feel my body. And they wouldn't let me out, they wouldn't . . ." She shook her head violently, her eyes squeezed shut, as if she was reexperiencing the discomfort.

"It sounds like they didn't know you can't tolerate the cold. I am sorry, what a bit of confusion while I was gone! I promise you that this will be the warm bath. I will see to it myself." Ruth smiled and grabbed Penelope's hand. "You just wait here, and I will take care of everything."

It was nine o'clock in the evening by the time Ruth and Robert were ready to leave the hospital. Ruth checked in on Penelope and was pleased to find her peacefully sleeping, back in her old bed in her elegantly appointed room. Her hair was washed, she wore a clean nightgown and robe, and there were no new scabs on her face. "Sleep well, my dear," Ruth whispered as she tucked the blanket gently around Penelope's slight frame. It had been a long but rewarding first day back.

Chapter Nine

"Oh, what a lovely floral arrangement. Ruth, can I assume that you have finally decided to let Monsieur Garneil add you to his schedule for weekly delivery?"

Ruth plastered a forced smiled on her face as she nodded at her mother. Ruth loved fresh-cut flowers. She had fond memories of collecting them with her grandmother Sophia in the gardens at Magnolia Bluff. Ruth and her grandmother didn't have much in common. Sophia was the archetype of a society lady and generally found Ruth's lack of interest in that world even more perplexing than Helen did, but she and Ruth had a shared love of nature. The only time Sophia allowed herself to get dirty was when she was out in the garden. When she could, she preferred to tend to her vegetables, herbs, and the many varietals of exotic blooms that she had planted there, herself—and Ruth loved to spend hours on end helping. She loved to feel the velvety softness of ripe peony petals, and smell their delicate perfume, to create rainbow arrays from the long stems of vibrant gladiolus, to nibble on freshly clipped mint and basil. But having blossoms delivered to your doorstep only to be tossed a few days later when they died seemed so excessive. She would much rather use her money to help people. Still, Robert liked having them in the house. And it pleased her mother when she and Bernard came for their now-monthly dinners. So, Ruth compromised. Each week, she gave the same amount of money that she spent on flowers to Susie, to distribute in the immigrant neighborhoods. This way, she was at least doing something worthy to offset the frivolity.

Ruth marveled at the many small ways her life had changed in the nine months she and Robert had been married. Although they lived together before marriage, they "officially" moved into her four-story townhouse when they returned from their honeymoon. The location on East Twenty-Sixth Street was ideal. It was an easy commute to the hospital and adjacent to—but still comfortably tucked away around the corner from—the action of Madison Square Park. When they sat in the interior garden, they enjoyed a quiet break from the bustle of the city. Now, thanks to Robert and Helen, the house had transformed from a casual place, haphazardly festooned with an eclectic mix of Helen's castoffs, into a proper home.

Robert felt that since they were innovators in medicine, their house should reflect their forward-thinking approach. He embraced the simplified furnishings of the Bauhaus school, which celebrated function over ornamentation, and he enlisted his new mother-in-law to execute his vision. Helen loved the idea of decorating a modern home. While this new trend was entirely inappropriate for her and Bernard's own houses, Helen agreed that it suited Ruth and Robert perfectly. So, with Robert's blessing and Ruth's reluctant agreement, she transformed Ruth's formerly hodgepodge house into a contemporary masterpiece.

Ruth liked that her home looked nothing like any place she had ever lived before. Chrome, leather, and lacquer instead of velvet, chintz, and carved wood. It felt like the heralding of a new era.

Robert also had the idea to host Bernard and Helen for dinner once a month. Helen was delighted that her daughter was finally assuming the role of a proper wife (even though it wasn't actually the case). Ruth had never entertained, and in spite of the fact that she had both a cook and a housekeeper, the evenings when Helen and Bernard came to dinner made her extremely anxious. She spent the entire week leading up to each of these meals planning a menu, deliberating over whether or not to include other guests, and determining what to wear. While she couldn't understand how her mother relished these banalities, she did gain a greater appreciation of the work that went into them.

With their shared love of design, Robert and Helen had become quite close. Unfortunately, the same could not be said of Robert and her father. Bernard had taken to Robert in the beginning, but in the past few months, Ruth had seen a change that made family visits even more unnerving. This evening, as they sat in the living room after dinner, with Helen and Ruth perched on the sleek, tightly upholstered sofa, and Bernard and Robert sitting in the leather and chrome Breuer chairs in front of the fireplace, Ruth felt an incredible tension building in the room.

"Father, you really should come to one of Robert's weekend lectures. They tend to be a packed house."

"Yes," Robert said proudly. "Apparently they've become a popular date destination for medical students in the area. The New York School of Medicine has had to start issuing tickets in advance to ensure that everyone has a seat."

"Tickets? For a medical school lecture? How absurd. Seems unlikely."

"Bernard!" Helen gave Ruth's father a disapproving look. "If he is telling you that it is the case, it surely is so. That's exciting, Robert. Perhaps I should come as well?"

"The more the merrier. Although I should warn you that they can be a bit gruesome."

"I am sure they would be of no interest to you, Helen," Bernard barked gruffly.

"Well, even if they aren't for Mother, you would surely enjoy them, Father. Robert puts on quite a show. It's amazing how completely he can engage these students."

"A show? Since when did medical school need to be a show?"

"Sir, it doesn't need to, but I have come to believe that the more absorbed the class becomes in my presentation, the more they retain. It is amazing how watching me dissect the brain of a cadaver goes much farther toward piquing their interest in neurological anatomy than the illustration in the medical textbook." Robert slid farther back in his chair, tugging gently on his goatee and taking a sip of his digestif.

"I would argue that only those who lack an ability to naturally engage their audience need to resort to shock to generate attention. But, if the college is pleased, it is really none of my business."

Ruth watched Robert's expression harden. It was as if, without lifting a finger, her father had smacked him across the face. She knew this feeling all too well, but she hadn't expected to see it elicited in Robert. She sat frozen, furious. She wanted to rail against her father but feared the consequences. Suddenly, her mother again stepped in.

"It *is* none of your business, Bernard." Helen gave her husband a light but chastising look. "A cadaver. Surely a bit much for me to see, but I can imagine it is quite an event." Ruth was overtaken by conflicting emotions: Gratitude that her mother took up Robert's cause. Resentment that she had never done the same for Ruth.

"My students say that it is indeed." Robert smiled at Helen. "Well, it is getting late. I would think you need to be getting home." Robert stood, his voice colder and harder than Ruth had ever heard it before. "Helen, so lovely to see you as always." He put out his hand and helped her up, ignoring Bernard as they made their way out of the living room and toward the door, leaving Ruth and Bernard momentarily alone.

"Father." Ruth hesitated. Did she really want to risk inciting more ire? When he didn't even look up, she continued. "That was a bit cruel. It would be nice to show Robert some support. He is a real asset to the hospital, you know."

"Please, when I am confronted with inanity, it is my duty to point it out. Any man who needs sycophancy to feel good about himself isn't much of a man."

Ruth simmered as Bernard stood and walked to the front door.

"Good night," he said stiffly and generally, not shaking Robert's hand, nor kissing Ruth's cheek.

"Good night, dear." Helen embraced her daughter awkwardly, and as her parents made their way down the steps into the chauffeured car, Ruth grabbed Robert's hand and held it tightly.

She knew that her father wanted to be the only titan in the family, but he was going to be challenged. Robert was on the verge of a breakthrough; Ruth was sure of it. The only question was when.

Chapter Ten

Ruth and Robert had fallen into an easy routine. During the week, they ate at the tulip bistro table in their small breakfast nook overlooking the garden and then traveled to the hospital together. Typically, they worked much longer hours than the majority of the staff—the evenings, with patients finally asleep, were the best time for Robert to work on his research. Since they married, they didn't frequent the El Morocco or Stork Club often, but Robert still adored a night on the town and, truth be told, Ruth had come to love the evenings of dinner and dancing almost as much as he did. So, occasionally, when Benny Goodman or one of the other big band orchestras played, they would treat themselves to a break from work and indulge in an evening out.

On the weekends, they retreated to Magnolia Bluff. The summer season hadn't yet begun, so they didn't have to worry about her parents. On these quiet weekends, Ruth would bundle up and go for long walks while Robert worked.

On a blustery spring day, she returned to find Robert pacing the length of the main hallway. His hair was unruly, which only happened when he ran his hands through it, deep in thought. Papers were strewn in piles all around the leather wingback by the fire. His shirt was wrinkled and untucked, and his suspenders hung down against his thighs.

"This is it! This is it, Ruthie. I am certain." Robert kept pacing and looked up at her, shaking the thick journal in his hand. "Moniz has done it. Remember the chimpanzees? Moniz has used human subjects. Twenty patients. Twenty!"

"Robert, what on earth?"

"What? Here is what: Moniz has performed a surgery on the brains of twenty patients. I told you at the congress last year that he was planning something. I could just tell. And as I suspected, it is what I've been circling around. He has proven it!"

"Proven what, exactly?"

"The frontal lobe connection. He's figured it out!"

Ruth walked the length of the large oriental rug and stood squarely in Robert's path to stop his perpetual motion. "Can we sit? So I can warm up and you can slow down and explain?" She grabbed his hand and led him back to the study, where she poured them each a snifter of brandy to sip by the fire. "Now what, exactly, has Dr. Moniz done?"

"Remember the presentation we attended in London? Fulton and Jacobsen's chimpanzees?" Ruth nodded. Of course she did. "Well, Moniz has performed his own procedure—a leucotomy, he called it—on twenty patients with varying degrees of psychosis and agitated depression, and not only did every one of them survive, their conditions all improved—less violent, more placid, happy even. This is it, Ruth. The answer is surgical. We have to do brain coring. Emeraldine Hospital can be the place to bring leucotomy to the States and I the one to do it!"

"Do you really think?" Ruth's pulse quickened. Robert's enthusiasm was contagious and she couldn't help but begin to get excited.

"I don't just think, Ruth, I know!" Robert stood up abruptly, shattering the snifter he had placed on the floor.

Ruth looked down at the shards of splintered crystal in a pool of deepening crimson, as the remaining brandy soaked into the rug. The last time broken glass had littered the front of this fireplace was Harry's final visit to Magnolia Bluff. He was so angry when Bernard told him he had to go to Payne Whitney for treatment that he had thrown his glass at the hearth. Ruth hadn't ever seen him snap at their father before.

She wondered now, if this leucotomy had been a possibility for Harry, would the whole course of her life have been different? Would he still be here with her today? She shook off the thought as Robert continued on, oblivious to her momentary lapse into melancholy.

"We need to hire a neurosurgeon . . . as soon as possible. And I think I know just the man for the job. While I understand and can likely navigate every corner of the brain, I'm not equipped to open the cranium of living people on my own. Oh, but once we have this surgeon . . ." Robert turned to Ruth and grabbed her in a hearty embrace. "This is it, my darling! I can feel it in my bones."

Dr. Edward Wilkinson was a young neurosurgeon who had worked under Fulton in the primate lab at Yale. He was particularly interested in Robert's line of inquiry and had sought Robert out after a guest lecture in New Haven. Robert enjoyed the adulation and, sensing a protégé in the making, had stayed in touch with the young doctor over the past several years. He was sure Edward would make the perfect partner for the new project.

While Dr. Wilkinson didn't have much of a professional track record yet, he had glowing recommendations from his professors and a deep determination that, Robert told Ruth, reminded him of his younger self. As soon as Robert had decided that neurosurgery was the key to his new treatment for mental illness, he knew Edward Wilkinson would be the perfect man for the job. Nevertheless, Ruth insisted on a complete search process, interviewing dozens of doctors to ensure she had properly vetted all available candidates. In the end, she agreed Edward was the one.

"He is entirely unlike most of the others I have interviewed, in the best possible way," Ruth said excitedly to her boss.

"Ah yes," Charles Hayden said with a grin. "These neurosurgeons tend to be a rather arrogant bunch, don't they?"

"Spectacularly so! Each one has been more impressed with himself and his accomplishments than the next, and none have seemed to have any interest in the work we are trying to do here. Whereas not only has Dr. Wilkinson worked in the primate research lab, he was the sole applicant to know about Dr. Moniz's leucotomy study."

"Well, to be fair, most in the field wouldn't know about that study. If it weren't for you and your husband, I would be among the men bumbling in the dark on that one."

"You're right, I suppose." Ruth paused thoughtfully. "Perhaps Robert's rubbed off on me too much. I used to tease him for assuming the cutting-edge research that he studies is common knowledge. And now, here I am doing the same!" Ruth smiled at that idea. "Nevertheless, I think Dr. Wilkinson is the man we have been looking for."

Edward Wilkinson carried himself so inconspicuously that it took careful scrutiny to realize how tall and handsome he actually was. His unassuming manner, combined with his obvious intellect, made him stand out to Ruth and, in the end, impressed Hayden in equal measure.

"Dr. Wilkinson, I would love to hear from you directly as to why you are interested in this role, as it is far from a traditional one for a neurosurgeon."

"Yes, sir. Of course. I suppose my interests aren't entirely traditional." He looked up from his fidgeting hands directly at Ruth and Charles, and as his floppy blond hair moved away from his eyes, Ruth was startled by the brightness of their blue hue. "Mr. Hayden, Mrs. Apter, I am endlessly fascinated by the puzzle of the mind. I want to touch it, and to heal it. I want to be the safest, most accurate, most effective surgeon I can possibly be. But I want to use my skills in the name of progress."

"I see. Wonderful. What type of progress do you mean?" Charles nodded encouragingly.

Ruth smiled to herself. She appreciated that Dr. Wilkinson spoke as if performing brain surgery was no more remarkable than delivering milk in the morning, and she knew this would appeal to Charles as well.

"Dr. Apter's research, the studies you are making possible, sir, essentially surgically rewiring the brain for better health, well, it just seems like the greatest use imaginable of any neurosurgeon's training and skill. Dr. Apter has incredible ideas and . . . with his ability to take what he knows from neurology and psychology and marry it with my surgical expertise, why, I believe we might really find new ways to help people. And that is the most I could ever hope for in a career."

"In that case, we would love to have you, Dr. Wilkinson." Charles stood up and walked toward the young man with his hand outstretched. "When can you begin?"

Chapter Eleven

Edward had not been born into a world of privilege. He grew up in the cornfields in Iowa, the third son in a farm family of seven children. From a young age, Edward was interested in the way things worked. He became the farm's go-to mechanic when equipment broke, as he had the patience and meticulousness to carefully take it apart and put it back together again. As he got older, this interest transferred into the field of medicine. It was a great sacrifice for his family to send him to college, let alone medical school, but it was Edward's calling. He worked tirelessly to secure his place at Yale—as well as the scholarship funds to ensure he could assume it—and while his family could offer little in the way of financial support, their pride in his accomplishment was limitless.

Ruth had never met another doctor as indefatigable as Robert—until Edward. The two men immediately fell into a tireless work routine, often remaining at the hospital late into the evening, lost in refining their leucotomy technique.

Edward was shy, but he quickly grew comfortable around Ruth. In spite of the chasm between their backgrounds, they had similar values—helping others was their number one priority—and within a few months, they had developed an easy rapport. He listened to Ruth in a way that Robert sometimes didn't, and he soon became a valued colleague and friend.

Ruth always remained at the hospital until Robert was ready to go home, and with Robert and Edward working so closely, this meant that the three of them usually departed together.

"Robert tells me your surgical technique is unlike anything he's ever seen," Ruth said to Edward one evening as they waited in her office for Robert. "I imagine you have already learned that he does not give a compliment lightly, and he is emphatic that your knowledge of not just the location but the function of every fold and crevice of the brain is moving your research forward at an unexpectedly rapid pace."

Edward blushed. "I think the credit for our progress should really go to your husband."

"Well, it is clear to me that he couldn't do what he is doing without your skill. I do worry, though . . . It is one thing for Robert and me to spend all our time at the hospital, but you." She paused and smiled at him. "You know it is all right for you to have a personal life too?" Ruth couldn't believe she was suggesting this. She sounded like an old-fashioned aunt.

"You don't need to worry about me. I've never been one for much socializing. And our research is moving so quickly, it's exhilarating. It feels like every day brings us nearer to offering the treatment in the hospital. It would be so incredible to change lives this way, to use a surgery to heal an illness that's physiologically imperceptible, but psychologically so apparent. Some days in the lab with your husband, I feel like I'm on the frigid waters of the Antarctic with Roald Amundsen, about to find the South Pole for the first time."

Ruth looked at Edward and knew she'd found a kindred spirit. Pushing him to date would be useless because no woman could rival the allure of their cause. Still, she wanted Edward to have someone of his own. She was about to say as much when Robert came bursting in the door excitedly.

"Eddie, I've received another letter from Moniz. What a generous man he is!"

"Generous?" Ruth laughed. "He might be many things, but Dr. Moniz never seemed the slightest bit generous to me."

"I have to give this one to your husband, Ruth. I'd heard many unpleasant things about Dr. Moniz before Robert started to correspond with him, but he has been incredibly forthcoming with his research."

"Indeed. And this is the best letter yet! Look here—" Robert thrust the paper in Edward's face. "He hasn't only given us the precise details of his surgery; he is supplying us with an introduction to the French manufacturer of his leucotome!"

"That's terrific! I have been struggling to get a proper cut in the lobe with the instruments we have at hand." Edward looked at Ruth to explain. "It's hard to keep the insertion as small as we'd like and still be able to maneuver the instrument the way we need to inside the brain."

"Exactly! Have a look at this." Robert unrolled the diagram. "Moniz is quite clever. The wand has a retractable loop at the tip so, it seems, you can insert it, open and then close the loop, and remove it from the cranium."

Ruth moved to look over Robert's shoulder as he and Edward studied the pages excitedly. "You know, Robert, with all this information, we could start real experiments soon," Edward said.

Robert clapped Edward on the back. "Well, of course, I want to move on to living subjects as soon as we can. But we need a great deal more practice before I would feel comfortable recommending that the hospital begin to experiment on patients."

"Yes, of course, of course." Edward's ears turned red. "I am not saying we begin tomorrow. But I am sure that, with this detailed information, our own leucotomy won't be far off."

"How wonderful that would be," Ruth exclaimed excitedly.

"Shall we head home?" Robert put his hand out for Ruth's.

"Edward, it's so late, would you like to stay over?" she asked, given that their house was nearby and his apartment a long ride on the El.

"I wouldn't want to impose." Edward looked at them sheepishly as he flipped his hair from his face.

"Nonsense, we insist!" Robert smiled, patting his young partner on the back in reassurance as they walked out of Ruth's office.

Ruth had a spring in her step as the three of them exited the building together. Finally, she felt like everything in her life was falling into place.

Chapter Twelve

Ruth flinched as Penelope walked into the recreation room. For several months she had really seemed to be improving, but today, the already-slight woman looked positively skeletal, and Ruth could see scratches on her face from across the room. Ruth stood, trying to hide her disappointment and fear as Penelope made her way closer to the bay window, her favorite seat, for their weekly game of chess.

"Hello, Penny!" Ruth tried to sound light, deciding not to draw any more attention to Penelope's caved-in cheekbones or the deep gashes on her face. She glanced at Penny's fingernails to see if they were long enough to make such marks, and noticed her cuticles were raw and bloody, her hands cracked and dry.

"Stop looking at me!" Penelope snapped.

"Oh, Penny, I am sorry. I am just concerned. Does your face hurt? Have you been eating like we talked about?"

"Stop with all the questions!" Penelope dragged the chair from the small game table with such force that several of the other patients turned to see what caused the commotion. "What are you all looking at?"

"Penny—calm down." Ruth tried to keep her tone firm but soothing. "You know you can't be in here if you behave that way." She felt her stomach tightening as she flashed back to visits with her brother when his behavior was unexpectedly hostile. "I've been looking forward to our game all week. I even practiced with my husband so, perhaps, you wouldn't be able to beat me so terribly this time." Ruth smiled falsely as she started to line up her pieces on her side of the board. Penelope silently arranged hers as well. "Penny, have I done something to upset you?"

"Just play." Ruth had never seen Penelope behave this way. It was as if all the progress she had made in her time at Emeraldine had disappeared, and then some. She had never seen Penelope in worse shape. She refused to accept the backslide.

"Since you were last week's winner, you choose whether to take the opening move or not." Ruth kept her tone steady and upbeat, a skill she had long ago perfected during visits with Harry. Penelope slid her pawn out one space in petulant silence. "I have a feeling you are trying to draw me out already. You are very clever. That's why I love to play with you." Ruth looked up at Penelope and reached to gently pat her arm, testing to see if her anger had abated.

"Take your turn." Penelope withdrew her arm to dodge Ruth's touch. Ruth moved her pawn out two spaces. "I knew you'd do that."

Ruth wouldn't have been surprised if Penelope stuck her tongue out; her behavior today was that childlike.

As their game continued, Ruth grew increasingly concerned. Had Ruth failed her? They had tried every tool available, even psychoanalysis, and still Penelope deteriorated. Ruth had been sure that her patience and steady presence combined with the latest developments in treatment would cure Penelope. She was a smart and well-off woman who just needed help getting control of herself again. Yet, here she was, clearly not eating, tearing apart her own body, and nothing Ruth had done had made a difference.

"Perhaps you are tired today. Maybe we should stop playing and go for a stroll. Or do you want to take a rest?"

"NO!" Penelope yelled. "JUST GO!"

"You want me to leave?" Ruth recoiled slightly.

"No!" Penelope started picking the chessmen off the board and throwing them at Ruth. "I"—she threw a pawn, which bounced off Ruth's chest—"meant"—the knight hit Ruth's shoulder—"make your move! But you ruined it!" Rook, queen, and king all came at Ruth's face rapid-fire, clipping her cheek, and two orderlies ran over, forcefully grabbing Penelope to immobilize her.

"It's all right, I'm okay." Ruth stood, holding her cheek, where one of the pieces had made a small gash. "Penny." She looked sharply at the woman. "You need to go have a rest." Turning to the orderlies, she said quietly, "Please be sure someone stays with her. I will send the doctor shortly."

"I spent three hours this afternoon reading diagnostic profiles for Penelope's condition, and I am still not sure what is causing her to decompensate this way," Ruth lamented to Robert and Edward over dinner in the small garden behind their townhouse. "She's becoming angrier and more self-destructive. Her obsessive and manic episodes continue to intensify, in spite of adding fever chambers and metra-zol-induced shock to her treatment regimen. How can none of this be helping her condition to improve?"

"Ruth, you need to temper your emotional attachments to every patient. Your oversized heart is part of what makes you so beloved with them, of course, but it is your oversized brain that makes you good at your job. You know patients like her are easily triggered. And, the unfortunate fact is that often, once deterioration begins, there is almost no known treatment to reverse the effects. Well, no treatment as yet, right, Eddie?" Robert looked at Edward, the corners of his mustache turning up in a tentative smile.

"Robert? What are you suggesting?"

"We have seen in Moniz's latest work that his greatest successes have been treating obsessive tendencies and agitated depression. So, we have been thinking that perhaps Miss Connor is the one for us."

"Edward?" Ruth looked to him for confirmation. "Do you think Penelope should be your first subject? Are you ready?"

"The primate experiments we've conducted in Yale's lab have had even better results than Drs. Fulton and Jacobsen."

"Don't let them hear you say that," Robert chided playfully.

"True." Edward smiled. "But, if we can perform this procedure on a flailing ape, I do feel confident that we are ready for live subjects."

"I can't believe the two of you are just telling me this now. You didn't say as much when you returned from New Haven!" Ruth looked accusingly at both men, slightly hurt to have been left out.

"Calm down, dear. We needed to wait for the longer-term results, and they just came in a few days ago. Meanwhile we have been discussing various patients at Emeraldine while we work, so we would have a good list of candidates when we felt ready."

"And you both feel ready? Really?" Ruth looked more at Robert than Edward.

"We do," Robert said emphatically.

Ruth took a deep breath. "Oh my, this is exciting. Unimaginable. And Penelope! If this worked, she could have a chance at a real and full life." She paused, considering the true implications of this conversation—imagining, for a moment, how the course of her life might have shifted if this had been available to Harry in his darkest days. She shook away the fantasy. Dwelling on the past was useless. "But I thought you wanted to begin with a more extreme case?"

Edward jumped in. "Ruth, I know much less about the nuances of the clinical psychology in this case. But I do know that Miss Connor fits the profile identified by Moniz almost exactly, and from what I've heard about her assessments, leucotomy could significantly improve her quality of life."

Robert applauded. "Exactly. Well said, Eddie!"

"I will add, Ruth, that Miss Connor's youth is helpful—her brain matter is likely healthy, and her system strong." Edward smiled reassuringly.

Ruth stood from the dining table and began to pace. "We will, of course, need to get Charles's approval. And ready the hospital. And then there is Father . . ." Ruth turned ashen; she knew that Bernard had become more skeptical of Robert's research. She couldn't imagine trying to convince him to let Emeraldine be the first hospital in the country to conduct surgery on a technically healthy brain.

"Ruth, your father may be the chairman of the board, but it is Hayden's go-ahead that we truly need. Your father and the board should simply be presented with the positive results after the fact."

Ruth thought about it. Technically, it was true. Her father did not need to know in advance about every new treatment they tried. Still, this was brain surgery. Could they really proceed without telling him? If he found out . . . She had done her best to establish a firm division between her personal relationship with her father, as his daughter, and her professional relationship as a representative of the hospital. But, technically, in her professional role, it wasn't necessary to get his approval, unless Charles asked her to. She looked to Edward, hoping he might offer her some sense of comfort, or an opinion, but he simply shrugged. He knew better than to weigh in on this.

"Okay, I suppose that makes sense. Then we just need to get Charles up to date on your progress. Shall I set up a meeting for the three of you next week?"

"As soon as his schedule allows. And, Ruth?"

"Yes?"

"You should, of course, plan to be there as well. This is our big moment, and we wouldn't be here if it weren't for you."

Ruth's heart warmed even as it pounded fiercely in her chest. She was acutely aware that her hospital stood on one side of the line between being mildly progressive and entirely radical. Although terrified to make the leap, she couldn't wait to jump across to the other side.

Chapter Thirteen

Ruth gently patted the sweat from her brow as she, Robert, and Edward walked from Charles Hayden's office back to her own to regroup.

"Well, that was more challenging than I anticipated." Robert lifted his eyebrows for emphasis. He was right to be angry.

"I should have realized," Ruth said apologetically. "I've been giving Charles periodic updates on your progress, but he hasn't been with the two of you every evening to hear you debrief on your day as I have. I can see now that it was too large a leap for him to go from preliminary results of lab and primate research to suggesting brain surgery on one of our patients. I'm sorry."

"You shouldn't apologize, Ruth." Edward looked at her, the kindness in his eyes offsetting the disappointment in Robert's. "It is our job to make the case for this next step, not yours. Mr. Hayden was right to be concerned. There are risks inherent in any brain surgery."

"Nonsense," Robert snapped. "We have performed this surgery flawlessly on so many cadavers *I* could even do it. And with the primates, it was impeccable. Jacobsen was kicking himself for not snapping Eddie up for his permanent team. We are ready."

"I agree. Which is why I said as much in the meeting." Edward spoke calmly and evenly, a good counterbalance to Robert's fire. "But we knew we would encounter some resistance; this is radical stuff, Robert."

"Well, I surely could have prepared Charles better. Helped things to go more smoothly. Assured him that you'd already considered all the gravest risks." Ruth put her hand gently on Robert's back. "But he came around eventually. That's the important thing, right? The two of you are going to perform your first leucotomy!" Ruth's heart raced as she said this out loud. She believed unequivocally in Robert. Edward was a gifted surgeon, and she was sure he wouldn't push forward if they weren't ready. Still, this was brain surgery. On a real live patient. On Penelope. What if it didn't work? Or she died? Ultimately it was Ruth who was bringing this radical treatment to Emeraldine, and she would be to blame if anything went wrong. "Really, it's a good thing that Charles questioned you so intensely. It's his job to be skeptical, and if he was convinced, then there is no doubt this is the right thing to do."

"True, true . . ." Robert's demeanor suddenly brightened, his mustache lifting as he smiled. "No point in dwelling on an uncomfortable meeting. We received permission from Hayden. We don't need to notify the board or your father. We simply have to formalize Miss Connor's consent. Once she agrees, the era of lobotomy will begin!"

"Lobotomy?" Ruth tilted her head as she looked at him, confused by the unfamiliar term.

"Yes. Our methods are different from Dr. Moniz's. We're only taking small corings of the frontal lobe, while he severed the connections entirely. Our unique version of the procedure deserves a distinct name, don't you think? And anyway, lobe-otomy is a more accurate description."

"All right then." She nodded, smiling. "To the era of lobotomy!"

Ruth entered Penelope's room tentatively with Robert close behind her. He suggested that he and her regular psychiatrist get Penelope's agreement, but Ruth insisted she do it. It had been a month since the chess incident, and while Penelope's condition hadn't otherwise improved, she was again affectionate with Ruth. Penelope trusted her, almost like a mother. Ruth had to be the one to get her consent. To explain how this surgery would change her life for the better. Still, Ruth was nervous.

"Penelope, how are you today?" Ruth was disheartened to see little improvement in her appearance, in spite of strict orders to feed her extra portions to put some weight on her.

"How do I look?"

"Truthfully, you don't look well. Have you been eating like you are supposed to?"

"All the food here is vile. It will just make me worse."

"Penny, if you don't eat, you'll die. I can't think of worse than that." Ruth's voice failed to hide her frustration.

"Perhaps this would be a good time for me to introduce myself?" Robert jumped in.

"Yes, I was coming around to that. Penny, I have some very good news for you!" She softened her tone again, and Penelope looked at her expectantly, like it was suddenly going to be Christmas morning.

"I'd like to introduce you to my husband, Dr. Robert Apter." Ruth gestured to Robert as he moved closer to Penelope's bedside. "Robert is a doctor here at Emeraldine, and he has developed a very exciting new treatment that I think might actually cure you."

"Cure me? Really?" Penelope's face suddenly eased, and she began to cry. It was as if all her recent hostility was just a mask to hide her fear.

"Well, we don't know if it will be a complete cure, of course," Robert interjected, "but we know this treatment is particularly suited to patients with your diagnosis."

"Yes, Penny, after you heal from the operation, it's quite possible that you'll be well enough to leave us here and go back to your regular life!"

"Operation?"

"Yes, it is a surgery. Very simple really, we will just drill a small hole in the top of your head, right here"—Robert tapped the top of

Penelope's head, just above her hairline, and she winced—"and then we do a small procedure to help your brain function better. You won't feel a thing, and afterward, you should be much happier, more relaxed, and less preoccupied with these things that are preventing you from eating and causing you to scratch yourself up like that."

"Then, a few weeks after that, when we are sure the wound has healed, if you are up to it, you will be able to go home." Ruth looked up and saw Penelope's face frozen in terror.

"A surgery? In my brain?"

"I know it sounds scary, but Dr. Apter is a brilliant doctor, and his partner, Dr. Wilkinson, is a gifted surgeon." Ruth waved Edward forward and he stepped to Penelope's bedside.

"Miss Connor." Edward reached out his hand and shook hers sweetly. Penelope tilted her head almost coquettishly. Ruth had never seen her this engaged with anyone else. "I want you to know that I would only ever consider performing this surgery if I was absolutely, completely confident that it was the right thing to do."

"Okay, Doctor." Penelope blushed, smiling at Edward as she seemed to struggle to hide her fear. "But I'm scared of surgery."

"I understand." He sat on the edge of her bed and looked directly at her. Ruth had come to know the comfort of looking into Edward's eyes. His presence was like a salve, a perfect counterpoint to Robert's endless energy. "Penelope, can I tell you a secret?" He leaned in toward her slightly and she nodded, seemingly entranced. "Dr. Apter and I have been practicing for many months now. This is a simple procedure that they have been doing in Europe with great success, and we have brought it here. Just for people like you! It is really easy to do, even though it sounds scary. And we are more than ready to use it to help you. Will you let us help you?"

Penelope gazed at Edward as he smiled at her reassuringly. Then she turned her gaze questioningly back to Ruth.

"I wouldn't recommend this for you if I didn't know you were in the best hands."

"I'm scared."

"I know you are, but, I promise, you will be just fine. More than fine, you will be better than ever! Can you trust me?" Ruth took Penelope's hand.

The women looked at each other.

"All right." Penelope nodded tentatively. "If you think it will cure me, and he will do it"—she pointed at Edward—"I'll do it."

Ruth walked down the hall of the ladies' wing as quickly as possible. She was panic stricken but had to appear undisturbed. The echoes of Penelope's screams were frightening enough; any sign of fear from her might create chaos among the other patients in the ward.

"What happened?" she asked in a sharp whisper to Nurse Riley, who was standing watch at Penelope's door.

"I'm sorry we had to call for you, Mrs. Apter. She needs an enema before her surgery, but she won't let me near her. The doctor is supposed to be here to administer the rectal anesthesia in ten minutes. This should have been completed an hour ago but . . ."

"It's all right, I'll sort it out." Ruth looked into the room at Penelope. She was facedown on her bed, both arms pinned in place by nurses. Still, she kicked wildly and thrashed her head from side to side, screaming, "Keep that dirty thing away from me! I won't do it! You can't make me!"

"Let's give Penny a moment to pull herself together, shall we?" Ruth sounded much calmer than she felt. The nurses hesitated but slowly released Penelope from their grasp as Ruth rushed to her side and wrapped the woman tightly in her arms.

"Shhhh, shhhh. It's okay, Penny. You are okay."

"They wanted to disembowel me!"

"No, they didn't, honey. They just need to evacuate you down there before the surgery. Remember, we talked about this? That is where they put the medicine so you can sleep."

"No! I won't do it. I can't do it. It isn't clean. I have to be clean. If I'm not clean, I will get sick. I can't get sick. I won't get sick."

"I know you are frightened right now." Ruth looked out the window to steady her own fear. The leaves on the trees were beginning to turn into the reds and yellows of autumn, and it made her feel calm in spite of the anxiety and near chaos in the room. "Remember this is going to be so wonderful for you!" If this was a success, it would mean they could treat psychiatric disorders in just a matter of hours; fix people who would otherwise be relegated to life in a psychiatric hospital, with a small surgery on the frontal lobe. Penelope would likely be cured and go home in just a few weeks.

But what if it didn't work? As long as Penelope supported having the surgery, Ruth felt confident, but to see the terror in her eyes now, irrational as it might be, opened the door to all of her own worst fears. If the surgery went badly, Penelope might not improve—she might lose control over her motor functions or her ability to speak. She might bleed to death on the operating table.

There were institutions who treated their patients like rats in a laboratory, who saw their inmates as expendable. Emeraldine was not one of those places. Emeraldine Hospital put patient well-being first, always. What would it mean, then, if something happened to Penelope and Ruth had allowed it?

"Mrs. Apter." Nurse Riley touched her tentatively on her shoulder. "Dr. Apter and the anesthesiologist are here."

"No! No!" Penelope wailed. "Don't let them in! Please don't let them in!"

"Penny." Ruth took Penelope's face in both of her hands, looking right into her green eyes, puffy and bloodshot from so much crying. "You are going to be okay. Do you hear me? You will be fine. You are going to do this, and when you wake up, I will be right here beside you smiling about how well you did. And you will tell me how you already feel so much better." Ruth had to believe what she was saying was true; the wheels were set in motion now and nothing could stop them.

"Okay." Penelope took a big, jumpy breath.

"Mrs. Apter." The anesthesiologist stuck his head into the room. "Sometimes it helps if we start with a little nitrous oxide."

"What a terrific idea! Penny, this nice doctor is going to give you something to breathe that will make you feel wonderfully happy. It only lasts for a short time, but I think it will be just what you need to relax before they begin." As she spoke, the doctor and two nurses held Penelope down and quickly placed a mask over her face, and Ruth watched her body ease onto the bed.

"We have it from here, Ruthie." Robert grabbed her elbow and led her to the door. "I'll call for you as soon as the surgery is over."

It felt like days went by as Ruth waited in her office for the surgery to finish. Paperwork usually required all of her attention, and she had planned to distract herself today by studying the hospital's ledgers to prepare for a board presentation later that month. There were several increases in spending that she and Charles would need to justify. Still, she could barely focus. After three trips to the kitchen for coffee that she did not need, several trips to the washroom, and even a brisk stroll along the boardwalk, she had still heard nothing. She stood up again, preparing to walk over to the hospital and see what was taking so long, when her phone rang.

"Mrs. Apter, it's Nurse Riley. Dr. Apter asked me to let you know that Miss Connor is back in her room."

"She's back?" The tension in Ruth's body eased slightly. "How is she?"

"The doctors are pleased. But she is still asleep."

"All right, thank you. Tell them I will be there momentarily!"

Ruth raced excitedly to the ladies' ward.

"She's all right?" Ruth asked Robert, who was standing outside Penelope's room when she came flying down the hall.

"Well, we still have quite a bit of recovery to manage but, yes, the surgery couldn't have gone better. Eddie was brilliant. I was able to get quite a good view the entire time and helped ensure that he severed the proper white matter. I have already done a postoperative evaluation of her basic reflexes, and her eyes, hands, and feet are all responsive to stimuli."

"Is she already awake then?"

"No, no, not yet. Let's see, it is 1:30 now. We began at 10:18, finished at 11:22. Anesthesia was administered at 10:03, so she should be recovering from her sedation by 1:48, at the latest."

Ruth laughed nervously at her husband's precision. She knew that he had not only already written down all the details of the exact times he had just recited, but he had surely taken photos to accompany his notes.

Please, please let her be okay. Her heart thumped as she entered Penelope's room to find Edward and Nurse Riley by her bedside. "Any change?" Robert asked.

"She is beginning to come out of the anesthesia," Edward said. "Moving her limbs a bit. Temperature and pressure steady. No other bleeding than the one vessel we encountered during the surgery." He gestured encouragingly to Ruth. "If you squeeze her hand, she should respond."

Ruth approached and gave Penny's small hand a gentle squeeze. Penelope returned the gesture as her eyelids fluttered open. She blinked several times, as if trying to find her focus, and then stared directly at Ruth. "Ruth." She smiled. "You've come to visit."

They let out a collective sigh of relief.

"Of course." Ruth's face relaxed into a broad grin. "I told you I'd be here, didn't I?"

"Miss Connor"—Robert moved closer to the bed—"I am going to ask you a few questions, all right?" Penelope nodded her head. "Do you know who I am?"

"Dr. Apter. Ruth's husband."

"Very good. And what is the day today?"

"Mon . . . no, Tues . . . it is Wednesday! I know because I wasn't allowed to eat dinner last night because of my surgery and it was the only thing I like—shepherd's pie!" Penelope frowned.

"As soon as you can eat again, I will make sure you get a special shepherd's pie feast!"

Ruth's face stretched into an even wider grin.

"And what is your name?"

"Penelope."

"And your family name?"

Ruth watched as Penelope seemed to struggle for a moment to recall and then said proudly, "Connor. You know that already, silly." She giggled. "You just called me Miss Connor!"

"Right you are." Robert looked so happy he just might have giggled himself. "Miss Connor, how do you feel today?"

"Great."

"Are you happy? Sad? Angry?"

"Oh, happy, happy, happy," she said and clapped her hands together.

"Wonderful. Dr. Wilkinson"—Robert turned to Edward—"make sure you are getting all of this."

Edward nodded, already writing.

"You had surgery today, do you remember?"

"I sure do. It was awfully fast."

"Yes, well, it feels that way because of the anesthesia." Robert smiled at her encouragingly. "And why, Miss Connor, did you have this surgery? Do you remember that?"

Penelope looked to Ruth, and Ruth grew tense. Penelope was still in such a fragile state. After the scene she had caused this morning, why would Robert try to stir up these emotions now?

But instead of another outburst, Penelope gazed at them placidly.

"I can't say that I do, Doctor. Can't have been very important, I suppose?" Ruth was relieved but also a bit surprised. Could she really have forgotten her terror this morning? Her behavior these past years? Still, she was calm and, by her own reporting, happy. That wasn't something she had claimed to be in as long as Ruth had known her. "I am very sleepy all of a sudden. I think I will rest now." Penelope closed her eyes and peacefully nodded off to sleep.

Robert had left the room momentarily and returned with his camera to take a photo. Ruth worried that the snap of the flash would wake her, but she slumbered deeply.

"Don't worry, I'll be checking on her hourly." Nurse Riley ushered them out of the room. "Now go and let the young lady rest!"

Ruth, Robert, and Edward walked quietly from the room and straight to Charles's office.

"Hayden—we've done it!"

"Is the surgery finished?" Charles looked up at the three eager faces in the doorway.

"It is. And I believe it was a terrific success. She is already awake and speaking, and reports that she is happy!" Robert began to applaud himself and his team.

"Excellent work, gentlemen. Ruth, I trust that you will keep a close watch on the patient's recovery over the next few weeks and keep me well apprised." Charles smiled at her. "Very exciting day, congratulations to all."

"Of course, sir. Thank you." Ruth waved her arm, indicating that they should move toward her office, where they shut the door.

"We've done it!" Robert leapt onto her desk gleefully. "We've done it!"

"Congratulations, Robert. Very promising initial results." Edward's response was, as usual, more measured. Ruth sensed a small note of relief in his voice.

"We must, of course, observe her over the next few weeks, but I don't think it is too soon to call this a brilliant success!" Robert jumped down, grabbing Ruth's face in his hands and kissing her excitedly on the lips. He then turned to Edward, who was awkwardly looking over his notes, and gave him a generous pat on the back, which somehow morphed into the three of them in the center of the room laughing in a gleeful scrum at their incredible accomplishment.

Chapter Fourteen

"Now, Robert, even if he provokes you, you know you cannot speak about lobotomy tonight, right? And, Edward, you will step in if necessary?" Ruth tapped her foot nervously as the taxi took them to her parents' for their annual holiday dinner. She had put off seeing them as long as possible, but this was the last weekend before Bernard and Helen went south for the winter. Unfortunately, the hospital's final board meeting of the year would be on Monday, which meant they would see her father before Charles could present their findings.

Robert had convinced both Ruth and Charles that they couldn't discern the full implications of the new procedure until they had a full data set. Moniz had performed twenty leucotomies in his first study, so they set that number as their goal as well. They had been working feverishly in the two months since their first surgery and had finally reached their target, collated their data, and deemed the procedure a success. They had also finished a paper that they would submit to the Medical Society of the County of New York after the presentation to the board. But tonight, they needed to behave as if nothing was about to happen and that made Ruth worry.

The evening started off in its typical fashion with Bernard still in his study and Helen holding court. Fortunately, for once, Ruth found the topic of conversation of interest.

"Mrs. Emeraldine, I was really impressed with the cubism and abstract expressionism show at the Museum of Modern Art. Robert said you were involved with that exhibit?" Edward asked deferentially.

"Indeed, I was! As you know, I quite appreciate the arts and I do believe it is so important to embrace the currents of contemporary masters. Fortunately, a few of my more forward-thinking friends agree, and I assembled a dedicated committee to fund the show. Mr. Barr, the curator, is rather a genius, and together, we were able to offer the public a truly spectacular exhibition."

"It really was, Mother. Robert and I particularly appreciated the parallels drawn between cubism and African art—"

"Yes, it was an impressively avant-garde experience in every way," Robert added.

"Well, the *New York Times* agreed, they described it as 'a thousand thrills to the minute, and not a single footnote.'" Helen sat taller, preening like a peacock, seemingly enjoying the unusually engaged conversation centered around her. "You know, Edward, if you had told me when you were attending, I could have arranged to have one or another of the eligible young daughters of the Metropolitan Club's membership accompany you. There are so many lovely girls looking for husbands right now."

Ruth watched Edward's ears turn red and could feel Robert's gaze imploring her to get her father, so they could get on with the evening.

"I am sure Edward can find his own dates, Mother." Ruth prickled as she stood, smoothed her skirt, and crossed the room to look down the hallway. "It is getting late. Might you go see what is holding up Father?"

"Oh, Ruth. You know your father operates at his own pace. If you are in such a rush, perhaps you can go retrieve him from the study yourself?"

"Yes, darling, why don't you go get your father? We do have so much to discuss with him this evening!"

Ruth shot Robert a look of warning. They decidedly did *not* have anything special to discuss.

She made her way down the hallway, feeling as always like that intrusive little girl about to get scolded as she tentatively knocked on the door. "Father, we are all in the library waiting for you." She heard the rustling of pages, the closing of a book. Her thumping heart vibrated through her body as she stood still, waiting. Listening. Feet shuffled. A glass clinked. Liquid poured. Was he getting himself a drink?

"You never have been very patient, have you, Ruth?" She startled as the door opened suddenly. "I was just finishing up some reading." Bernard Emeraldine had begun to age. He stood with a slightly stooped spine, which now set him at eye level with his daughter, rather than the imposing several inches above her that he once had. His knees had become arthritic, and he compensated by shuffling along the floor in his slippers. Still, he remained terrifying.

"Good evening, Father. Sorry, it's just that, well, Mother called dinner for six thirty, and it's nearly eight. We have Edward here as well, and I just feel awful to make him wait and . . ."

"Stop your equivocating. I'm here, aren't I? Come then."

Ruth followed her father down the hall, past the library where she momentarily stopped to gather the group. Bernard continued on directly to the dining room and sat in his oversized chair at the head of the table. The others took their seats, sitting in strained silence. Ruth almost felt as if her father knew that the three of them were hiding something and was testing her, challenging her compunction to address him head-on like a proper professional. Of course, he couldn't know anything. She hadn't told him, and she knew Charles had intentionally remained vague.

"Dr. Wilkinson, how do you feel about your post at our hospital now that you have nearly a year with us?" Bernard turned to Edward almost warmly.

"It has been terrific, sir. Everything I could have ever wanted."

Ruth saw Edward pulling at his napkin under the table.

"I must say I am still surprised that you were interested in the position. I know my son-in-law has his outlandish ideas about treatments that alter the brain somehow, and that's all well and good for a researcher, but I would think a true surgeon would want to pursue a path that enabled him to use the knife for real work, outside the lab."

Ruth watched Robert bristle at Bernard's condescension and began to panic.

"Not at all, sir. Working with Dr. Apter—Robert—has been even more rewarding than I could have ever imagined. He is quite a genius."

Robert smiled tightly and Ruth held her breath, fearing that Robert might say more. Thankfully Arnold entered the room with the soup, and as the sweet-spicy smell of pumpkin bisque filled the room with notes of Christmas, Ruth took the opportunity to change the subject to something entirely banal. "Mother, I was surprised that the two of you are heading south so early this year. I thought you never miss the holiday party season?"

"Well." Helen took a dramatic breath. "We felt that the warmer climes would be best for our ailments." Helen looked pointedly at Bernard, intimating that his deteriorating health was to blame. "Of course, there is quite a festive season in Palm Beach as well."

"Mr. Emeraldine," Robert cut in jarringly as his knee bounced under the table, rattling the china charger and nearly spilling the soup. "I'll have you know that I am not simply doing lab research on cadavers."

"Robert, Father is aware that you have now spent several years studying the brains of patients." Ruth reached out under the table to try to hit Robert's foot with hers and gave him a look, admonishing him to stop.

"You mean that rogue theory about brain connections and mental illness?" Bernard chuckled.

"It is hardly rogue," Robert retorted. "I know you believe in the biological approach to treatment. And there is cutting-edge research that proves, unequivocally, that altering the connections in the brain helps to address a host of previously uncurable mental diseases. I have been working with a highly respected doctor in Portugal, Egas Moniz, who has been very generous with his own research. In fact, we are now performing a brain surgery based on Dr. Moniz's leucotomy that seems to be nothing short of a miracle at the hospital. Our lobotomy—"

Edward dropped his spoon with a loud clank. Ruth felt sick. How could Robert be so reckless?

"I am sure I understood you incorrectly. It seemed like you said that you have performed brain surgery at my hospital?" Bernard asked in a voice all the more menacing for its measured tone.

"Gentlemen," Helen interjected with some force, "I don't believe this kind of business belongs at the dinner table, particularly during our holiday meal! Honestly." Helen lifted and refolded her napkin and looked at Bernard and Robert with a sharp warning before taking a graceful and deliberate spoonful of soup.

"You're absolutely right, Helen. I apologize for steering the conversation in this direction. May I just say, sir"—Robert turned back to Bernard—"that it's not exactly *your* hospital. Of course, you paid for the wonderful facilities but—"

"That's right. *I* paid for the facilities, *I* run the board. I might not have a degree in medicine, but make no mistake, as long as my name is on the door, it is most certainly *my* hospital."

How could he? Ruth began to sweat and felt her stomach folding in on itself. She had hoped her mother's admonition would have saved them, but now she feared Robert had reached a point of no return. "Father. Please. Of course it is your hospital. That is why Charles and I are preparing a detailed presentation for you and the rest of the board at Monday's meeting. You will see all the data to support the impressive results of Robert and Edward's work. They have made an incredible breakthrough, one that could put Emeraldine at the forefront of the most revolutionary care for the mentally ill—"

"Yes, Mr. Emeraldine," Robert cut her off again just as she found her voice, "my lobotomy is a marvel of a surgery that promises to tame even the most violent patients. Since the surgery, our patients report less anxiety, less mania, a cessation of aggressive thoughts and impulses, and our caretakers are able to do their work with fewer interruptions. I daresay this might just be one of the greatest surgical innovations of our time." Ruth braced herself. She would not have given this level of detail to her father even if she had planned to tell him about the lobotomies tonight.

Bernard's face turned red with fury. "Your *patients*—plural? I cannot believe that you have the audacity to risk the reputation of my hospital!"

"Hardly, sir. We are simply and effectively drilling into the brain and taking the core of some tissue in the frontal lobe. That is why we call the procedure a 'lobe-otomy.' This will soon become commonplace, I can assure you."

"Enough." Helen tapped her spoon on the edge of her china soup bowl. "Robert, I am surprised at you. This is simply gruesome. How will we ever have the stomach for our lovely stuffed squabs if you continue on with this?"

"Just a moment, dear. If I understand correctly, you are sitting at my holiday table telling me that you decided to take it upon yourself to intentionally damage healthy brain tissue, to alter the very human essence of a person, obliterating all that distinguishes us from the animals." Bernard looked on in disbelief, and Ruth felt her heart fall to her ankles. She took a deep breath to calm her panic and fury. Yes, they shouldn't have broached this subject tonight, but still, her father simply refused to see the point, to appreciate the progress they had made.

"Father, we all want nothing more than to find a real, long-term cure for mental illness. That is why Charles Hayden and I are so excited about this incredible breakthrough. I am not sure why you refuse to even listen . . . If only . . ." Ruth's eyes welled with tears. "If only Harry had been here now, he might . . ."

"Enough!" Bernard bellowed. Ruth startled, almost knocking over her wineglass.

"Father, I lost him too, you know."

"You leave him out of this." Bernard's voice caught in his throat, and Helen reached to grab hold of his hand, scowling at Ruth. Just the mention of Harry elicited more emotion from her parents than they had shown for Ruth over her entire lifetime.

"Mr. and Mrs. Emeraldine, if I may." Edward cleared his throat nervously and Ruth watched his ears turn red. "This was an inappropriate moment for you to learn about lobotomy, that is certain. However, as a doctor with a naturally conservative orientation, I can assure you that what Robert has pioneered has proven, in initial results, to be both safe and effective at treating severe mental illness. I think we all wish that you were not learning about it at such a lovely dinner"—he smiled sheepishly at Helen—"I know that was not your daughter's nor Mr. Hayden's plan. But I do want to reassure you that when you learn more on Monday, I believe you will be quite pleased."

"I doubt it." Bernard wouldn't yield, and Ruth had had her fill.

"All right then, it is getting late and clearly we aren't going to be able to move beyond this tonight." Ruth stood, grabbing Robert's hand. It was time to accept defeat, at least for today. There were so many things her father would never acknowledge: for Bernard, Harry's death would always be about the loss of a rightful heir. No one to take over the family business. No one to carry on the Emeraldine name. But she would show him.

"Please do not blame Charles for your learning of this tonight. He has a thorough report that will explain every benefit, including the thesis of the paper Robert and Edward will be presenting to the Medical Society of the County of New York. I imagine when they laud this great achievement, as they most certainly will, you will feel compelled to do the same. Mother, I apologize for ruining your meal. And safe travels."

"Helen. Mr. Emeraldine." Robert gave a small and obsequious bow as he stood.

"So sorry for the commotion, you are a wonderful hostess." Edward shook Helen's hand awkwardly. "Mr. Emeraldine, thank you and sorry." He stooped his head as he followed Ruth and Robert out of the dining room.

When they got outside, Ruth's whole body wilted. Robert scooped her up and whispered softly, "Darling, it's okay. If your father would rather sit idly by as we change the world, let the codger do just that. Once the medical board praises our discovery, it will usher in a new era of lobotomy and leave narrow-minded men like your father looking the fool."

Ruth held tight to her husband, her anger at his recklessness transforming into appreciation for his unflappable confidence and unbridled genius. He was right; they didn't need her father's support. They had each other, and together, they were going to change the world.

INTERLUDE
MARGARET: 1952

Margaret roused suddenly. Had she heard a thud? She was disoriented, and as she turned on her side, the plastic edge of a curler hit her cheek. When had she set her hair? Her mouth tasted sour and felt pasty, like someone had painted stale coffee onto her tongue.

She was so tired. She would just close her eyes again and stay in bed a little longer. As she nestled herself deeper into the pillows and began drifting back to sleep, she could make out the sound of a baby wailing in the distance. It was far enough away that she was certain she didn't need to worry about it. She would just pull the covers up, surrender to the pull of exhaustion, let the clouds carry her back to sleep. Back to sleep.

"Margaret Abigail!" Her mother threw open the door of her bedroom, William crying in her arms. "What in heaven's name are you doing in here? It is two o'clock in the afternoon! Your son is starving." Sara Davidson stomped toward her daughter, whipping the coverlet off and giving her a firm tap on the cheek. "You're still in your housecoat? Have you even left your bed since I was here this morning?"

It took all Margaret's strength to move into an upright position, and the moment she got there, her mother thrust her hungry son into her arms. Her breasts were full and burning and starting to leak as William writhed and pawed at her. She was still groggy and struggled to prepare herself to feed him. "Hold on!" she snapped angrily, momentarily tempted to fling her son across the room at the dresser. In the same instant, he desperately latched on and began to pull at her with a ferocity that made her feel used.

Her mother angrily hmmed as she aggressively opened all the curtains. The sunlight made Margaret's head throb. She shifted to shield her eyes without disturbing William's powerful sucking, even though what she really wanted was to thrust him off of her.

"Maggie, this is becoming unacceptable," her mother said sharply. "I know you're tired, but that's motherhood. Now, I've put a pot roast in the oven—it'll be ready by the time Frank gets home—and brought you some groceries, but you need to get to the market and fill up your refrigerator yourself. It just isn't right for a husband to come home to a kitchen that looks so bare."

Margaret nodded, remembering last week when she tried to do her own shopping. Her mother had stayed home with William and she had felt so ecstatic, so free, as she drove away. Even if it was just the mile to get to the market. But then she was there. Walking up and down the aisles aimlessly. Did Frank prefer the creamed corn or the kernels? How could she not remember? It was peak season for raspberries, and she had the idea to bake a cobbler, but she couldn't for the life of her remember what other ingredients she needed. Did she have butter? And which day did the milkman come so she could ask him to include heavy cream?

She stood paralyzed in the middle of the aisle, unable to think; her red fingernails chipped on her keys as she dug desperately through her purse to find her shopping list. How could she have forgotten it? Head hung low, hoping no one would recognize her, she began frantically loading her cart. When she finally returned home, her mother berated her for wasting Frank's hard-earned money on such nonsense. Three bags of sugar? Five pounds of cornmeal? In the end, she took the two full bags of items that Sara insisted she return and hid them in the corner of her garage. They still sat there, tucked behind the bicycle that she hadn't had the opportunity to ride in years.

"Maggie!" Her mother shook her. "Were you dozing off again?" Margaret worked hard to keep her eyes open. Why was she still so tired? "Maggie, you've got to pull yourself together. For the kids. For Frank."

"I know." She felt like she had to dredge her voice up from a great depth. She dropped her head in shame, waiting for the tears to come again, but they didn't. She just felt cold and dead inside. "I am trying. And Frank loves me—"

"Of course he loves you. But you know how hard he works. To live here in your own house, with your own yard and bedrooms for your children. You could be in a two-room apartment in the Bronx like I was when you were born. With a bathroom down the hall. Frank is a wonderful provider. A loving husband and father. You can't ask him to hold you up more than that."

Margaret nodded.

"Honey, I know how hard it is to have babies." Sara sat on the bed next to her daughter, softening a bit. "Especially once the third comes. Your brother, John, was a handful, believe me. But it is our greatest role in life."

"Don't you think I know that?" Margaret asked plaintively, the words instantly draining all her strength. She wanted to let William slip from her arms onto the bed and join him in sleep. Instead, her mother took hold of him in one hand and pulled Margaret up to standing with the other.

"Maggie, Maisy and John will be home from school soon, for goodness' sake. Now, go wash up, put on a summer dress, and make up your face. I'll get the baby in the pram and we can go outside for a bit. The fresh air will do you both good."

Margaret felt nearly catatonic as she followed her mother's instructions. She splashed icy water on her face, but it did nothing to chase away the heavy blanket of fatigue. She hadn't felt this way with John or Maisy, and she didn't understand what was different now. But, for the first time, it dawned on her that there might be something really wrong.

PART 2

RUTH: 1941–47

Chapter Fifteen

"You'll never guess who I just got a call from!" Robert bounded into Ruth's office, grinning.

"My father?" Ruth asked, a bitter note of sarcasm in her voice. In the five years since Bernard learned about the first lobotomies performed at Emeraldine, he had all but stopped speaking to Robert. The family had long ago ceased to have their monthly dinners, and Helen made sure to seat the men as far apart from each other as possible when they were obligated to be together at holiday gatherings. It was difficult for Ruth to feel the sting of Bernard's disapproval yet again, particularly when it wasn't directed only at her but also at her husband. Though that feeling was more than offset by the positive reception lobotomy had received by the hospital board and the medical community. It had become an increasingly sought-after treatment for severely ill patients, and Robert and Edward, having now lobotomized more than three hundred people, were the go-to experts to perform it.

"No, not your father. Why would I want a call from the daft old man anyway?"

"Robert." Ruth gave him a sharp, pleading look. She understood Robert's disdain, but still, this was her father, her family.

"Sorry. The man I just spoke to is a contemporary of your father's but, I dare say, he's even more important than Mr. Bernard Emeraldine." Ruth tilted her head quizzically and gave Robert a look somewhere between a grimace and a smile. Robert was so dramatic. "Joseph Kennedy," Robert continued as he lifted his eyebrows, looking to Ruth to share his excitement.

"Joseph Kennedy? From Boston?"

"Yes, indeed."

"What would he call you for?"

"Well, as it so happens, he has a very confidential assignment for Eddie and me. If I were inclined to sell stories to the papers, this would be a juicy one. Of course, I would never violate the confidentiality of a patient."

"A patient? Joseph Kennedy is a patient?"

"No, no. He isn't, but he . . ." Robert paused. "Before I tell you more, you must understand that this is truly top secret."

"Robert! Have I *ever* been one to gossip? Anyway, if it's a medical issue, I have an ethical responsibility to protect the information. So, what is it?"

"Well, you know that Joe Kennedy has a very large family, nine children?" Ruth nodded. Of course she did, the Kennedy clan was very well-known. "But I bet you didn't know that one of his children is very ill." Robert raised his eyebrows as if to underscore the significance of the confidential information. "Apparently, his eldest daughter, Rosemary, has always been mentally unstable. Difficult. The family has kept this private—in fact, even when she met the king of England, they managed to hide it."

"How sad for her, and for them."

"Yes, well, things have gotten very bad. She has been having periodic convulsions and violent outbursts; she is generally irritable and irrational, and has become impossible for the family to handle. Their doctor suggested she would be a strong candidate for our lobotomy."

"Really?"

"Indeed. Joe called me himself because he wanted to explain the delicacy of the situation and the urgency of the matter. Afterward, I spoke to the family physician who recommended me, and he gave me more of the medical details of the case. Ruth, she would benefit so greatly from lobotomy, and they want me and Eddie to go to Boston as soon as possible and perform the procedure. Just think of the publicity for us!"

Ruth felt momentarily overcome. Here was a family much like hers, suffering as she and her parents had with Harry, but with the hope of a cure. This was really happening. Her greatest dreams realized. "The publicity isn't the point," she said, smiling, "but how wonderful for them. We're really doing it, offering a new way to heal people. When will you leave?"

"I need to confirm it all with Eddie and clear my calendar, but if we can make the arrangements work, Joe would like us to be there Monday."

"I am sure I can help shift your schedule here for something so important. This poor girl. This poor family. How marvelous if you can help them all."

"Not if—*that* I can help them. And how about that vote of confidence for such a high-profile family to embrace lobotomy? Now remember, no one knows about Rosemary, and Joe doesn't want anyone—even his wife—to know about the procedure until afterward; so we must keep this between us."

Ruth was surprised. Why wouldn't Joseph Kennedy want his wife to know? Surely, she would want to be there with her daughter? Still, it wasn't her family, and it wasn't her business. "Of course."

Ruth had asked her cook, Liana, to prepare lobster thermidor as a celebratory dinner for Robert and Edward. She was planning for the best, even though she feared the worst. They had been in Boston for nearly two weeks—a week longer than planned—with no explanation beyond that Joe had required them to stay. Not every lobotomy was a success.

She knew that. They had had some failures, even a few deaths. But, overall, most patients improved and only 5 percent died. She imagined if this had happened to Rosemary, Robert would have told her immediately. Still, she worried. Something must have gone wrong. She paced in the parlor, back and forth in front of the fire, anxiously waiting.

When the men finally walked through the door, she was taken aback at the gray pallor of their skin, their eyes ringed with black circles. They seemed much more exhausted than what she would have expected after a few hours in the car. She braced herself.

"Robert, Edward—what happened?"

"I don't want to talk about it," Robert answered flatly as he ushered Edward into the parlor to sit down. "I need a stiff drink. Eddie?"

Edward nodded.

"I had planned on champagne but—"

"This is not a moment for champagne, I'm afraid," Edward said wanly.

"Scotch then?"

Both men nodded. Ruth poured them all drinks and then sat beside Robert on the sofa across from Edward. "Please, tell me. What is it?" she asked as softly and gently as she could.

"It didn't go well." Robert looked at the floor and Ruth took his hand.

"How badly? Is she—"

"She's alive," Edward interjected. "But we didn't help her. We thought that maybe, after the cerebral swelling went down, we would see a better result, but unfortunately, we did not."

"Oh my. Do you know why? What went wrong?"

"Nothing went wrong!" Robert snapped. "We performed the procedure as we always do. We had her awake, so we could be certain how deep to cut. She was speaking to us the whole time as per our usual protocol—reciting 'God Bless America' and counting backward—and we stopped our incision as soon as she started to become the slightest bit incoherent."

"Yes, I am certain that we didn't go too deep. I think she was just incurable."

"Eddie keeps trying to make me feel better. And I know you are right, Ed. It is not as if this is our first disappointing outcome. But . . . if this one had been successful, it would have catapulted us into a new level of notoriety and influence."

"Maybe, but that's not why we are doing this. Mr. Kennedy wasn't angry with the result. Very upset and disappointed, understandably, but he knew the risk." Ruth had never heard Edward use such a short tone before.

"Robert, Edward, please! What, exactly, happened?"

"Rosemary Kennedy has not regained her mental capacity. At all. In fact, she is worse. We stayed for an extra week hoping that she was just slow to heal, but there was no change. Her intellect has diminished to that of a toddler. Needs constant care. Can hardly walk. Is incontinent. Joe insisted that we transfer her to an institution, so we moved her to Craig House before returning home. Really it is nothing so out of the ordinary. We've seen this before in the spectrum of our results. I just really didn't want it to happen to her." Robert hung his head.

"We don't want it to happen to anyone," Edward said pointedly. "But it was a particularly hard blow given who the family is."

Ruth's eyes welled with tears. Of course, lobotomy didn't always work perfectly, but this seemed such a tragedy. For the family to go through all that just to have poor Rosemary end up in an institution, worse off than before. Still, this wasn't a moment for her to feel downtrodden; she clearly needed to stay strong for Robert and Edward. They had tried their best. "Well, at least she will be well cared for. And she has her family to support her. That is more than so many patients have."

"Yes. Well, her parents anyway. They are not telling the other children. And Joe made it very clear that we are never to speak of this."

"Not telling them?"

"Ruth, this is not our affair. Joe wants to handle this his way. He knows what is best for his own family. Anyway, we will stay in touch with the family doctor, who will monitor her condition. Such a disappointment."

"You two are the country's greatest experts on this procedure. So, I am certain that if you weren't able to produce a successful result, no one could have." She stood, feeling shaky and a bit hollow from the false cheer she was putting on. Her confidence was rattled, but it wouldn't do for these men to know that. "I know this was a blow, but it was only one bad result—after five years of so much success. We need to put this behind us and look forward to the bright future you two have enabled for so many. Liana has prepared a special meal, so come, let's eat and drink and toast all the progress that we have made instead of wallowing in one of the rare bad outcomes."

She started walking toward the dining room, looking behind her with an overly enthusiastic smile. "I have some good news, actually. I had a visit last week from Penelope Connor and her aunt. You wouldn't believe how well she is. Full-figured and rosy cheeked. Not a scratch on her. She was so pleasant and calm and happy. Her aunt couldn't thank us enough for giving her niece back her life. So, you see, you two really are working miracles."

Ruth felt terrible for everyone. Robert, Edward, poor Rose and Joe Kennedy and, most of all, for Rosemary. But sadness had to be cast aside. Nothing in medicine was 100 percent successful and, overall, lobotomy was doing so much more good than harm. They were making progress, helping so many. That was what really mattered.

Chapter Sixteen

"I still can't believe he is really gone." Ruth dabbed her eyes with Robert's handkerchief as they walked the few blocks home from her family's Gramercy Park mansion.

"Your heart is too big, Ruth. I know he was your father, but even in death he managed to stick it to you."

"That's not true. He left us Magnolia Bluff!"

"Yes, but to appoint his board seat to your mother? It is unconscionable. What does she know about the hospital?"

"I suppose but—well, I couldn't very well sit on the board as the assistant superintendent of the hospital."

"Perhaps not, but I could."

"Robert." Ruth looked at him askance. She knew he was almost as eager for Bernard's approval as she had been. It was hard for both of them that he had died without ever acknowledging the huge contribution lobotomy had made to the treatment of mental health; still, it was entirely inappropriate to be so arrogant in a moment like this.

"Ruth, I know this is hard on you. That, in spite of everything, you loved the man. But your father hasn't really been a part of our lives in a meaningful way for some time now." Ruth could hear the strain in Robert's voice as he tried to sound supportive. She knew he was relieved that Bernard was gone. His presence at the hospital had been nothing but an obstacle to Robert's progress, as her father was always the dissenting voice on the board in matters related to the advancement of lobotomy.

"I know you're right. I just—poor Mother. She has lost so much."

"She has. But she still has a lot." Robert pulled her in toward him and gave her a gentle peck on the cheek. "She has us. And, you might not have noticed, but she seemed thrilled to be able to relocate to Palm Beach."

"You're right, I suppose." Ruth smiled softly. "She was always much happier there than Father was."

"Yet another reason why I don't understand the board seat. It isn't as if she will be here to attend meetings."

"No, she won't. She will likely vote in absentia. Or appoint someone proxy. She has made it quite clear that her preference is to remain in Florida most of the year."

"Exactly, I'm not sure why she is even keeping the Gramercy Park house. Perhaps we should see about moving there ourselves?" His eyes lit up slightly.

"Robert, it was their family home. I don't want to live there! We have more than enough space in our townhouse. And that is actually *ours*."

"Of course, darling. I love our townhouse, you know that. I was just thinking, if we lived in the mansion, I could convert a portion of it into an office for my private patients. It would be an efficient way to be near to home and manage all my work at the hospital and privately."

Ruth stopped walking and looked at Robert for a moment. The idea of his having an office at home for his outpatient psychiatry practice was intriguing. But she decidedly did not want to live in her parents' mansion, a place that had never felt much like a home to her to begin with.

"I think it would be too much for Mother not to have Gramercy Park waiting for her when she returns on visits. And, with the demands on all of us now that the war is escalating"—she took a sad, deep breath—"I don't think there is any reason to make any changes. Anyway, if I were to move anywhere, it would be Magnolia Bluff."

"Now there's an idea! Why, I could convert the carriage house into a whole office suite!" Robert smiled as they began walking again. "And you are so happy there. You need a place that calms your nerves with the hospital being what it is these days—all the soldiers. I know it is hard on you." He squeezed her hand tightly; he didn't ever mention Harry directly, but she appreciated this subtle acknowledgment of her lingering pain. "I think a move to the beach might be really extraordinary for us."

Ruth pondered the idea. Magnolia Bluff *was* the place where she was most at peace in the world. And with her father gone and the war raging, her emotions were ragged. At Magnolia Bluff, she could take solace in the happiest times of her life: the carefree days with Harry, the quiet weekends with Robert. It could be a wonderful salve to the pain she witnessed at the hospital.

"I say we do it!" She smiled and turned back to Robert, momentarily gleeful. "Of course, there will be times where work makes it impossible to commute—but we will have the townhouse for that. I love the idea. A peaceful retreat at the end of each day at Magnolia Bluff. Robert, yet again, your brilliance amazes me. Thank you."

Chapter Seventeen

"Goddamnit! Goddamn them! Look what they've done to him. We have to help!" Estelle Lennox stood in Ruth's office yelling and waving her arms to flag down imaginary aid for an imaginary patient.

"She's been like this for months," her father said quietly as he sat in the chair beside her, the eggplant-colored circles under his eyes revealing the toll his daughter's behavior had taken. "I thought she'd improve when the navy discharged her, when she was no longer taking care of all these wounded soldiers. But it's been two months and she's gotten so much worse. Sometimes I even wonder if she'll hurt someone—me, or herself." He placed his face in his hands and took a deep breath. "I'm a widower, Mrs. Apter, and I need to work. I just don't know how to take care of her on my own."

Ruth nodded as she frowned sympathetically. "I know how difficult this is, Mr. Lennox." *You have no idea how well I know.*

Ruth kept expecting to feel less pained with each new veteran that came to Emeraldine Hospital but, instead, every time she did an intake like this one, she felt the agony of all that she went through with Harry as if it were happening for the first time. Emeraldine was now 30 percent over capacity with veterans unable to function in the world. Each time a new patient arrived, she wondered how her family would have felt if there hadn't been a bed for Harry. So, she took them all. She made more space. And she experienced anew the heartbreaking loss of two decades before as if it had just happened. She was emotionally and physically exhausted. Still, she had a job to do. One that was more important than ever.

"We are very experienced with the various psychoses that this awful war has brought about. Estelle has done such a noble thing serving as a nurse for our soldiers. Let us help her heal now."

"Do you really think you can help her?"

Ruth knew this desperation. This need for hope. She so badly wanted to embrace him tightly and tell him with certainty that she would make his daughter well. This was the true test—if she and Robert and Edward could weather this storm, treat these broken men and women, give them back their lives, then it wouldn't be all for naught. Harry would have died for a reason—to pave the way for progress. For healing. For better lives for so many. But she didn't say any of that. Instead she remained composed and professional.

"I do, Mr. Lennox," she stated as evenly as she could. "I really do. We've developed something of an expertise in this area. I can assure you both that Miss Lennox will be in the best hands here at Emeraldine." She smiled at the young woman.

"Oh, Estelle, please. I'm Estelle."

Ruth thought the beautiful twenty-three-year-old could be mistaken for someone in magazines or pictures, were it not for her incoherent ramblings. She was a stunner, with a heart-shaped face, perfectly plump pink lips, and thick brown hair.

"All right then, Estelle, would you like to see your room?" Ruth stood and gently took her arm. "You'll be rooming with several other military nurses. I think you'll be in perfect company." Estelle nodded tentatively as Ruth turned to her father. "Mr. Lennox, you can just head down the hall to Mrs. Cathers. She'll get you all squared away with the paperwork while I get your daughter settled.

"I do want to draw your attention to one item in our admissions document." She spoke quietly, so that Estelle wouldn't hear her. "We use the most progressive treatments here at Emeraldine, including, in extreme cases, lobotomy. In fact, my husband, Dr. Robert Apter, is the man who pioneered the procedure. While I can't tell you that Estelle will need an intervention of this magnitude, I do want to be sure you are aware that our paperwork permits us to perform any treatment we deem necessary to optimize her health and chances to be released. So, please make sure you are comfortable with that before you leave. I'm happy to discuss it with you further if you like, when I return."

Mr. Lennox seemed stunned, his eyes widening momentarily as he swallowed awkwardly and then nodded. "Whatever you need to do to help her." He looked away from Ruth for a moment as if he was ashamed and then turned back. "She sings, you know. Voice like an angel. Used to be a soloist in the church choir."

"Wonderful! We have a band that performs at our monthly dances. Perhaps you can sing with them, Estelle?" Ruth smiled encouragingly and then turned back toward her office to give Mr. Lennox a final reassurance. "She'll be very well taken care of. I give you my word."

Chapter Eighteen

Ruth entered Charles Hayden's office casually. The two of them had worked together for nearly twenty years, and she never gave a second thought when he requested a meeting with her. But today, as she sat across from him, she saw a wistful look on his face that unnerved her. He, too, had been working much too hard due to the influx of veterans. Perhaps that was what she saw in his eyes. The same fatigue they all felt.

"Charles, is everything all right?"

"Yes, yes. Not to worry. Please, have a seat." He motioned to the chair across from him and watched as she got herself settled. "Ruth, from the moment I began here at Emeraldine, you've been an invaluable and exceptional partner to me."

"I've only done what you've given me the opportunity to do." She looked at him, surprised. *Could this possibly be what he called me in for?*

"Not at all. From the beginning, you cared about every aspect of the patient experience in a way that few people do. You helped me to plan the design of our wards and common rooms so that Emeraldine feels warm and welcoming, while still offering the highest standard of care; you have stayed abreast of the latest advances in our field and encouraged the hiring and adoption of the most innovative thinkers and treatments—your husband at the top of the list. And, you have enabled me to make sure that Emeraldine runs smoothly while your personal, loving touch has helped each and every patient at this hospital feel like they are part of a family instead of an institution."

Ruth blushed. Such unmitigated praise made her uncomfortable. She didn't see anything she had done at Emeraldine as singularly extraordinary. She knew that Charles appreciated her. She agreed that they were a good team. She was simply doing her job as best she could. *What is this really about?*

"I'm sure you have wondered for some time when I might step away from my role as head of this hospital. I am getting up in years after all." He smiled.

"Not at all, actually. I can't imagine Emeraldine without you. You've made it what it is." Ruth felt a nervous sweat beginning to form under her blazer, in the pits of her arms. "Please don't tell me that you are planning to leave?"

"Not leave. Retire. It is time, Ruth. You've more than proven yourself capable to take the helm of this hospital. I cannot think of anyone to whom I would rather pass on my title."

"Charles, I'm honored and so appreciative of your support, but— it's simply too much." Ruth held her face in a tight but controlled smile, trying not to reveal the excitement she felt. She had, of course, wondered what it might be like to be the head of this entire hospital, but she'd never allowed herself to believe it was possible. It would be an incredible accomplishment for anyone—but especially a woman. Even if her name was on the building. Still, she knew much of Charles's day-to-day was administrative in nature. How could she possibly take on all of his responsibilities and still have time for the patients?

"I don't think I would be very good at the bureaucratic aspects of the job. The finances and the operations, the relationships with the major donors, legal protections and accreditations? You know my strength is with the people inside this hospital: the patients and the staff."

"I do indeed. But I also know that there is nothing you can't accomplish if you set your mind to it. I have begun to cull a list of candidates to replace you as assistant superintendent. People with backgrounds in just the type of administrative duties you are discussing. All with strong track records at other hospitals. And, of course, I won't go until you have found your replacement."

"But, the patients, Charles. What if I don't have enough time for the patients?"

"I will be candid with you, Ruth. You won't have as much time as you do now. You will have to sometimes trust reports from your assistant, as I have from you. But if you hire carefully, you can structure your position so that you have more time to be in the wards than I have. I ceded that part of my job to you because you are so exceptional at it."

Ruth looked down at her hands, embarrassed.

"Also, I will still be available to give you guidance and advice. Your mother has asked me to assume her seat on the board."

"She has?"

"Yes. Your father had only appointed it to her in an interim capacity, until you were ready to take over the hospital, at which point, he had intended for it to go to me."

Ruth looked at Charles with wide eyes. Had her father actually anticipated she would run Emeraldine one day?

"Ruth, I know he didn't say so, but your father was very impressed with you and your work at the hospital. I can assure you this was his plan all along."

"It was?" She couldn't imagine that was true. Bernard was so meticulous about all his plans. Certainly he would have spoken to her about it if he had seen her running Emeraldine in the future. "No, it's not possible—"

"Not only is it completely possible, it's the right thing to do. And now is absolutely the right time—past time, if you ask me." Charles stood and pulled Ruth into a fatherly embrace. "Congratulations on a job exceptionally well done, and a promotion long overdue. I can't wait to see what the next chapter of Emeraldine Hospital will look like with you at the helm."

Ruth stood in shock. It was all so much. But if Charles and her father believed in her, she had to be up for the task. "Thank you for your faith in me. Now and always. I have never taken for granted how fortunate I am to have had such a forward-thinking and supportive superior, and such a true friend. I will miss seeing you every day. And I can't even imagine how I will begin to fill your shoes."

"You don't need to fill anything; you just need to be yourself. Now, if this is settled, would you like to have a look at the résumés for your replacement? The sooner we get you sitting in this chair the better."

Ruth took a deep breath and nodded. The next chapter of her career was about to begin whether she wanted it to or not.

Chapter Nineteen

Ruth sat at her new desk, eyes burning. She had been officially running the hospital for three months now. With Charles's help, she had hired Roy Haddington to replace her as assistant superintendent. Roy came with several letters of recommendation from a small hospital in California where he had primarily been responsible for their finances and operations—the areas most anathema to Ruth—and she and Charles agreed he would be a good complement to her areas of expertise. Still, she constantly felt as if she was drowning in paperwork. The managerial aspects of her new role, which would have been overwhelming in quiet times, were exacerbated by the influx of war veterans.

It was already nine o'clock, and she needed to approve four requisition requests for equipment upgrades and read at least three more patient evaluations before she could consider going home. It was no matter. She had to wait for Robert and Edward to finish their last surgery of the day. Robert's days were busier than ever with his work at the hospital, a full lecture schedule at the university, and an ever-growing caseload of private patients at his offices in Manhattan and at Magnolia Bluff. He and Edward tended to perform surgeries first thing in the morning or later in the evening, when they'd finished the rest of the day's work. In spite of their best efforts, the wait list for lobotomies continued to grow.

The overcrowding was no different at psychiatric hospitals across the country, and Ruth felt proud that their pioneering work eased the suffering of so many. Nevertheless, she could hardly keep up with the scores of men and women who needed their help. She felt her eyelids drooping as she read the same line a fifth time and was jolted by a tap on her door.

"Edward." She smiled. "Finished for the day?"

"Yes, finally. Robert is just writing the last of his notes and then he should be ready to take you home. You look tired. You need to get some rest, Ruth."

"Oh, please, I do nothing compared to you and Robert. The two of you are the ones doing battle to repair the damaged. You're kind to worry about me, but I'm just fine."

"You don't give yourself enough credit. Our work wouldn't be possible if it weren't for you. You made this place. You keep it going. You have managed to accommodate two times our planned capacity and still seem to know the ins and outs of every single patient in every single ward. You're incredible. But even God needed a day of rest!"

Ruth looked at Edward, her eyes bloodshot and rimmed with purple circles. Perhaps it was the sleep deprivation. Or maybe the file she was reading about another suicidal soldier. Or the fact that Edward's genuine concern reminded her, yet again, what it felt like to have a brother. But suddenly Ruth felt her eyes filling with tears she couldn't tamp down.

"Ruth, what is it? You're doing all you can. We all are." Edward crossed the room and touched her back tentatively, like an awkward boy looking to comfort his mother.

"But what if it isn't enough?"

"What if what isn't enough?" Robert asked as he bounded through the door. "Eddie, my boy, what on earth have you done to bring my wife to tears?"

Ruth chuckled at what she realized was the absurdity of this moment. She shouldn't be the one crying. Robert and Edward worked nonstop for their patients. When they weren't treating people at Emeraldine, they traveled to other hospitals to train their doctors in lobotomy. They had even begun to consult for the Veterans Administration. These two men were swimming in a sea of mentally ill soldiers, and she had to stay strong and support them and her hospital. "Sorry, dear. Edward just caught me having a moment. Time to go home?" Ruth stood, gave Edward's arm a grateful squeeze, and neatly restacked the remaining files on her desk. She could read them first thing tomorrow morning.

Robert helped her with her coat and turned out her light, then the three of them walked down the dimly lit corridor toward the exit.

"Eddie, I think it is time that I tell Ruth about my new idea, don't you?"

"You haven't told her yet?" Edward sounded surprised, perhaps relieved. "I thought you told Ruth everything the moment it entered your head."

"Yes, yes. I usually do." Robert inclined his head toward Ruth and gave her a little smile. "But we've been so busy lately that we haven't had time for a proper conversation. And, with her being the final decision maker on all matters at the hospital now, I need to be careful to present to her professionally." He laughed. Robert had been thrilled about Ruth's promotion both for her success and because he knew she was the greatest champion of his ideas. "In fact, Eddie, why don't you come back to the house with us? We are staying in the city since it is so late. It will be the perfect time to begin to explain my idea to Ruth. The three of us can talk about it while we eat. You can spend the night."

"Edward, you are always welcome to stay with us, of course. But I am too exhausted for any sort of presentation tonight. I plan to head straight to bed when we get home." Ruth was comfortable enough around Edward that she didn't worry about offending him.

"Come now, Ruthie, you need to eat. And I promise this will be worth staying awake for."

"Frankly, I don't even know if there's anything in the house for supper. But I suppose Liana can make some sandwiches."

Once they were seated at the dining table with a simple supper of omelets, greens, and French baguettes, Robert excitedly began. "What if I told you I've come up with an adaptation of our lobotomy that could exponentially grow the number of people we can treat?"

"Exponentially?" Ruth knew Robert had been struggling with the constraints that prefrontal lobotomy presented. Emeraldine currently had a backlog of patients still waiting for the treatment because the hospital didn't have the capacity to administer the care required for so many. It was even worse in the overcrowded and less well-funded public hospitals that Robert had been visiting. If they could perform more lobotomies, it would be a boon to mental health.

"You heard me correctly." Robert smiled and stood, preparing for what Ruth now thought of as his "professorial mode" of conversation. "Amarro Fiamberti." He paused for dramatic effect or, perhaps, because Liana had arrived with a tray of food for them. As she left quietly, he continued. "This Italian doctor has been accessing the brain differently, without disturbing the skull. Through the upper membrane of the eye socket."

"Through the eyes?" Ruth didn't understand. "For lobotomy?"

"Well, he isn't using the access point regularly for lobotomy. But I think we can."

"But, how can you . . ."

"We've been doing lobotomies for nearly a decade now. We understand where we need to be in the brain. Eddie could do them blind at this point. Not that he ever would." Robert laughed, turning to Edward. "Perhaps you should try that first."

"Robert, how can you joke?" Ruth admonished.

"I'm not joking, *exactly*. If we enter up through the eye socket—transorbitally—we would essentially be performing a lobotomy with no view of the brain. But we can do that, I think, because we know that part of the brain so well now. Plus, there is some margin for error. Right, Eddie?"

"Well." He looked at Ruth, seeming a bit uncomfortable. "Robert believes that since none of the patients from whom we've taken samples have shown any difference in result from those who we haven't, that if we weren't perfectly precise in the transorbital approach, the patients wouldn't suffer."

"Samples?" Ruth sought confirmation.

"Yes, the live tissue we've periodically collected for our research has helped our progress tremendously."

"Right, of course." Ruth wasn't certain she knew about this, but she assumed they had told her at some point, and she simply hadn't thought to make a note of it. It was a common enough practice for patients to serve the double duty of research subjects. "So, what is the benefit of this new point of entry for lobotomy? How would it change anything?"

"If we can go up through the eye socket, we don't need general anesthesia. I can simply knock people out with a few jolts of electroshock. No drilling into the skull. Minimal to no bleeding. No shaved hair. No stitches. Almost no recovery time. Lobotomy could become a simple office procedure."

Ruth took a bite of her eggs and then turned to Edward. "Do you think this could work?" While Robert was a brilliant doctor, when it came to matters of neurosurgery, she trusted Edward more. He did not look nearly as sure.

"Frankly, I'm just beginning to wrap my arms around the concept. I can't imagine I would feel comfortable performing a lobotomy outside of a hospital under any condition, but I do think that a transorbital approach might be more efficient—"

"Which would enable us to treat more patients!"

"*If* we can master the conditions in a hospital setting."

"Details, details!"

"Boys!" Ruth laughed, standing from the table. "I am too tired for details. Please, let's talk about it some more in the morning, okay?" And, with that, Ruth gave her husband a kiss and Edward a pat on his shoulder and went to bed.

Chapter Twenty

Ruth drove through the gate and up the gravel drive, feeling the tension in her body release at the smell of the salty air, overjoyed to be home. Now that they had moved full time to Magnolia Bluff, they had purchased a second car and often commuted to and from the city separately. She missed her drives with her husband, but with Robert spending entire days seeing psychiatric patients in his private office in the carriage house, and so busy with patients and lobotomies at the hospital that he sometimes didn't come home until after midnight, it was simply impractical to travel together.

As Ruth approached the porte cochere, she saw a car parked at the far end of the circular driveway. Did Robert have a patient at the cottage? He had left the hospital hours before her and she was certain he hadn't mentioned any patients in the afternoon. They were supposed to have dinner together. Work had been so all-encompassing lately she couldn't remember the last time they had shared a proper meal. She felt low, and really needed a dose of Robert's determination tonight. He was excellent at reminding her that things would be better for the men in their care than they had been for Harry.

She gathered her things from the car and walked through the grand marble foyer, past the dining room, and into the kitchen where she found the cook. "Liana, it seems that Dr. Apter is going to be working later tonight than I thought. Can you please keep dinner warm? I'll let you know when we're ready to eat."

Without waiting for a response, she exited the kitchen's back door and crossed the stone path to Robert's office. As she briskly approached, she saw a man sitting on the chair outside the carriage house. His pained face was illuminated by rays of the sun as it made its way lower in the sky. "Do you have someone inside?" she asked, her tone soft.

The man began to nod. "My wife is in with the doctor." His face was drawn, and his jaw clenched. She felt a wave of sympathy run through her.

"What time was her appointment?" He gave Ruth a distrustful look. "I work with Dr. Apter, at Emeraldine Hospital in Manhattan. You can talk to me, it's okay."

"Three o'clock," he said, looking relieved to have a professional to talk to. "I didn't want it to come to this, I really didn't. But last week she locked herself in her room for two days, and when I finally got her out, she came at me with a knife." His eyes filled with tears. "I've always treated her like a princess. How can a wife do that to her own husband? I just want her back again, back the way she was."

Ruth shifted her gaze away from him and down the lawn to the water's edge, to hide her shock. She had assumed Robert was simply in the midst of a session, but he was fastidious about keeping those to a single hour, and it was almost five thirty.

Was it possible that he was performing the new transorbital lobotomy?

There was no way he would attempt this, for the first time, without even telling her, was there? And, if he was, what about Edward?

"Sir, may I ask your name?"

"Darner. Thomas Darner. My wife in there"—he gestured toward the closed cottage door—"is Alice."

"Mr. Darner, did Dr. Apter tell you how long to expect the appointment to take?" Ruth tried to sound casual in spite of her now racing heart.

"He said the procedure would be quick, and then maybe an hour for her to recover enough to walk to the car. I know I have been here for quite a bit longer than that . . ." Mr. Darner's tears started to flow, and Ruth grabbed his hand in her own as much to soothe him as to steady herself. She knew Edward was teaching today in his new position at Columbia and she didn't think Robert would consider performing a lobotomy without him.

Still, she was always a hospital superintendent first, and she knew that this moment required her to reassure the family of the patient. She looked Mr. Darner squarely in the eye for the first time. "I am certain that Dr. Apter will help your wife. He can work miracles. How about if I just pop in and check on her progress for you?"

Even with the shades drawn, she could see the outline of her husband standing above Alice Darner, and he seemed oddly still. She knocked gently on the door so as not to startle him. If he was performing the procedure, she knew it required delicacy and a steady hand. In a calm and even tone, she asked, "Robert, everything okay in there?"

"Ruth?" he confirmed. "Excellent! I need a second pair of hands. Please, please come in quickly!"

"I'll just be a moment," she assured Mr. Darner as she fumbled slightly to open the door while obscuring his view. She slipped inside, taking a deep breath to slow the throbbing in her temples.

"Ah, thank goodness!" Robert said excitedly. "I've done it! I am essentially finished, just have to remove the instruments, but I need to take a photo. I've been standing here for what feels like forever trying to calculate how to keep these things in place and reach the camera."

Ruth sucked in a short, sharp breath, feeling as if she might faint. She had heard Robert describing the surgery endlessly for the past six months, but somehow, she hadn't imagined it would look quite like this. There he was, her husband, standing over an examination table. On it, Alice Darner was draped in a floral sheet from the neck down. Was this one of their guest linens? And the "instruments" Robert had chosen—those couldn't possibly be the ice picks from Ruth's own freezer? Had he decided to perform this procedure on a whim? And did he really leave this poor woman in such a state for even one second more than necessary, simply for a photo?

"Can you just steady these for me for a moment, darling? So I can take a few shots?"

"Robert, I . . ."

"Actually." He was so caught up in the moment that he seemed not to notice her hesitation. "I need to hold them. You take the photos. This way, you can capture the full insertion, and an image of me removing the instruments. Just remember, the removal is quick, so be ready!"

Ruth steadied herself. She knew this was a pivotal moment in her husband's work, and not only was she here to witness it, he was counting on her to capture it for the world to see. He needed her. She walked to the table and picked up the camera.

"Ready," she said flatly as the room moved in and out of focus.

"Get in close enough to see how the instrument inserts," Robert reminded her. A clammy sweat formed on her upper lip and brow, but she took the picture.

"Great. Now, here I go removing them . . . steady . . . okay, shoot." Robert turned his face toward her, beaming at the camera like a movie star on the red carpet. Then the flash went off, and Ruth, unable to stomach the sight for a moment longer, collapsed on the floor.

Chapter Twenty-One

The following evening, Ruth walked to the carriage house excitedly. Robert had completed his first successful transorbital lobotomy and he was telling Edward the details about it before Edward's new girlfriend arrived for their weekend stay. They knew better than to talk about lobotomy in front of her (it was a bit gruesome for those outside their line of work), and her train was due to arrive soon.

Ruth had been surprised by what she had witnessed yesterday—particularly Robert's chosen instrument to perform the procedure—but the end result had been a success. She was sure Edward would be as excited as she was. As she approached the door, she heard Edward yelling. She knew Robert was quick to rage, but never, in the ten years since Edward had become part of their lives, had Ruth heard Edward truly raise his voice. Until now.

". . . after I expressly told you over and over again that I didn't agree with this!"

Ruth stood frozen outside the door, unable to stop herself from listening.

"I didn't perform it in the hospital. You don't have to have anything to do with it."

"Please, Robert, we're partners. And I'm supposed to be the surgeon. It's one thing for you to take the scalpel in an operating room with me, and back up nurses and medical interventions in case of an accident. But here?"

"What about here? I am perfectly capable of treating my patients in my office and how dare you insinuate otherwise."

"This is an outpatient office for psychiatry. It isn't sterile. You don't have the proper equipment. What would you have done if she'd had a seizure? An uncontrollable hemorrhage?" Edward's tone shifted from angry to pleading.

"Those risks are rare anomalies. Alice Darner skipped out of here smiling."

"Here we go again with your anomalies."

"*This* is the future of lobotomy. The beauty is that I *can* perform it myself, any doctor can. And I *can* perform it here, in my office. I don't need a hospital and I'm free to save as many people as there are hours in the day."

"Robert, please. You need to hear me. I am not trying to stop progress. I just want to make sure what you're doing is safe."

Ruth was suddenly unnerved. Why was Edward reacting this way? Was he right that the procedure should not be performed in an outpatient setting? Should Ruth be more concerned?

But she had questioned Robert extensively over the past few weeks, as he discussed preparations to shift to this new technique. He assured her that the procedure was safe to perform in an office, and she had seen Alice Darner walk out of the carriage house with her own eyes. If Robert could continue to treat patients with the transorbital lobotomy, he could heal so many more people. Why, with the right press and attention, Emeraldine could grow to be one of the nation's leading facilities for research and advancement on the treatment of mental illness. They might even attract enough funding for national expansion. Imagine how much good they could do with Emeraldine treatment facilities across the country! Ruth generally trusted Edward, but his response didn't make any sense. Was it possible that something else was motivating it? Edward was always relegated to the second chair, tucked away behind Robert's shadow. Could it be that his anger now was an expression of years of hidden resentment? It seemed so uncharacteristic, but Ruth couldn't think of another explanation.

Suddenly the door slammed opened. Edward strode angrily in the direction of his car. "If that's what you want, fine!" he called over his shoulder.

He jumped in and started the ignition.

"Edward!" Ruth called frantically. She couldn't let him storm off. They needed to talk. But the ocean breeze carried her voice away.

Surely, he was just going to collect Rebecca at the train. This was simply a fight between colleagues, after all.

The car tore down the drive and out of sight.

Ruth ran inside the carriage house and found Robert standing by his desk, collar undone, looking deeply shaken. "I don't understand, I thought he'd be thrilled. We can now help everyone who needs it."

"I know, I know," Ruth whispered, squeezing his arm.

"People who can't afford a hospital stay can now be cured."

"Sh, sh, sh, yes," Ruth said. Were there tears in the corners of his eyes? "Robert, listen to me." She looked at him. "You have made a tremendous breakthrough. We need to spread the word far and wide about your radical innovation. I am going to make sure that everyone will know what you have pioneered. This new treatment of yours . . . it's going to change everything."

He wrapped his arms around her. "I love you, my darling," he said ferociously into her hair.

"I love you too," she whispered back.

Chapter Twenty-Two

Six months later, Ruth sat at the kitchen table with a cup of black coffee. Usually, the bracing bitterness was the perfect jump-start to the day, but on this particular morning, no stimulant was needed. If anything, she might require something to slow her racing heart. The morning papers, piled neatly for her when she came down to the kitchen, were now scattered everywhere, folded open to the relevant pages. The date at the top of each one, January 23, 1947, was one they would remember forever.

She looked out the window toward the water, but even the tranquil view was not enough to calm her excitement. Her body vibrated to the rhythm of her bouncing foot, and at the sound of footsteps, she nearly leapt out of her chair. "Robert?"

"Expecting someone else?" He was dressed for the day in a three-piece suit, with his walking stick. Ruth wasn't sure the apparatus added the gravitas that Robert believed it did, but like all his flamboyant affects, she was powerless to change it, so she chose to find it charming. She smiled at her husband and stood to pour him a cup of coffee. As she crossed the kitchen, she dropped the *New York Times* in front of him, open to the headline: "The Ice Pick Lobotomy: A Ten-Minute Miracle Cure for the Insane."

Ruth watched Robert as the corners of his mustache lifted and his entire face expanded into a triumphant smile. He began to read aloud, "'Earlier this week I was one of a select group of reporters invited to a special presentation at the Emeraldine Hospital . . .'" Robert muttered, skimmed the next bit, and then read on. "'This is not the first time that I have written about the promising work of Dr. Apter in his quest to find a more effective treatment for mental patients.'" Robert lifted his eyes to Ruth to be sure she was listening and then continued. "'He is the man responsible for the prefrontal lobotomy, a surgery that involves drilling into the brain . . .' Oh, I think I know how it's done," Robert murmured good-humoredly as he continued to scan the article. "'. . . For a decade, Dr. Apter has been using his lobotomy to help the most violent and incurable patients at the Emeraldine Hospital here in New York.' Yes, yes. More about the old procedure. Ah, here we go, a direct quote from me in the *New York Times!*" Robert straightened up as he read his own words to Ruth. "'For several years I have believed that there must be a more effective way to enter the brain. One that would have the same efficacy as the prefrontal lobotomy but that was not a surgery. This new method is a simple procedure that can be performed in any office in the country.'" Robert paused and looked across the kitchen to catch Ruth proudly smiling at him. His own smile grew as he continued to read, half to himself and half aloud. "'Dr. Apter explained that the patient arriving in the operating theater had, just the day before, tried to stab a nurse with a fork she had stolen from her lunch . . . The entire procedure took less than a few minutes and, other than the unavoidable residue on the "ice pick," there was virtually no blood . . . When the patient, an attractive former nurse who had developed violent fits of rage after the war, regained consciousness, Dr. Apter, to our horror, offered her a Waldorf salad with a fork—' I hope Edward sees this, wherever he is."

"You know, Robert, I thought it was a bit much when you did that to poor Estelle after the procedure, but it seems to have made a strong impression. You really do know how to engage an audience." Ruth placed a steaming mug of coffee in front of her husband, who radiated like the sun in a cloudless sky. She paused to bask in his warmth and then settled herself in the seat across from him.

"'In all my years covering medicine,'" Robert continued, "'I can honestly say that I have never witnessed a breakthrough like this. The patient was giggling and gleeful as she calmly ate her salad and declared to the room that she felt better than she had in years. Dr. Robert Apter is undoubtedly a medical genius who has found, in his new "ice pick" lobotomy, a miracle cure.'" Robert slapped the paper down as he stood up. "A medical genius. A miracle cure!" Beaming, he grabbed Ruth by the hand, pulled her from her chair, and twirled her around the room before dipping her with dramatic flair and kissing her deeply. Ruth, as always, flooded with that feeling of gratitude for this exceptional man.

"All right, time to head to Emeraldine. I am sure the operators will be overwhelmed with calls from hospitals across the country looking to learn how to perform my 'miracle.'" His smile stretched from ear to ear. "Ready, my dear?"

"Robert?" Ruth gave him a prompting look.

"What is it, dear? You look radiant as always. Now come along; if you want to drive together today, I need to get into the office tout de suite."

"I'm still in my dressing gown!"

"Ah yes." He chuckled as he actually took her in.

"I need a few minutes."

"Sorry, I can't wait. Work to be done, work to be done." He picked up his briefcase and gave her a theatrical bow, as if he were tipping his hat, and whistling the seven dwarfs' song from *Snow White*, he walked out the door.

Chapter Twenty-Three

"Our socials won't be the same without you. It's like we had our very own Andrews sister, right, Albert?" Ruth gave Estelle Lennox a heartfelt smile as she turned to Albert Burdell, one of the inmates with whom Estelle had become very close. "I know you are going to miss your singer a great deal." He smiled and nodded with tears in his eyes.

Albert had been a patient at Emeraldine for nearly a year now. His family had him admitted for schizophrenia, although it was clear to Ruth that was not the malady he suffered from. Certainly, he'd experienced traumatic stress; that was evident from the scarring on his back and thighs, the flinching behind the eyes at sudden movements, his proclivity for nightmares. Still, he was a highly engaging and competent man. He was quite good-looking, tall and lean with thick brown hair that he slicked into a fashionable soft wave; he dressed impeccably and had an air of sophistication that reeked of generations of wealth. Yet, he was unpretentious. He never looked down upon the hospital's other patients regardless of their background and was a kind and sought-after friend. He played the piano beautifully and had become Estelle's accompanist and near-constant companion from the moment they met in the music room. At the monthly socials, all the patients congregated around Albert and Estelle, and the two seemed as if they had been friends for years.

Initially, Estelle's father worried that they might have romantic feelings toward one another, but Ruth assured him Albert didn't pay that kind of attention to the women at the hospital. Ruth did not judge Albert for being homosexual. In fact, when she understood that this was why he was at Emeraldine, she tried to convince him that he should leave the hospital to enjoy his life in the world—perhaps in Europe. In spite of what his family thought, Ruth knew all too well that it was possible to rise above that disapproval. She knew that one could still make a good life. Although, thankfully, when it came to her interests, no one had ever tried to "beat it out of her."

"All right, well, that is the last of it. I'm afraid it is time to say goodbye, Albert."

Ruth had allowed Albert into the women's quarters to help Estelle pack, in part because she hoped that with his best friend leaving, he would be more inclined to follow after her.

"Estelle, my beauty, go share that voice of yours with the world." He gave her a gentle hug.

"Oh yes, I'll be singing!" Estelle giggled. "Just, now it will be at my new job at the school. I'll miss you, Albie!" She smiled easily as he walked with her and Ruth to the end of the corridor and then turned left, back toward the men's wing, while they turned right, to meet Estelle's father in the front hall.

"I don't know how to say goodbye." Estelle fidgeted. She seemed anxious to get the farewell over with and go back to the world.

"You don't need to. You can come back and visit me. I am very proud of you."

Saying goodbye to patients healthy enough to be released was one of the pure joys of Ruth's work, and thanks to lobotomy, she was having more of these moments. She understood that she was not sending her patients home the same as they were before. Estelle's speech was less sophisticated than it had been before the procedure, and sometimes she had a bit of a twitch, but she could function outside of a hospital. Be with her father. Have a regular life. It was a triumph.

Ruth would genuinely miss Estelle. She had been a challenging patient at first. So capable and lucid at times, and then suddenly deteriorating into moments of unexpected violence. Like that fork incident, which had not happened the day before her lobotomy, in spite of what Robert told the press. Sometimes he was like a carnival barker embellishing and creating drama to intensify his impact. Still, Ruth couldn't deny that since her lobotomy, Estelle had been just wonderful. Placid, even-tempered, happy. Ruth could see that she had surely been a good nurse at one time. She didn't have the mental capacity for that kind of work anymore, but the Veterans Administration had helped her secure a job as a music teacher at a small school, and she would be well suited to that.

"Mr. Lennox, we are quite sad to say goodbye to your delightful daughter. But we are overjoyed to be able to return her to you."

"Mrs. Apter, I don't know how to thank you." He shook Ruth's hand a bit too long, overcome with emotion.

"There is no need, sir. This is my job. Anyway, Estelle's health is more than enough thanks for me."

"For all of us. I just can't believe it. I have my girl back." He turned to his daughter and she embraced him.

"Let's go, Dad. I wanna see my room and my bed. And I'm hungry."

Ruth laughed. "Estelle, stay in touch with us! And, please, do let us know how she is doing," she said to Mr. Lennox as she handed him his daughter's few belongings. "We wish you all the best of luck."

"We don't need luck. We have you." He smiled. "C'mon, Stelle, let's go home!"

Chapter Twenty-Four

Ruth shut the door to her office and sat down next to Susie in the other Barcelona chair. She had been running Emeraldine for eighteen months now, and Robert had finally convinced her to redecorate Charles's office to both make it feel like her own and give it a more modern aesthetic. She would have happily stayed in her old office, but she knew it would have set the wrong tone with Roy Haddington, her assistant superintendent, to put him in the larger corner office. As a female in charge, she needed to do everything she could to ensure that others recognized her authority. Unfortunately, as she sat down with Susie to look over the inconsistencies in the annual budget, she worried she hadn't done enough.

"I'm going to tell it to you straight, Raffey, this looks bad."

"So, I'm not wrong?"

"Well, I don't work with budgets of this scale at my little women's health organization, but an increase in spending of twenty-five percent? I'd lose my job over that."

"I just can't make sense of it. I've been over every line a dozen times. Our patient load is actually down year over year. We've started to send veterans home." She smiled in spite of herself. "Suze, do you see anything I might have missed? I was hoping to solve this myself before getting the accountants involved, it being my first full fiscal year as the head of this hospital."

"I wish I did." Susie flipped the pages of the reports in front of her and started entering numbers into her adding machine. "Did you put in new heating this year?"

"No. Charles had all that upgraded right before the war. It's been just over five years. We might have needed some repairs but certainly not an entirely new system."

"Hmmm. Did you get all new mattresses?"

"No! What do you see?" Ruth leaned over to look at the pages Susie was examining.

"Look at this: the monthly spending on these six line items . . . it goes up a little bit each month this year. I think this is your culprit." She flipped back and forth through the pages of the Facilities Management section of the budget. "None of the expenses are that large on their own, but they add up to a big increase in spending if you combine them."

"But we didn't upgrade any of these things. At least I didn't authorize it." Ruth looked at Susie, scrunching her eyes to makes sense of what was dawning on her. "Roy handles this part of the budget. He's supposed to clear any significant increases with me, of course. But, I've been overwhelmed. You know I like to visit with the patients as much as I can during the day—could he have made all these decisions without me knowing? Have I been so remiss in doing my job that I missed this?"

"I honestly don't know, Raff, but there is one easy way to find out. Go ask the man."

"Thank you for your help, Suze." Ruth stood up. "I don't want to take up more of your day and I think, now, I have enough to get to the bottom of this."

"Are you kidding? I want to know what the hell happened. I'm not going anywhere. I can wait."

"You are too much." Ruth laughed. "Thank you."

She made her way to Roy's office filled with a mix of anger and shame. She had given Roy a lot of latitude over the budget so that she could maintain her close patient relationships. That was a big part of why she hired him. Charles had encouraged it. But had she let him do too much unchecked? At the end of the day, the fiscal management of the hospital was her responsibility. She had to ensure funds were properly allocated.

"Roy, do you have a moment?" She walked into his office without knocking. Roy was an unremarkable-looking man. He stood an inch or two shorter than Ruth, a perfectly average height, and had light brown hair with eyes to match. He made up for his average looks by always dressing exceedingly well—his hair Brylcreem-combed to perfection, his suit and tie always the latest fashion. Ruth found it perplexing given that most of his days were spent with patients, but she hadn't given it much more thought than that.

"Of course." His tone was not entirely welcoming. "What do you need?"

"Well, I'm going over our year-end fiscal reports, and I see a large increase in spending that I don't remember authorizing."

"And?" he snapped at her, almost impatient.

"And"—she looked at him sharply—"I need to understand what these purchases were."

"I make numerous facilities purchases over the year, Mrs. Apter. If I came to you for approval on every one, neither of us would get any other work done."

"I appreciate that, but these are steady monthly increases that simply make no sense. I know you are fastidious about your record keeping, so I imagine it should be no problem to find the receipts for me. I just need to understand what we bought and why so I can explain it to the board."

"That's a ton of paperwork. Seems like a waste of time to me."

"Well, I'm afraid it is necessary. Please gather the receipts and bring them to my office as soon as possible."

"Yes, ma'am." Roy looked away from Ruth and started rifling through drawers. Though he had never been the warmest man, today he was rude to the point of insubordination. Something was not right. She hoped she had just caught him off guard, but she worried there might be more.

Several hours later, with Susie long gone, Roy came to Ruth's office with an update. She had gone in search of him twice, hoping to assuage her growing concerns, but both times he was nowhere to be found.

"Finally! Do you have the receipts for me?"

"I don't." Roy looked away from her, his lips set indignantly.

"I don't understand."

"I searched everywhere, even went down into the archives, and I couldn't find anything. They must have been thrown away by accident. Honestly, I don't understand why you need to see them anyway. If there were spending increases, it was because we needed items purchased. Heating vents, linens, there are many things that require frequent replenishment in the hospital, you know. I buy things all the time."

"Of course, but that wouldn't change dramatically from one year to the next, would it? We didn't do any major capital improvements. It simply isn't making sense. Are there other receipts missing as well? Or just these?"

"I'm not sure what you want me to say." Roy was defensive as he looked Ruth in the eye with an aggressive scowl, challenging her to push him on this. She remained undeterred.

"I want you to track down the items that drove a twenty-five percent increase in our year-over-year budget. I need specifics to explain this kind of irresponsible spending to the board."

"Are you calling me irresponsible?"

"You're misconstruing me, Roy. I am not trying to place blame; I am simply saying that this is not an acceptable increase. I need an explanation for the board, and since this was under your purview, I expect you to provide one."

"Well, I can't do more than I already have. So that'll have to be enough." Roy turned away abruptly and slammed Ruth's door behind him. She was stunned. He was acting like a petulant child. Once she got through this board meeting, she would have to put him on notice. This behavior was unacceptable, and if he couldn't show her more respect, he would need to be replaced.

As it turned out, she never had another conversation with Roy. When Ruth arrived at the hospital the following morning, she found his office cleared of all personal items, as well as any paper trail that might have directly indicated him for his thievery. Ruth felt destroyed by his violation of her trust and, even more, by the fact that she had let such a thing happen. Her first major contribution as head of Emeraldine was an embezzlement scandal. How could she have been so blind?

One thing Ruth now knew for certain—while budgeting, requisitions, and financial planning were not her favorite parts of the job, they were critically important. She could never again lose sight of the administrative underpinnings of her hospital, even if that meant losing some of her day-to-day contact with her patients. This was her job now, and if she survived this scandal, she would never again risk failing at it, no matter what.

INTERLUDE

ROBERT: 1952

Robert placed his portable electroshock machine on the floor beside him and knocked forcefully on the door. As he looked around for signs of life, he noticed the trash lining the stairwell and the paint peeling from the doors. This single-room occupancy hotel was not the type of establishment he would stay in, that was certain, but then again, Robert would never be hiding out from a court-ordered lobotomy like this man was.

It wasn't the first time that an involuntary case hadn't shown up for a scheduled appointment. Robert could have left the man to another doctor, but he didn't want any patient to miss an opportunity to have their procedure performed by him, if possible. And he would only be in Ohio for one more day. So, there he stood, at the man's door. Robert knew a little dose of electroshock would likely be all the patient needed to assuage his jitters, and Midwestern Regional Hospital didn't have a portable electroshock machine, so he made the trip to this awful place himself.

"Mr. Orenbluth, it's Dr. Apter. We spoke on the phone this afternoon." Robert heard shuffling behind the door. Was he really going to have to coax this man like a stray alley cat? "Sir, I am only here to help you. I drove out of my way after a long day of work so that we could talk. Please, open the door."

"Just talk?"

"Yes, sir, just talk."

The door opened a crack, with the chain still on. "Then why do you have that thingamajig machine next to your feet?"

"Don't worry about that; I have that with me in case you'd like some help to feel calmer. I know that this procedure can seem frightening, but there really is no reason to worry." Robert leaned in, toward the small opening, and forcefully whispered, "Sir, I am sure you do not want the other occupants of this establishment to know your business so, please, let me in and we can go over this in private." He heard the chain slide, and the door opened. An overwhelming stench of mold, cigarette smoke, and stale alcohol immediately hit him. The man sat down on the unmade bed. "Mr. Orenbluth, I can tell that you are suffering. Lobotomy will make you better. Isn't that why you agreed to have it done?"

"Yeah, it is." He looked down at the ground and kicked a beer can under the bed. As if he could hide it there. "But I dunno. Cuttin' into people's brains. Doesn't seem right somehow. It's ungodly."

Robert winced. He detested that turn of phrase. God had given man the ability to reason, and Robert had used this gift of reason to develop a miraculous way to ease suffering. It was religious poetry, that's what it was.

He noticed an overflowing ashtray on the small desk. He needed to get out of this filthy place as soon as possible. "Mr. Orenbluth, may I call you Sam?" The man nodded. "Sam, did your doctor at the hospital explain the reason for lobotomy to you?"

Sam nodded again slowly—it seemed he was hesitant to admit too much.

"From what I see in your file, there is a strong chance that you will be placed in lockdown at an institution based on your recent behavior. Did the doctor tell you that?"

More nods.

"So, you understand that this is going to help you? To let you have a life? To keep you out of prison?"

"Yeah. But what kinda life will it be without all of my brain?"

"I think you misunderstand. You will retain your brain. You will just lose the connections that make you do the bad and violent things, like breaking a beer bottle and holding it at the bartender's throat for giving you the wrong change."

Sam looked down in shame. "I wasn't really gonna hurt him. Just wanted him to know he couldn't mess with me."

"Whatever the details of that event, they led you to the hospital where you ended up on my schedule. I am only in town for one more day, Sam. And I am the man who invented this procedure. I have performed more of them than anyone else in the country. My understanding is that the state wants you to have a lobotomy one way or another. So, would you rather come to the hospital tomorrow and have it done by the country's expert, or wait longer and let one of the staff members, who I will have just trained, stick an ice pick in your brain?"

"Stop! Stop talking about it! I don't want it! I'll be better. I promise."

Robert looked at the man in front of him. He wasn't tall, but he was quite solid and a bit overweight. He could hurt Robert badly if he wasn't careful. Robert bent down and opened the top of his electroshock machine and plugged it in. It began to hum.

"What's that? Whatcha doin'? Don't hurt me!"

"It's okay, Sam. It's okay." Robert looked at him with his kindest and gentlest smile. He needed to get him sedated before things got out of hand. "This is simply a tool that I use to help patients who are feeling very worried. Come sit here on the floor with me and have a look. See, these coils hold electricity, like inside of a light bulb. Sometimes I use it on myself for a headache; it feels lovely, really. A small tickle that just makes my body relax." He lifted the two metal cups and held them on either side of his temples. "I just place these little cups here, like this, step on that pedal there, and the next thing you know, you will feel calm and peaceful. You probably won't even remember what you were worrying about." Sam seemed to be calming down just by listening. "This is such a good treatment that you will feel relaxed and fearless all the way until tomorrow, when I will see you at the hospital, and if you want, I can use this again. Would you like to try it?"

"Will it hurt?"

"You won't feel a thing. I promise." Robert leaned over to Sam and, in one deft movement, placed the electrodes on his head and stepped on the pedal. Sam convulsed momentarily and his upper lip curled as a shot of current ran through him. When Robert released the pedal, along with his grasp on Sam, the man slumped over onto the floor, unconscious. Robert unplugged the machine and packed it neatly back up. He thought it might be better to leave Sam in a prone position, so he grabbed under his armpits and drew his torso long. Sam was so listless that Robert might have worried he was dead if he didn't see the man's chest rising and falling with breath. *Well, that should keep him until tomorrow.*

Robert stood to go and, as he reached for the doorknob, noticed the white cuff of his lab coat. He had come over in such a hurry that he hadn't yet removed it. Placing the electroshock on the floor, he sat in the small vinyl chair next to the desk, the seed of an idea taking root. A brilliant idea, actually. He slid his hand into the lab coat pocket and fingered the orbitoclast—the metal "ice pick." He didn't have a mallet, but he could probably quickly run to get one from his car. He'd rather not take the chance, though. Perhaps there was something in the room he could use. He scanned the area, looking through the mess for some-thing heavy and blunt enough to act as a surrogate hammer. An empty bottle was too risky; the glass might shatter. His eyes landed on the nightstand. Smiling at his cleverness, he walked toward it, opened the drawer, and removed the large book that sat inside.

He locked the door and knelt down next to Sam on the filthy carpet. He straightened Sam's undershirt, and then carefully laid the orbitoclast and the book on his stomach, amused that Sam made such a fine instrument tray. Then he deftly flipped open Sam's right eyelid and went to work. The book was a bit more unwieldy than a mallet, but it did the trick. And Robert did love the poetry of it. "I'll show you ungodly," he muttered as he gave the metal stake its final tap.

He watched Sam for five minutes after he had finished, to make sure his breath remained steady. And then he placed the Bible back in the drawer and went into the hallway bathroom to give the orbitoclast a thorough rinse. By the time he returned, Sam had started to stir. Robert settled himself in the chair and calmly waited. Slowly, Sam moved his body a bit more and then turned to his side, curling up in a fetal position with a soft smile on his face.

"Sam," Robert said gently. "Sam, don't fall back to sleep there. Can you sit up for me?"

The man complied, pushing himself to a seated position. His face contorted into a look of confusion and he brought his hand to his head.

"Yes, you have a bit of a headache, I imagine. That is the most unpleasant aftereffect of the procedure. But it will recede in a day or two. Can you stand up, maybe lie down on the bed?" Robert offered Sam his hand in case he needed assistance. Sam grabbed it gratefully, and as Robert helped him up off the floor, he fell into a bear hug, hanging on Robert. "Okay, now. Let's get you into bed."

As Sam settled himself, Robert searched the desk for a piece of paper and a pen. Unable to find one, he turned to Sam. "I am going to be right back; I just need to go to my car for a moment. I am going to leave the door open. You can call for me if you need me. Just say 'Doctor,' okay?" He propped the door open with the electroshock machine and hurried out the door. When Robert returned, moments later, Sam was more awake, staring at the door blankly. "Good, you're becoming more alert. Can you tell me your name?"

"S-S-Sam." He smiled.

"Very good. And my name?"

"DOCTOR!" he shouted proudly.

"Yes." Robert gave an encouraging nod. "Sam, you had a small procedure today. It should make you feel much happier, but it might be hard to remember some things. And your head is likely to hurt for a bit. Does it still hurt now?"

Sam looked quizzically at Robert and then nodded.

"That's all right, it will get better. I am going to take a photo now. You will see a flash, so don't be startled." Robert snapped a shot with the camera he had brought back from the car and then removed a piece of paper from his pocket and handed it to Sam. "I need to go now, but if you feel sick at all, just walk to the desk downstairs and hand them this paper. Okay?"

Sam looked at him, perplexed.

"Let me read it to you: 'My name is Sam Orenbluth. I had a state-ordered lobotomy on April 22, 1952. Please call Midwestern Regional Hospital in case of any concerns.' You understand?"

Sam looked blankly at Robert.

"There is an attendant at a desk just down there." Robert pointed out the door and down the stairs. "You give them this paper if you need anything. Okay?" He placed the note in Sam's hand as he nodded. "Okay, Sam. You take care."

Robert turned toward the door, grabbed the handle of his portable machine, and was on his way. It had been a long day and he was ready to celebrate with a nice glass of Bordeaux and a steak.

PART 3

RUTH AND MARGARET: 1952–53

Chapter Twenty-Five

"He's still crying, Frank. He's still crying." Margaret paced back and forth in their small living room, her whole body tense, as she waited for William to fall asleep.

"Mags, Dr. Spock says to say good night and leave them. You know that. Worked like a charm with John and Maisy. And they were a lot younger than six months. Come, sit. We can watch *I Love Lucy*, that'll distract you." Frank turned on the new television set.

"Turn it down!" she snapped sharply at Frank. "What if he hears it?"

"So what if he hears it? He needs to learn to fall asleep with noise. That's part of life, honey." Margaret knew Frank was right, but every time William cried, her skin crawled and her pulse raced. She just couldn't tolerate feeling so on edge.

"Mommy, is William ever going to stop crying?" Maisy emerged in her nightgown, her golden curls framing her head like a halo. "John and I are trying to read."

I agree, Maisy. It is torture. Why can't William be more like the two of you?

"I know it might be hard to believe"—Frank grinned as he scooped up his daughter to take her back to the bedroom that she now shared with her older brother—"but you used to scream even louder than that. Let's ask your brother if he remembers."

"I did?" Maisy looked at her father with shock.

"Babies cry, Maisy. It's simply what they do. We all just have to live with it."

Margaret sighed. *How I live with it, I'm not sure anymore.*

By the time Ricky had forgiven Lucy for another one of her foibles, the house was silent. "See?" Frank stood, putting his hand out to lift his wife from the sofa. "Everything works out over time. You just need patience and faith. That's what got me through in France."

"Faith in God?" Margaret scoffed. She had prayed. It hadn't helped.

He took her hands. "Faith that you would be waiting for me. Faith that I could expand Dad's hardware store, that we would have our own house. This third child is a gift, and we will manage just fine."

Margaret smiled and nodded at her husband. *Can't you see I'm not managing? That my life is unwinding more and more all the time? Do you not see the black rings around my eyes? Notice the clumps of my hair that litter the bathroom floor, even after I vacuum?*

"Let's go to bed. You know they say Mommy should sleep when Baby does."

Margaret managed to smile as she followed her husband to bed. William was asleep; the house was calm. For the moment there was nothing for her to worry about. Maybe tonight she would finally get some much-needed rest.

Margaret awoke with a start and looked at the clock. It was 3:00 a.m. and the house was silent. Too silent. She shivered as she realized that her nightgown was soaked in sweat. Again. Had she had a nightmare? She sat up, suddenly feeling wide awake. Three-cups-of-black-coffee awake. Why hadn't William woken up? He usually still had one feeding in the middle of the night. *Another failure to train him properly.* She leapt out of bed in a panic, racing out of her room and down the hall.

As she stood at the side of her son's crib, she watched his stomach rise and fall, his breath rapidly filling his tiny lungs. He was so small and fragile, so helpless. How could she possibly protect him? She placed her hand on his forehead, certain that it would feel hot. He must be sick. But he wasn't warm at all. Was he too cold? Did he need another blanket? As he began to shift in his sleep, she was overcome with a wave of elation. He was waking up! He was waking up! But then he settled again, and his breath steadied. He was six months old. It was possible that he could finally be sleeping through the night. More than possible, it should have happened already. Should she just go back to bed? Why didn't she know the right thing to do?

She sat on the floor of the nursery, leaning against the changing table.

How did she manage to take care of her other two children? She was such a dreadful mother. No instincts.

She didn't remember drifting off, but suddenly she startled, momentarily disoriented. Where was she? Then she saw William unmoving in his crib. She leapt up. *Oh, my goodness, he isn't breathing.* Her heart raced; her body seized in panic as she touched his stomach. She started to shake him. Lightly at first and then harder. For a moment she felt like she couldn't stop. Like the rhythm of her hands was out of her control. *Wake up, William. Wake up.* He began to squirm and cry, and Margaret, overcome with relief, scooped him from his crib and held him tightly in her arms. As the tears fell down her own face—she was sobbing hysterically now—she suddenly realized what she had done: woken her peacefully sleeping baby for no reason. And now she would have to get a bottle, get him quiet, put him back to sleep, and, probably, be awake for the rest of the night herself. Yet again, she had made a complete mess of things. She would be exhausted again tomorrow. And it would start all over. The endless cycle of crying and feeding and changing and sleeping. Why did anyone want to be a mother? If this was life, perhaps death would be better.

Chapter Twenty-Six

"Come out already, Maggie!" Carolyn called.

Margaret stood frozen, looking at herself in the three-way mirror of the dressing room at Lord & Taylor. Frank was taking her out for their anniversary, and she had nothing to wear.

She wished Lucy hadn't invited Carolyn along. Carolyn, with her perfect figure and coordinated outfits and, now, her job selling cosmetics. As if Margaret didn't feel like a failure already.

"Just come out and *show us*. The last two that you said looked awful were knockouts, so I don't trust your eye," Lucy cajoled, and Margaret saw her trying to peek through the crack in the dressing room door. "Please. I promise we won't make you try on anything else after this!"

"Yes, please come out, Maggie! I just know you will look gorgeous. That cerulean color is such a perfect complement to your eyes." Carolyn always had to mention something about color, like her new job suddenly made her an expert.

"I really can't. I look like a Studebaker," she replied in a soft whisper.

"Oh, Maggie, stop. Please just let us see?"

She knew her friends meant well, but she was so humiliated at what she saw in the mirror. How could she show them? Her eyes filled with tears. *No, not more crying. Not while I'm wearing this silk shantung.*

"Margaret Davidson Baxter, I am a mother of four children who wears a size fourteen dress, and Carolyn over here, with her straight up-and-down figure, would look like a coatrack in a sheet in that. So don't even try to tell us you look anything but terrific!"

"Sadly, she's right, Maggie." Carolyn giggled. "I would kill to have the hips and bust to fill that out."

Margaret smiled in spite of herself. Were they being honest? "Okay. Please just be kind." She opened the door tentatively.

"Ooh la la!" Lucy whistled. "That's the one!"

"You'd better buy it, because if you don't, I will be forced to. And Dick will kill me if I come home with one more dress. Even though I am helping to pay for them now."

How nice it must be for Carolyn to have some sense of independence. Margaret couldn't even imagine what that felt like.

"Darlin', that is lovely on you." The saleswoman came barreling into the dressing area. "It looks like couture, made just for you!"

Margaret recoiled. "Oh, I don't know." She used to love the attention, but now, she knew it was all lies and flattery to convince her to buy something she couldn't even afford.

"It's perfect on you. Don't you think, girls?" Her friends nodded their heads in violent agreement. "And, you know, boxy jackets are very chic right now. We have a lovely one with a fur trim that would be perfect for this dress. In case you ever need to be a bit more modest." She winked. "Let me run and grab it."

Once again, a deep melancholy engulfed Margaret. Who did she think she was? She couldn't afford a fur-trimmed jacket. They now had three children to feed. And the Tupperware had been a disaster. She felt the tears welling up again and knew she wouldn't be able to stop them. "Get me out of this thing. I need to get this off." The tears started coming fast, and she tilted herself forward so that they would land on the carpet instead of the dress. "Please, Lucy, just take it off before I ruin it!"

Lucy had known Margaret since they were ten—she was as close to her as a sister. Still, Margaret was humiliated. When did the head cheerleader, who had climbed to the top of the three-tier tower of bodies, become the mess of a housewife who had to be cleaned up by her best friend?

"Okay, honey, okay. Let's just go back into the dressing room." Lucy gave her a nudge inside the safety of the closed cubby as she unzipped the dress and delicately placed it back on the hanger. Then she turned to her friend, who was sobbing now, and took her in her arms. "How can I help, Mags? How can I help?" she whispered into her hair.

Margaret just shook her head no. There was nothing anyone could do.

"You know, Maggie," Carolyn said from outside the door. "I read an article in *Better Homes and Gardens* about the 'baby blues.' It said you need to get out on your own. Have a few hours a day away from the baby. That's why we thought this shopping trip would help."

It seemed like there wasn't anything in the world that made her feel better. Her life was now a series of battles to fight off the darkest moments and try to put on a good face. "I know you are trying. And I appreciate it," she said in between sobs. "But . . ."

"This was probably too much in one day. William is only six months old. Let's go home. Maggie, I am sure you have something in your closet already that will look just as stunning on you!"

Margaret nodded appreciatively as she tried to wipe away the unrelenting tears.

"Oooh, yes! And I can do your makeup to complement your outfit. I have loads of samples you can take for free! C'mon, let's go before that bossy saleslady comes back!"

Margaret gathered herself and, feeling both defeated and grateful, left the store with her friends to return back to the safe, suffocating world of her home.

Chapter Twenty-Seven

The Copacabana was even more extravagant than Margaret had imagined, and she felt awestruck as she and Frank entered. No wonder this
place was almost impossible to get into.

As they arrived at their table, she could hardly focus her eyes, dazed
by the phantasmagoria of Brazil all around her. The horns and the
drums of the lively Latin band, the Copa girls twirling on stage in
sparkling headpieces, the enormous fake palm trees—ten feet at least—
creating the feeling of a party in a tropical paradise.

Frank gave Margaret an adoring once-over. "Pretty incredible." He
beamed.

"Yes, it is." Margaret was so overwhelmed and grateful that he had
brought her here that she felt almost unable to speak.

"I was talking about you. I feel like I'm here with Rita Hayworth."
Frank smiled at her with a grin that had been melting her heart since
they were fourteen years old. "You look spectacular tonight." He gave
her a loving peck on the cheek and then pulled out her chair. They
hadn't been out like this in so long that Margaret had forgotten she
could actually be in the world as a woman, not just a cook, laundress,
and mother of his three children.

"How about two Piña Colada Copacabanas?" Frank raised his eyebrows to confirm with her and then turned to the waiter. They were
seeing Harry Belafonte. Carolyn had told her that this was his "return

debut," after having been banned in 1944 for being African American. Margaret vaguely remembered reading something in one of the gossip rags about this but had been too busy with her studies to pay much attention. Anyway, this night probably cost Frank a week's wages, and the headliner made it even more special. She needed to appreciate every single moment.

When their drinks arrived, Frank lifted his daiquiri glass. "Nothing like a paper umbrella to make an evening feel really special." He smiled and put his hand on Margaret's knee as she giggled, nuzzling into him. She loved the strength of his chest. And his spicy-sweet smell, so comforting and familiar; for a moment, she was that brazen young girl again who asked him to the homecoming dance. Back then she had picked him. She knew he would be too timid to ask her on a date, even though she could feel him looking at her differently. She wanted to be more than just the friend down the street who used to beat him in sprints. And she was pretty sure he wanted that too. She had been right.

So why, now, did she feel like she had to hide herself from him? Why did she have to pretend everything was okay when it wasn't?

The waiter arrived with spareribs, egg rolls, pork chop suey, and even Cantonese lobster—Chinese food in a Latin-themed club! How perfectly exotic.

Everything was delicious, and the two of them ate as if they hadn't had a meal in weeks. Margaret would normally have worried that her dress would burst, but right now she didn't care. She didn't know if it was the loud music, or the rum, or just being out alone as husband and wife but, for a moment, she felt like her old self: happy, carefree, brave. She threw down her napkin and turned to Frank. "Should we dance?"

"Absolutely." He stood, holding out his hand to her, and then they made their way to the dance floor. The music was fast and the Latin rhythms unfamiliar to them both. Margaret tried to mimic the hip swings of the dancers onstage and failed miserably, which left Frank nearly doubled over in laughter. And then the music slowed. Finally, they could actually hear each other speak, and Frank held Margaret close.

"I think you know this already, but I thank my lucky stars every day that I got to have you as my own."

She moved even closer to him, so grateful.

"I know things have been hard on you lately, sweetheart—but don't worry, you're doing a great job with all three kids, and the sales at the store are better than ever. We are going to be just fine."

His words broke the spell. She was *not* doing a great job. She had actually made a terrible mess of things and was only hiding it from him with the help of her mother. Her nose began to tingle, and her lip began to shake, and she couldn't stop the tears as they started rolling down her cheeks. Frank didn't notice right away. But they quickly gained momentum, and before she knew it, sobs racked her whole body.

"Mags? What's going on?" Frank looked so confused.

"I'm sorry, I just need a minute," she managed to choke out, and then she ran across the dance floor and into the ladies' lounge, where she locked herself in a stall and let herself weep. *I need to stop this. I must stop this. Get yourself together, Margaret. Make this night okay. You're at the Copa . . . Harry Belafonte . . .* But the more she tried to calm herself down, the harder she cried. She felt like she had climbed out of her body and was an innocent bystander. She had so little control over her feelings right now.

"Honey, are you okay in there? Do you want me to go get your fella for you?" She saw a beautiful pair of pumps at the door of her stall.

"No, no." She tried to sound upbeat but was still crying. "I'm okay. Didn't mean to bother you."

"Okay, well, if you—"

"Mags, honey, are you in there?" Frank threw open the bathroom door and ran to the locked stall.

"I'm so sorry, Frank," she wailed.

"Mags, just come out, please. Come out. Let me help you." He reached his hand under the door, which made her cry even harder.

"I'm a mess."

"I don't care. C'mon, honey. Tell me what is going on."

"I can't."

"You can. Of course you can. And I think these nice ladies would like to get rid of me, so please, darling . . . open the door."

Slowly Margaret cracked opened the stall door. Frank stood in front of the round ottoman in the center of the lounge, while the bathroom attendant kept a careful watch on him. As did the women reapplying their makeup. Margaret saw her reflection in the mirror as she walked toward him, her lipstick smeared from blowing her nose, black lines of mascara running from her eyes, her cheeks red and splotchy.

He opened his arms to her. "What is going on, Mags?"

"Something is wrong with me, Frank."

"Okay. Okay." He stroked her head. "Let's get you home. And then we will figure out how I can help. You're going to be okay. I promise."

Chapter Twenty-Eight

Ruth saw the sun flash off the windshield as Robert's car made its way past the budding trees and toward the front door. There was a time that her first instinct would have been to run outside and greet him, but he had been traveling so much lately that she now treated his return from long trips as if they were any other day at the office. She knew to give him the space to reacclimate to being at home, to get his voluminous files sorted and his equipment unpacked, and that he preferred to do that alone.

But when nearly two hours had passed, she decided she had waited long enough. She wanted to hear about the trip! He had been enlisted by a group of regional hospitals to perform and teach them lobotomy, and she loved hearing about how much Robert's ice pick procedure helped overcrowded and underfunded hospitals in other parts of the country. Plus, he had visited old patients along the way, and she was eager to get updates on their statuses. So she made two cups of tea and carried them from the kitchen, across the stone path, to Robert's office.

"Ruth!" Robert turned, smiling distractedly at her as she entered the carriage house. He sat on the floor, surrounded by piles of papers and photographs. Ruth was taken aback by their sheer volume. "Have you been waiting for me, dear? I'm so sorry, I was just trying to get myself organized."

"I was waiting, yes. I missed you! Oh, my goodness, are *all* those from this trip?"

"Yes! It's remarkable really. Once I get the doctors trained, my lobotomies run like automobiles in a Henry Ford factory." His face lit up with pride as he stroked his goatee. "Guess how many procedures we performed?"

"Let me think." She stalled, trying to calculate a number that would seem both reasonable and impressive. "You were there for fourteen days—"

"Actually twelve, two were spent on the road visiting other patients. Ah, I must tell you about dear Mr. Barney; he's doing so well! You should have seen how he smiled and ran to me when I got out of the car. Gave me a giant hug. He's a bit juvenile after the procedure, likes to play in the mud and that sort of thing, but Mrs. Barney is so happy. Freed from his psychotic episodes, she is able to live quite peacefully. Remember how nervous and beaten down she was when he came to Emeraldine?"

"Yes. I'm glad for her. But him? Playing in the mud?"

"You know there can be regression after lobotomy. But he's home and happy. That's what matters."

"I suppose. Well, I am glad you were able to visit with them. Did you see other patients?"

"I did, but more about that later. How many do you think?" Robert grinned like a schoolboy bursting with a secret. Ruth was more interested in the former patients than in getting a tally of the lobotomies Robert performed over the two weeks, but she knew he wouldn't relent until she played along. "All right, so twelve days. And I know that with the transorbital you can go much more quickly, so, six per day? Seventy-two?"

Robert stood and began tapping his foot.

"What?" Ruth was weary of the games. Had she overstated?

"Two hundred and twenty-eight! I transformed two hundred and twenty-eight patients from being the most difficult and taxing at their state hospitals, into the easiest. Some will even be able to leave altogether and no longer be a burden on the state!"

Ruth stood, mouth agape. "But how? That would mean . . ."

"Yes, I averaged nearly twenty people a day." He beamed. "It wasn't that consistent, of course. One day it was actually closer to thirty, some days more like fifteen, but I really do have this down to a science now." He paced triumphantly. "The first day at each hospital was the slowest, because I had to train the staff. But that really only takes an hour or two, unless the doctor is very clumsy and ignorant about the brain. Not every psychiatrist is as well versed in neurological anatomy as I am. Still, the landmarks are fairly obvious even if you aren't a neurosurgeon.

"I read the patient files the night before, so I was able to get right to work. And, since there were so many patients, I quickly adapted to work on multiple people simultaneously. It was brilliant, really. We would bring in six or eight at a time, and once they were all strapped in, I'd shock the first one and then begin, while the other doctors would shock the next one. We continued on down the line like this until everyone in the group was finished. Then a few minutes to recover from the grogginess before they were escorted out and the next group brought in."

Ruth walked to the small kitchen and poured herself a glass of water before sitting down in Robert's chair. She had a hard time making sense of this. She understood that the transorbital technique was fast; nevertheless, was it really possible to perform this many safely in such a short amount of time?

Robert lifted Ruth from the chair and placed his strong hands on her shoulders. "Ruthie, you *do* understand what an accomplishment this is, right? What we've done for the world?" She looked at him searchingly. "Our lobotomy has been liberated from the operating room and is radically altering the treatment of patients across the country.

With fewer violent inmates, hospitals for the mentally ill can raise the standard of care for all."

Ruth smiled and nodded. She was heartened by the idea of doing so much good, but the number still seemed disquieting.

"My love, I know that we haven't been spending much time together lately with me on the road so much. We're overdue for a night out. How about we clean up and head into the city?"

Numbly, Ruth nodded. It had been a long time since she and Robert had enjoyed a frivolous night out together, and maybe that was what they needed. Maybe if she could hear this all, in detail, it would seem as commonplace to her as to him and she'd feel like a team again. "Yes, Robert, that sounds lovely." She leaned against him, her head on his shoulder, and looked out at the gray, choppy water. "Let's go and have a proper celebration."

And if it didn't seem routine? Well, what then?

Chapter Twenty-Nine

Margaret sat quietly in the passenger seat. When she thought of doctors, in general, she thought of offices in skyscrapers in Manhattan or, perhaps, in a hospital. But here they were, driving through this tiny town only a few miles from their own. This was much more civilized than she had imagined. Frank slowed on a street adjacent to the water and began looking for the number.

"Are you sure this is right? These are mansions."

"Apparently this doc's office is on his property." Frank put his hand over Margaret's as he turned into the long, tree-lined drive. "I know you're nervous. I am too. But some guys from my unit saw him at Emeraldine and said he was the best."

Past the hibernating trees, Margaret stared at the sweeping snow-covered lawn, slowly sloping down to the gray water of the sound. The drive circled past a grand Tudor mansion the likes of which Margaret had never seen, and then on to a carriage house.

Frank turned off the car and they sat for a moment, taking in this unexpected setting.

She wasn't sure how any man who lived here could possibly make her feel better about herself. Rather, she felt even smaller and more insignificant in the face of such opulence.

"Take a breath, Mags. This is going to help. It will be good." Frank touched her cheek gently and smiled at her as Margaret's eyes welled with tears. At least she was able to cry in front of him now; she didn't have to hide it anymore.

Trying to look better than she felt, she had dressed for the appointment in a fashionable full skirt and coordinating jacket. Now that she saw where they were, where he lived, she was relieved she had made the effort. She smoothed her skirt and reapplied lipstick. "What time are we due for the appointment?"

"You," Frank corrected her, "are due at noon."

"So, what do we do for the next ten minutes? Do we sit here and wait? How does he know we've arrived?"

"If you like, I can go and knock."

"Well, didn't he tell you what we're supposed to do?"

"He didn't, baby." Frank smiled. "I'll just go and check. Stay here where it's a little warmer and try to relax."

As Frank walked along the bluestone slabs toward the small building, his breath making a cloud of smoke in front of him, she saw him slip and catch himself. "Frank, watch out!" she cried, too vehemently, she knew. But if he fell, how would she help him? What would she do? She was wearing pumps—what if she slipped too?

She knew she needed to get control of her thoughts. Apparently, this "therapy" would help her understand herself so she could get better. Feel what she was supposed to feel instead of always being so overcome.

Frank returned down the path, giving her a thumbs-up. How was he always so calm, so even, so patient? She wanted desperately to feel that way. Instead of being a constantly agitated wreck.

"He's ready." Frank opened her car door and extended his hand to help her out. She looped her arm in his and they walked side by side until they reached the copper-roofed carriage house. Inside the open door, she saw what looked like a pleasant-enough sitting room with a modern, amoeba-shaped coffee table, a reclining chaise, a love seat, and a leather chair. At the sound of their footsteps, the man inside turned and walked to the door. He wasn't tall. Compared with Frank, he was, in fact, quite small. But something about the way he carried himself gave him an air of authority. Like a school principal. She immediately wanted him to like her.

"You must be Margaret." He smiled, extending his hand as he took her in with his gaze. His hands were soft and warm, and she immediately felt a bit more at ease. "I'm Dr. Apter. Why don't you come sit down, and we can get started?" He waved her in with a rather grand gesture, almost a bow, and then turned to Frank. "We'll be finished in fifty minutes."

He shut the door and told Margaret to sit wherever she liked. She chose the end of the sofa, farthest from his leather chair. And then, just like that, her whole life began to change.

Chapter Thirty

Ruth made her way nervously up First Avenue toward the restaurant. In spite of the bitter cold, she decided to walk, both to calm her nerves and to ensure that she wasn't early. Normally she took great pride in her tendency to be punctual, but today, she decidedly did not want to arrive first. They had chosen the bistro on Fiftieth both because it was rumored to have excellent food and because it was well out of the radius of the hospital—she wanted this meeting to be discreet.

Since learning about the 228 lobotomies performed last year during what Robert now referred to as "Operation Ice Pick," Ruth had a niggling unease about Robert's trips. The holidays put a temporary stay on his travel, but since the New Year, Robert spent more time than ever touring the country in the car he had dubbed his "lobotomobile." Ruth needed to assuage her concerns.

She was so bundled up that, by the time Ruth reached La Toque Blanche, she was damp with perspiration. She stood outside briefly, attempting to dab herself off, which made her feel silly. She'd never given a second thought to her appearance around Edward in the past. Why was she so nervous?

Calm settled over her the moment she entered the dimly lit restaurant and locked eyes with him. Something about his whole essence gave Ruth comfort—it always had. He had reached out to her after Dr. Moniz had won the Nobel Prize, about four years ago, but she was still hurt by his sudden and complete break with them, with her. She had thought they were closer than that. Truth be told, she also still felt humiliated by the embezzlement scandal at the hospital. Edward had become established and successful in his own right, as both a professor and chair of the Neurology Department at Columbia. Meanwhile, she had taken over Emeraldine's operations only to have her first assistant superintendent, Roy Haddington, steal from the hospital under her watch. She felt more than fortunate that Charles had helped convince the board it had been as much his mistake as hers, but Ruth knew the truth. She hadn't spent enough time doing what she needed to do to keep the hospital running. After Haddington disappeared, she doubled her efforts to appease the hospital's donors and replenished much of the loss from her own pocket. At that moment her job really changed. She hated that she didn't see her patients much, but it was necessary to keep Emeraldine running smoothly. Making sure that Emeraldine stayed open for her patients was vastly more important than spending time with the patients themselves.

Ruth settled into her job and now had the support of a reliable assistant superintendent, Jeremy Mandrake. His presence allowed her to return her focus to the specifics of her patients. She had noticed that more patients who had lobotomies remained at Emeraldine than she'd expected. It didn't make sense. If lobotomy was less effective than they had thought, Robert surely wouldn't continue performing the procedure on hundreds of people across the country. She had tried to reconcile these seemingly discordant facts with Robert, but he had brushed her off. Which led her here. Edward was the only other person she knew who could help her make sense of what she was starting to fear. Maybe lobotomy wasn't all they hoped it would be.

"Ruth, you have no idea how wonderful it is to see you. I was over-joyed when you called." Gone was the awkward man-boy who had first entered her office nearly two decades ago; in his place stood a distinguished gentleman, even more handsome with the sprinkle of gray in his temples, the scattering of lines at the edges of his eyes, his fuller, more solid figure. He immediately drew her into a strong embrace. Ruth was taken aback. The Edward she knew was much more tentative and cautious.

He released her, his gaze filled with an adoration that disarmed her. "You look well. Very well. How are you?" He looked affectionately into her eyes and pulled out the blue vinyl chair for her to sit.

"Edward, it is really lovely to see you again." She took a deep breath and looked down at her hands and then around the room for their waiter. She needed a drink. "Tell me everything. How is Columbia?" She glanced at his left hand and noticed, to her surprise, it was bare. "Still with Rebecca?"

"Rebecca and I broke things off years ago. Soon after—" He looked down awkwardly as if he knew Ruth had heard his fight with Robert that evening so long ago. "After Robert and I parted ways, I never got to apologize for my abrupt resignation. I just felt it would be easier for everyone if I made a clean break."

"It was a difficult time. And we missed you at the hospital. I missed you. But I came to understand that it was what you had to do. And now you're chairing the department at Columbia. How wonderful!"

"Yes. My teaching post turned out to be an excellent career decision. But now that I am running the department and still practicing surgery, I am busier than ever. Hence, no ring." He held up his hand, seeming to know that she had looked. "The truth is that I have found neither the time for a steady girl nor a girl who warrants the time."

Ruth smiled. She was surprised a part of her felt relieved.

"As you know, I certainly understand. But I can also tell you that a partner in life is a welcome salve to the intensity of our work."

"Yes, of course. But we can't all be so lucky as to find a partner who is as like-minded as you, Ruth." He looked at her earnestly. "Now

I am, of course, happy to spend the afternoon divulging the details of my nonexistent romantic life, but when you called, I had a sense there was more reason for this meeting than a social visit. I know you like those less than I do."

"You know me too well," Ruth said with a laugh. "Although it does feel more like a family reunion with you."

"That's a really nice thing to hear. I feel the same. I've really missed our talks."

"Me too." She took a deep breath. "All right, I will just get to it then. I wanted to get your opinion about something. It's a bit awkward."

"Please, Ruth, there is nothing you could say that will offend me. I hope you still know that after all these years?" Edward smiled, and the sincerity in his face gave her strength.

"Edward, you should know that I overheard you and Robert that night . . . fighting about transorbital lobotomy." She paused again and saw Edward's face harden slightly. "I don't want to revisit that evening. It's just that these days Robert is spending more than half of his time traveling around the country performing these lobotomies. He's doing so many so quickly, and when I look at the statistics at the hospital, I just wonder . . ."

Ruth watched Edward stiffen to attention, his body language betraying an overeager interest. "Oh, Edward." She sighed, still not sure how to put these words together. "Things just feel different."

"Different how?"

"Well, Robert was always so concerned with the patients. With the cure. He was working miracles. But now." The waiter set a martini in front of her. "Something feels off to me about it all. The sheer volume—last year he apparently performed two hundred and twenty-eight lobotomies in twelve days. Twelve days? Is that even possible?"

Edward winced at this piece of information and then took a deep breath. "Ruth, there are a lot of things I want to say to you at this moment, but it really isn't my place. Robert and I parted ways because we no longer saw eye to eye. I had concerns, and he didn't want to hear them."

He was interrupted by the waiter, and they placed their order. When the server was gone, Ruth continued.

"What kind of concerns did you have, exactly?" She leaned in closer to him as she took a long sip of her drink.

Edward stood and moved his chair around the table right next to hers. "We both know Robert is a brilliant man," he said, his voice low and intense. "But he is also prideful and stubborn. And from the moment he performed his first transorbital lobotomy, he decided that this was going to be his legacy. He believed this method could be used even for less serious illnesses, and could be performed anywhere. I didn't agree, on either count. And nothing I said could change his beliefs."

"But he was right. Moniz won a Nobel Prize for lobotomy, thanks to Robert's nomination. Robert is in high demand all over the country."

"Yes. But—" Edward paused again. "Let me just say that lobotomy isn't all that we'd hoped it would be. And Robert's transorbital"—he shook his head—"well, I haven't actually been with Robert when he is performing one but . . . I cannot conceive of how it would be possible to safely perform more than two hundred of any type of procedure in such few days, I really can't." This was what she had come to Edward for, but she realized she wasn't prepared for his answer.

Their appetizers arrived. She watched him lift his small fork and stab one of the escargots floating in butter. She sensed that he was trying to stall. She took a bite of her salad, realizing she was grateful for the pause as well.

She finished off her drink and then decided to get to the point before she lost her nerve. "Do you think he's becoming reckless? Could what he's doing be dangerous?"

"I think it's possible that he's become unwilling, or perhaps unable, to see the facts for what they are."

"But, surely, he would never risk the well-being of a patient?"

"I hope not. But, even when we worked together, he managed to see every failure as an exception and every success as the rule." Edward looked up at her and then glanced suspiciously around the restaurant. It was empty except for one table in the opposite corner. "Remember Rosemary Kennedy?"

"Of course I do. But those were still early days, and that was one bad outcome. Broke my heart, but I know there were some of those, especially before Robert transitioned to the transorbital approach."

"Yes, we had some bad outcomes. But this one could have been avoided."

"What do you mean?"

"When we got to Boston and evaluated Rosemary, it seemed that some form of mental retardation was impacting her behavior, and I suggested that she might not benefit from a lobotomy. But Joseph insisted. And Robert was so anxious for the publicity, I let him convince me. So, to help save the political ambitions of the famous Kennedys, we took a young woman with a lower-than-average IQ and some mild behavioral problems and reduced her to a near-mute toddler in the body of an adult." Edward looked away, but Ruth could still see the shame and fury on his face.

She reached for her martini glass and, realizing it was empty, signaled the waiter for a second drink. "Surely that can't be right?"

"I wish it weren't. The thing is, there are many others like her, Ruth. Men and women who, yes, were somewhat unstable before, but were still functioning at some basic level until, until . . ."

"Until?" Ruth felt her head swimming.

"I'm sorry." He gently took her hand in his. "The last thing I want is to upset you. I am sure you see evidence of what I'm talking about at Emeraldine." The faces of some of her old patients flashed before her as his eyes locked onto hers searchingly. She held his gaze for a moment and then looked away, overwhelmed by his seeming sincerity, his intensity, and the implications of what he alleged.

"Of course, there are patients who have remained at the hospital after lobotomy, more than I anticipated, to be honest. But their lives within the hospital are so much better. Aren't they? You saw that when you were there—"

They were interrupted by the arrival of a bright blue enameled Dutch oven filled with rich coq au vin. The signature dish in this rustic Provençal restaurant was meant to be eaten family-style. Normally Ruth wouldn't have minded this in the slightest but, in the midst of this deeply unsettling conversation, the intimacy of it made her uncomfortable. She took a small portion of the red wine–braised chicken and ladled it over the roasted potatoes. And then she moved the food around her plate as Edward ate. After what she heard, she didn't have an appetite.

She allowed the conversation to veer away from Robert momentarily. She had such a long history with Edward, it felt good to have a more ordinary and banal discussion for a few minutes. To feel almost like the old days again.

As they finished their meal and ordered coffee to offset the martinis, Ruth turned back to the subject at hand. "Edward, please. I need to understand. My patients, they have been improved by lobotomy. Even the ones who remain at Emeraldine. You can't dispute that?"

"In some cases, yes, but . . . Listen, I have already said more than I intended, but I will say this: I believe there is a place for lobotomy in the spectrum of treatment, but it is far from the same as where Robert sees it. So, if you are concerned that he is performing more lobotomies than he should, at Emeraldine or elsewhere, well . . ." He looked up over her shoulder at the clock on the wall and then hurriedly waved for the waiter, getting out cash to pay the check.

"Well?" Ruth perched on the edge of her chair, and as she leaned closer to Edward in anticipation of his response, she nearly tipped it over. She steadied herself and tried to appear calmer as she looked at Edward and asked him pleadingly, "Well, what?"

"I can see that I am upsetting you. That's the last thing I want to do. Just know that I support you, whatever you decide to do. I'm so sorry, but I've already overstayed. I have a consultation and have to get back."

"Yes. Of course." Ruth was surprised to see it was nearly three o'clock and began to gather her things in a daze. *What does he mean "whatever I decide to do"?*

"I truly am sorry. It was wonderful to get to see you again today. I wish I could have been of more help."

Ruth stood at the door of the restaurant, putting on her wool coat and wrapping her fur muffler over her head, stupefied. She had long ago stopped scrutinizing lobotomy the way she had in the beginning. Was it possible she had also grown so distant from the day-to-day of the patients at her own hospital that she didn't realize how little improvement the procedure had made for them? The fact that she couldn't answer this question with a definitive *no* made her wince. It was time to get herself back to the core of her work, the reason for it all—the patients. The future of her hospital might depend on it.

Chapter Thirty-One

After her lunch with Edward, Ruth went immediately to the continuous care ward at Emeraldine, the quarters of the long-term lobotomy patients. Robert had always been honest about the fact that not every lobotomy had been a complete success. Some inmates remained at the hospital even after their surgeries. But typically, lobotomy freed them of the anxieties and aggressive behaviors that limited them before, and significantly improved their quality of life. They could move freely around the ward, enjoy the recreational activities that had been off-limits to them, even have friendships. That was progress.

It was around time for afternoon snack, so Ruth went to the dining hall, hoping to see several patients all at once, but she had miscalculated, and the room was almost empty. She scanned the tables and noticed a man sitting in the corner alone. He sat hunched over his tray, his gray hair untidily hanging down, obscuring his face. His long, elegant fingers rhythmically lifted a teapot that sat on the table in front of him, pouring imaginary tea into a cup and saucer. Ruth watched him do this for what felt like several minutes before she realized who she was looking at. Her chest tightened as a stunned panic rose inside her.

"Albert, Albert Burdell? Is that you, my dear friend?" The man looked up and squinted at Ruth, a blank expression on his face. "It's me, Ruth Apter. Remember?" She approached him tentatively. When she reached the table, she slowly pulled out a chair. "May I join you?" She tried to hide her shock at his unkempt appearance.

He looked at her with a vacant expression. Was it possible that he really didn't know who she was? Her heart sank. Had she abandoned him for so long that he didn't remember?

"Want some tea?" he asked her matter-of-factly.

"Oh yes, I would love some, thank you. Let me go and get myself a cup."

"No, here." He slid his cup toward her and began to pour from his empty teapot. "Careful," he warned. "It's hot."

She looked at him with a frozen smile. How could this be the same man she used to have intense debates with about Sartre and Camus, and the nature of human relationships?

"Thank you for the tea, Albert. Don't you remember me at all? We used to go for walks together in the garden and talk about all the books you've read. We were very good friends." She tried to lock eyes with him, but when she did, she saw only emptiness behind his brown irises. She racked her mind to remember when she had actually last seen him. His lobotomy happened during the height of the Haddington scandal. She had been so preoccupied. What an awful person she had become that she was so engulfed by her role as the new head of the hospital that she had all but forgotten about her most treasured patients. She was disgusted with herself.

"Nope. I don't go for many walks." He took the mug away from her and refilled it with more imaginary liquid.

Ruth watched him, her heart breaking. "You're sure you don't remember me? Ruth Apter?"

He shook his head no and looked apologetic, like a child who knew he had done something wrong.

"It's all right. I'm sure you see lots and lots of people in this hospital. It is a busy place."

"Yes, very busy. Lots of people. That's why I stay here. More?" He handed her the cup again.

Ruth heard the noise of the last few dishes being cleared from the dining tables, and then a nurse approached them. "Mrs. Apter, what brings you to us today?"

"Hello, Nurse Pauline. I came to visit with some of my old friends. It's been too long since I've seen them." She smiled at Albert and then stood. "Albert, thank you so much for the delicious tea. If it's all right, I would love to come back and have some more another day."

"Sure," he said flatly.

"Nurse, may I have a word?"

"Of course, Mrs. Apter. Albert, gather your things, I'll take you back to your room when I'm finished with Mrs. Apter, okay?" He nodded.

Ruth walked to the door of the dining hall, out of Albert's earshot. "What happened to him?"

"I'm not sure what you mean." Nurse Pauline looked at her blankly.

"Did he have a recent breakdown? He seems to have deteriorated significantly since I last saw him."

"Really? He seems the same to me. Same as he's been for years."

"Years?" Ruth realized it really had been years since she had visited Albert.

"Gentle as a lamb. Could spend all day every day with that teapot. We all do miss the piano, though. Tried to get him to play, but he just bangs on the keys like a child. It's a shame. But I suppose that's what happens."

"That's what happens?"

"Sure, most of the people who stay in here after are like this. Sometimes we joke that our job is more like baby nursing than taking care of adults." Pauline smiled as Ruth looked at her in shock. This was nothing like the reports she received from Robert about his lobotomies. Yes, she knew many patients remained at the hospital who hadn't been cured as entirely as they had hoped, but like this? Albert Burdell's personality was obliterated entirely.

"Is there anything else I can help you with, Mrs. Apter? I do want to get Albert back for a little rest. He tends to get quite fussy without enough sleep." She smiled. "See what I mean? Like a baby."

"No, no, nothing more. Thank you, Pauline. Keep up the good work. You are a gift to these patients."

Ruth immediately made her way back to her office in a stupor, feeling entirely unmoored. This wasn't how lobotomy was supposed to work. What had gone wrong?

Once in her office, she took out a pad and began to write a list. When she got to thirty names, she picked up the phone.

"Mr. Mandrake, I hope I didn't interrupt you in the middle of something," she said apologetically as her assistant superintendent entered her office.

"Not at all, Mrs. Apter. Was just some paperwork that can wait. What can I help you with?"

Ruth paused, looking at the list on her desk before taking in the man sitting before her. He was dressed, as always, in a sports coat and slacks, his tie complementing the muted palette of browns and beiges he favored. His personality matched his style—even-tempered, diligent, and thorough. He was a good man. In the several years he had worked for Ruth, he had always treated her with complete deference and respect, in spite of the fact that she knew it must be difficult for a man in their field to have a female superior. She believed him to be someone of strong moral character who genuinely cared for the hospital's patients, entirely unlike the scoundrel who had held the position before him. Still, she was nervous to ask him for what she needed today.

"Mr. Mandrake, I have a research project for you." She watched him perk up attentively. "It is a bit of a delicate one." Jeremy had developed a strong working relationship with several members of the hospital's board, something Ruth herself had encouraged, but now she needed him to help her collect information in strict confidence. She believed she had his loyalty, but if she was wrong, it could jeopardize her whole career. Still, she needed these answers, and she couldn't get them alone. He was the only person at the hospital with the access and understanding to help her. She had to trust him.

"Of course. What can I help you with, Mrs. Apter?" He held his pen at the ready, pad in his lap.

"Well, I've just visited with a patient of ours who had a lobotomy a few years ago."

"Yes, there are quite a few of those in our long-term care wards these days."

Ruth flinched. "I think it's time for us to do a bit of an analysis on them, well, on lobotomy." She paused, looking at Jeremy to see if this idea elicited any reaction in him. His expression, thankfully, remained unchanged. "I'd like you to collect the patient results from a good representative sample of the past few years. Visit with the ones who are still here, interview the doctors responsible for their current care, and if you can, contact the ones who have been discharged. I want to gather enough data to do a proper analysis of the spectrum of outcomes." Suddenly Jeremy Mandrake's face contorted into a look of confusion.

"You want me to do an efficacy report on lobotomy? I'm happy to do it, of course, but it will take some time to pull this together properly and . . . I assumed you have plenty of these from Dr. Apter?" Ruth froze momentarily, feeling goose pimples forming on her arms and the back of her neck.

"Robert keeps copious notes on all his patients. But I want something with more of an administrative bent. So I can tie outcomes to the hospital's financial results. I will involve Robert if necessary."

"I see. All right then." Jeremy nodded.

"And, Mr. Mandrake, this is of high priority. I might like to include it in the May report for the board if you can get it finished by then. Please come straight to me with your findings. We can decide together the best way to present it to other constituencies. If there is anything interesting to present." She didn't want to sound too desperate.

"Of course." Jeremy scribbled a few more notes on his pad and then stood up. "If there isn't anything else, I can go get started on this immediately."

"Terrific. Oh, just one more thing." Ruth tore the paper from her pad and handed it to him. "I made a list of patients I would love to have included in the report, some of the early transorbital recipients. Hopefully they won't be too hard to track down."

"Very good. Shouldn't be a problem, although it might take some time, slow things down a bit."

"I understand. Still, I think it will be important to include them if we can. Thank you. I look forward to seeing what you come up with."

Chapter Thirty-Two

Margaret sat in her usual seat in Dr. Apter's office, noticing the shadows cast by the bright spring sunshine streaming through the window. In the months she had been coming here, the place had become comfortingly familiar.

"How have you been?" Dr. Apter asked once she was finally settled, legs delicately crossed at the ankles, feet tucked under the sofa.

"All right, I suppose." She began fidgeting with the folds of her pleated skirt. Should she tell him? This seemed like such a repetitive conversation at this point.

He sat quietly, watching her. She hated these awkward silences. She knew he would let her sit this way for the entire session if she didn't speak again. But what could she say? She removed a cigarette from her purse. As she inhaled to light it, he suddenly spoke. "Do you really feel all right? I don't think I believe that."

She was momentarily stunned. How did he see her so clearly? "I don't know, Doctor. I just . . ." She couldn't say it.

"You just what?"

"I just don't think I'm getting better." She shivered, shocked that she had said this out loud. And then the tears started forming. Her nose pricked. She was furious with herself. If she started crying, she wouldn't stop. She could finally drive herself here and needed to remain composed enough to get herself back home.

"What is it that you are expecting to feel? What will tell you that you are 'better'?"

She didn't know how to answer that question. She had expected that things would start to change. That she wouldn't feel devastated and empty when William was asleep, and then miserable and put out the minute he awoke. She expected her saggy belly to tighten and her bust to perk back up—for her body to be as it was before. That's what had happened after John and Maisy were born. She expected not to feel filled with hatred for her husband every time he came home from a satisfying day at the store, where he scraped together enough extra money for this therapy that was supposed to be helping.

Nothing had changed, and she didn't know how she would ever get better if nothing changed.

But she didn't have the words to say any of this. So instead, she just let the tears take over. Dr. Apter sat calmly, watching her for nearly five minutes. He handed her a box of Kleenex. She felt like a circus act.

Finally, he spoke. "I see that you are feeling very upset. Do you know what is making you cry right now?" Margaret shook her head no. Even though she did. "Are you sure? I have a feeling that you actually do know, you just won't allow yourself to say it." He was baiting her. But he was right.

"Fine." She looked down at her hands like a petulant child. Embarrassed and ashamed. "I feel like I am hopeless."

"Nothing is hopeless."

She felt his gaze upon her and looked up to see his brown eyes piercing her, as if trying to look into her soul.

"What else do you feel? You often talk about failure but, I wonder, do you also feel angry? Resentful?"

Her stomach dropped. *Yes. Yes. Yes!* Could she really admit this, even to him? She nodded her head, a gentle yes. "I suppose." She took a deep breath. She couldn't possibly say more.

"Tell me about those feelings, Margaret."

She shook her head no, shrugging him off as the tears started to well up again.

"Margaret, if you can't tell me what is happening inside of you, I can't help you."

"Fine," she almost yelled, the dam bursting inside her. "I can't do it! I simply can't do it! I had a life once, you know? I was gonna be a nurse. I was gonna help people. But that doesn't matter, does it? That wasn't important once I got to do the most natural and significant job in the world. To be a mother. And I can't even do that right. I am failing at the one thing in the world that no one is supposed to fail at. I thought I would be something, that my life would mean something, and, instead, it just feels like I am tending to a never-ending hole of other people's need. I'm supposed to enjoy this, but I despise every minute of every day except when I'm sleeping. And sometimes I wonder if I should just let myself slip away forever, if everyone would be better off without me." She couldn't believe she had admitted this. Her darkest secret.

"Margaret, it's all right." She couldn't believe he was so calm and unfazed by her tantrum. "What you are feeling is not uncommon. In fact, there is a term for what you are experiencing."

"Yes, I know, the 'baby blues'?" She took a deep, ragged breath and looked at him. "It's not supposed to be like this, though."

"Well, baby blues might have been a trigger for you, but what you are describing is beyond the simple malaise of the postpartum period. Yours is persistent. And when these types of feelings linger and are accompanied by extreme anger, we call it 'agitated depression.' Left untreated, it can be quite serious." He paused, as if allowing the words to settle.

"Quite serious?" Margaret felt the color drain from her face. She'd suspected there was something really wrong with her. And now he confirmed it.

"Well, clinically, we worry that a mother who is unable to recover naturally in the immediate postpartum period suffers from underlying psychological conditions that could be very harmful to the healthy development of her children."

"My . . . children?" She startled.

"In extreme cases, we have seen mothers actually physically harm their babies. Even try to kill them."

"You think I would try to kill my children?" Margaret's tears returned with the force of a hurricane; she felt like she might vomit.

"I hope not. And I know you don't want to do that intellectually, in your brain." He tapped at his head. "But the emotional world sometimes runs counter to the intellect. That is why you are here." He stood up, poured her a glass of water, and smiled eagerly as he handed it to her. "There is hopeful news for you, though. I do know how to help you. Why don't you take a moment to gather yourself, and then I can tell you all about my miracle cure."

Margaret left her session in a daze. Yes, what the doctor suggested terrified her, but if he could cure her in a single day, with a simple office procedure? Was it too good to be true, or the greatest gift she could receive? Her head was spinning, and she had an odd sensation of elation alongside her confusion. Instead of walking toward her car, she began to wander deeper into the property until she spotted a bench surrounded by the sweetest-smelling lilacs. It wasn't appropriate, she knew, but she would just sit and get her thoughts in order before going home. Try to make sense of what the doctor had said. What it might mean. She tingled with fear, but for the first time in as long as she could remember, she felt full of hope.

Chapter Thirty-Three

Ruth wanted to cut some lilacs for the table before dinner. She found the fragrance relaxing and craved relaxation right now. She hadn't taken a proper vacation since she started in her new role, more than seven years ago. Robert was so often on the road, and they were both so busy, that time had just evaporated. But she had been unusually on edge lately as she anxiously awaited Mandrake's report, so when the board suggested that, in advance of their May meeting, she take a week for herself, she decided to do it. She had selected this week because Robert was home (seeing private patients, of course, but still present at Magnolia Bluff, at least). While he worked, she gardened to settle her uneasy mind.

As she rounded the hedge with her shears and basket, she found a woman sitting on the stone bench. She was a buxom blonde, her fashionable shoulder-length hair perfectly curled, her cheeks rosy from a dusting of rouge. She wore a simple but fetching shirtwaist dress, festooned with roses that matched the pink of her lipstick. Could this woman possibly be a patient? If so, it was a bit odd for her to be lingering on the property. Perhaps she was the mother or wife of someone seeing Robert for a session? Yes, that made more sense. Ruth had been in the business of mental health so long she could tell a patient almost on sight, and this woman did not fit the bill.

Perhaps she should turn back, give the woman some privacy? But she did look quite low. Ruth might be able to offer her some comfort.

"Hello there. Lovely afternoon, isn't it?" Ruth removed her wide-brimmed sun hat as she approached, so the woman could see her face.

"Oh my! I'm so sorry." The woman jumped up and backed away from the bench as if she had been caught trying to steal it. "I was just collecting my thoughts and I—"

"Please, stay. It's fine." She reached out her hand. "I'm Ruth Apter, the doctor's wife."

"Margaret Baxter." Margaret raised her hand but lowered her eyes, as if making eye contact with Ruth would be inappropriate.

"Nice to meet you, Miss Baxter."

"Oh no, it's Mrs.!" Margaret smiled. "I am a homemaker with three children, haven't been a Miss in forever. And, please, call me Maggie, everyone does."

"Three children! Sounds lovely . . . and quite tiring. Is one of your children seeing my husband now?"

Margaret looked at her furtively, like she had been caught at something.

"Don't worry," Ruth said comfortingly as she took a seat. "I can assure you I pass no judgment about his patients or their families. In fact, I am glad that you found a quiet place to wait. The lilacs smell wonderful, don't they?"

Ruth saw a look of panic cross Margaret's eyes and gently tapped the spot next to her on the stone bench. "Please, come. You're more than welcome to sit back down. No point in standing around waiting."

"I'm not actually . . ." Margaret hesitated. "I'm not actually waiting."

"Oh. You're a patient then?" Ruth said easily, sensing Margaret's discomfort.

Margaret nodded her head, looking as ashamed as she felt.

"Well, Dr. Apter is a very fine doctor. The best. You are in excellent hands."

"Thank you." She smiled weakly and began fiddling with the strap of her purse before turning her gaze down the hill toward the water. "You have such an incredible home, Mrs. Apter. I'm sorry for trespassing. I had a lot to think about today and, well, I just kind of found myself sitting here. It's such a beautiful spot, but I'm sorry. I'm so embarrassed." Margaret blushed.

"Don't be! I understand completely. In fact, if you'd like, I can show you around the property. There's a spectacular view of the ocean beyond the groves, and I find there's nothing like it to get one's thoughts in order. On a clear day like this, you'll see all the way across the sound to Long Island."

"Oh, I wouldn't want to impose."

Ruth sensed that this girl needed someone to talk to, and while she knew she shouldn't get involved with one of Robert's patients, she couldn't see what difference a short walk would make. She used to walk with patients at the hospital all the time. It would be a welcome distraction from the anxiety that gnawed at her mind.

"I insist. Join me. It's such a lovely afternoon and the sea breeze does wonders for clearing one's head. I imagine it must be difficult to leave here and jump right back into life with three children."

"Well, it certainly shouldn't be." Margaret's whole face seemed to fall, and she looked down at her feet.

"And whyever not? I think the work you mothers do is astonishing. It's impossible to give that much and never need a moment for yourself."

"Do you really believe that?" Margaret lifted her eyes to look directly at Ruth. She yearned for some kind of acceptance, understanding. If Ruth knew her better, she would have given her a motherly hug, but that would be entirely inappropriate under these circumstances.

"I absolutely do. Come, let's stroll."

"Well, if it really isn't an imposition. I have to admit I've been dying to see this place, Mrs. Apter."

"Please, call me Ruth."

Nearly an hour later, Ruth watched out the window as Margaret's green Chrysler Saratoga slowly pulled away. What an odd and unexpected afternoon. She knew it wasn't very professional to befriend a patient of Robert's, but from what she had observed, Margaret couldn't possibly be a patient for long. She had run-of-the-mill baby blues. Maybe a bit of insecurity. Nothing very serious. She wondered if this young woman had a mother to talk to or if, like Ruth, her mother didn't understand her for who she was. She felt for this young woman, for the pain she seemed to feel about her life. A life that, from what Ruth could gather, was terribly typical. For the first time in a long time, Ruth had that old hopeful feeling. Margaret could be easily cured, and she could help. The ability to have such a clear and immediate impact on a patient, even a patient technically not hers, lightened her mood so much that she decided she would do what she could to be home on Tuesday afternoons, when Robert saw Maggie. She looked forward to walking with her again.

Chapter Thirty-Four

Margaret was suddenly inspired to make a roast for dinner that evening, so on her way home she stopped quickly at the market. It had been some time since she cooked anything as elaborate as her mother's tenderloin, even though it was a family favorite. When she arrived home, she got to work peeling potatoes and carrots, salting the meat, and heating the oven. She was happily lost in her work in the kitchen when her mother arrived with William, and Maisy and John returned from school.

"Making my roast beef?" Sara seemed pleased as she followed the scent into the kitchen.

"I am!" Margaret smiled at her mother, taking the baby from her arms. "I felt in the mood today."

"How wonderful, dear. I'll set the table." All at once, Margaret realized her mother had grown used to filling in the gaps for her.

"That's all right, Mom. Maisy, John, and I can handle it. Right, kids?" she said enthusiastically to her older two as they sat at the table coloring.

"Well, then. If you don't need anything else, I'll go." Margaret sensed her mother's unease, as though she didn't trust Margaret to do all of this correctly.

"Thank you, Mom. We'll be fine. We really will."

By the time Frank arrived from the store, she had put the children's mess away and gotten the table set. Margaret met him in the foyer.

"Well now, this is a nice surprise." Frank embraced her as she gave him a peck on the cheek, handed him a freshly poured martini, and took his hat and coat.

"Maisy, John, wash your hands and come to the table! Daddy's home, it's time for dinner."

Margaret felt Frank's eyes on her, and she turned toward him with a reassuring smile. She was okay.

"Can I help?" He tried to follow her into the kitchen.

"Absolutely not! Go get settled and then have a seat and relax. I'll be right in."

"Do I smell roast beef?"

"Perhaps." Margaret glanced coyly over her shoulder.

"Maisy, John—I think Mommy made beef castle, you better get to the table before I eat it all!"

"She did, Daddy! It's beef castle for dinner!" Maisy cheered as she slid into her seat and anxiously awaited the meal. Margaret had renamed this dinner "beef castle" years before, to entice the children to eat it. Today, she couldn't imagine inventing a meal that encouraged playing with food so much—the slice of roast beef teetering on top of a large scoop of mashed potatoes, a moat around it of pearl onions, peas, and carrots. But Margaret had been freer when the children were younger. More fun. She knew that person still existed inside her somewhere; she just had to recapture that spark, and now she knew that she could.

"Are we celebrating something tonight?" Frank asked appreciatively. "Did I forget someone's birthday?" Frank looked at his son with an exaggerated quizzical expression.

"No, Daddy! It's not my birthday." John laughed. "You know my birthday is after the Fourth of July!"

"Of course." Frank mock slapped himself on the forehead. "We haven't seen the fireworks yet, have we? So, what could we be celebrating?"

"I think we are celebrating William's new tooth!" Maisy pointed at her baby brother, who was smearing potatoes around his high-chair tray. Normally this would have made Margaret rage inside, but for some reason, tonight she found it endearing. She was finding this whole dinner perfectly silly and joyous and . . . normal. Yes, it felt special because it was like it used to be.

"I suppose I am the only one who knows what we are celebrating tonight." Margaret smiled. "We are having a very special dinner to celebrate . . . nothing!" Maisy and John burst into hysterical laughter and she winked at them.

"And . . . everything." She raised her glass in Frank's direction and encouraged the children to lift their cups of milk. "A toast. To my wonderful family. And a perfectly regular family dinner!"

"To nothing, and everything." Frank beamed.

"Nothing and everything!! Nothing and everything!!" Maisy and John sang.

"Well, that was a wonderful evening!" Frank said kindly as he tentatively slid his arms around Margaret's waist. But instead of stiffening, which had been her instinct every time he had tried to touch her since William was born, she softened into him. She continued to wash the dishes, while she luxuriated in the soft kiss he placed on the top of her head, relaxed into his comforting smell, relished the weight of his body pressed against hers. She had planned to talk to him about the exciting news from her appointment with Dr. Apter, but her body suddenly yearned for something different. She hadn't had any desire to be touched by her husband in so long, she needed to indulge it.

"Everyone asleep?" she asked seductively, placing the last pot on the drying rack.

"In fact, they are." Frank eyed her cautiously. She knew he would never make the first move these days. She had read plenty about the fragile male ego in *Ladies' Home Journal* and she had rebuffed him so many times already.

"Perhaps we should make our way to bed too?" she said with a devious smile as she sashayed out of the kitchen, hoping Frank would follow.

Rummaging in the back of the closet, she found the sheer silk chemise and matching feather-trimmed robe that Frank had purchased for her several years ago. "Are you in bed?" she called out, desperate to seize this opportunity before the feeling went away again. Oh, how she missed actually yearning for her husband. Getting lost in his perfect muscular arms. Tasting the sweetness of his mouth. Smelling the musk that emanated from him as he began to sweat.

Tonight, she thought she might never have been more eager. And as they began to move together, and he caressed her soft middle, her drooping breasts, she didn't feel ashamed. When he sat up and grabbed her waist, whispering, "You are so beautiful," she even believed him a little bit.

Afterward, they lay together in serene silence, her head on Frank's strong, damp chest. He stroked her gently, and then whispered, "I've missed you, Mags. I love you so much."

The deep relief in his voice was clear and, suddenly, this simple phrase told her everything she needed to know. She couldn't risk the darkness creeping back in. She had to stay this woman for her marriage. For her children.

"Frank." She propped herself up on her elbows and looked at him. "I want to do something. It is a little bit scary, but Dr. Apter says it will help. Cure me. It's an easy procedure really, in and out in an hour, he says. I think I should do it."

Chapter Thirty-Five

Ruth shut the door to her office. As a general rule, she preferred to have it open, a signal to her staff that she was available as needed. But, right now, she required privacy and concentration. Jeremy Mandrake had finally finished his report, and now, on her desk sat a thick folder. As she put on her reading glasses, she chided herself for not having done this sooner. She was generally thorough and diligent about monitoring everything at the hospital. But with her bumpy start as head of Emeraldine and then with Moniz winning the Nobel . . . lobotomy had become so widely accepted that she had simply stopped following up on the recipients. She was nervous. She opened the report to the succinct summary of findings and read hungrily. What had he concluded?

> *Study conducted across 400 patients . . . variety of conditions prior to lobotomy, most commonly those who failed to respond to other treatments . . . overall finding is that baseline condition improved by lobotomy.*

Improved! Ruth breathed a sigh of relief. She began to feel her pulse return to normal as she turned to the data.

OVERVIEW OF RESULTS

Out of hospital	20%
In hospital: Good	29%
In hospital: Fair	24%
In hospital: Unimproved	25%
Operative death	2%
Total	100%

Only 20 percent of patients left the hospital? She knew some remained—more than she'd hoped—but still, one of the key benefits of lobotomy was its ability to return inmates to the world. Ruth remembered sending so many people home. She thought of sweet Estelle Lennox, who, last Ruth heard, was now married with two children. How was she part of such a small subsegment of results? Still, Mandrake had concluded that lobotomy led to improvement. Even if only 20 percent of patients left the hospital, more than 50 percent were better off. That was really an excellent result.

She turned to the detailed pages. What were Mandrake's criteria for classification? Who, she wondered, was considered a good outcome?

Classifications were developed as follows:

Good: those no longer requiring isolation, who have been moved from the secure wing to continuous care, and who have exhibited no violent or dangerous behaviors in the past year.

Fair: those who are generally able to cohabitate with other inmates in continuous care, but require periodic instances of isolation, restraints, or additional ECT.

Unimproved: includes both patients who exhibit symptoms consistent with their initial intake diagnosis without change, and/or those who have deteriorated since initial assessment.

Operative death has been very rare and is consistent with broader hospital surgical statistics.

She was slightly unnerved by his classifications. They weren't as promising as she had hoped. Still, Mandrake was a levelheaded and reasonable man; if he deemed these results appropriate, surely, she would agree.

She was about to move on to the individual patient descriptions, eager to see examples of the individuals who fell into each classification, when her secretary rang. She had been so anxious to receive Jeremy's report that she had completely forgotten her lunch with the president of the School of Medicine. Satisfied for the moment with Mandrake's encouraging conclusions, she closed the binder and gathered her things. The rest of the report would have to wait.

Chapter Thirty-Six

Margaret had been mortified when Dr. Apter's wife first discovered her lingering on the property, but Ruth was so kind. She felt like a long-lost aunt, and when Margaret saw Ruth waiting for her the following week, she was overjoyed. They quickly became friends. Ruth even confided in Margaret about the loss of her brother, Harry. Margaret was so lucky that war hadn't changed Frank one bit. No, she was the one who had changed. But Ruth made her feel a little brighter. Now the highlight of Margaret's week was when she and Ruth met on the bench in the lilac grove for their walks. Especially on a day like today, when her session with Dr. Apter had left her so on edge. Frank had made it clear that he was not in favor of the lobotomy. But he would support whatever she decided. Maybe his reluctance was the reason that every time she made up her mind to schedule it, she got cold feet. Whatever the reason, the doctor seemed to be losing patience with her wavering.

"Margaret, are you all right?" Ruth looked concerned. Somehow Margaret already felt calmer.

"I feel a little . . . unsure today. I'm worried I angered your husband."

"I doubt that." Ruth looked at her with surprise. "His role is never to be angry with you."

Margaret realized that wasn't how she felt in her sessions. Instead, she felt chastised and inspected for flaws that needed fixing. And there were many. But she couldn't say that to Ruth.

"It's funny, sometimes I feel more comfortable with you than in there. I'm so grateful that your schedule has allowed you to be here for me these past few weeks. When we take our walks, I actually feel like I might be okay. Like everything might be okay."

"Well, you are! And it will." Ruth smiled warmly.

"How do you know that?"

"I have seen what it looks like when it won't. You're strong, Margaret. You might not realize it, but to me, it was immediately apparent: you will find your happiness again."

"I just don't know. I've never felt like this before. I guess life came pretty easily to me, you know?" She looked at Ruth, feeling shy, worried she sounded like she was bragging. "After William, though, I don't know. I just haven't been able to feel good about anything. And I know it's me. Because nothing else has changed." Margaret paused and looked down the slope of the hill. "This might sound odd, but when you told me about your brother . . . I understand him. Feeling like all that pain and the darkness is too much, being powerless to make it go away." Nervously, she lit a cigarette. She needed to control her mouth better. It had felt so special when Ruth shared that awful experience with her, such a tragedy. How could she have compared that to her own feelings? "I'm sorry, I shouldn't have made that comparison."

"No. It's all right. It must be a very frightening way to feel." Ruth paused, looking off at the horizon, and then turned back to Margaret, gently taking hold of her hands. "I wonder, though, what would happen if you stopped expecting yourself to be so perfect?"

"I'm hardly perfect." Margaret laughed, feeling awkward. Could she really let herself off the hook that way?

"Well, of course not. There's no such thing. But you're clearly a very bright and capable woman."

"Really?" She flushed with pride and, for a moment, she remembered her days in nursing school, when her life was filled with so much possibility.

"Absolutely." Ruth nodded her head reassuringly. "You know, it isn't unusual to feel like you aren't good enough, especially when you have children. Sadly, I don't know this from personal experience—Dr. Apter and I met too late in life for that—but there are many new studies about postnatal psychology that suggest a lot of what you are feeling is very natural."

"I know all about the baby blues, but if that was it, I should be better by now. I should appreciate the time I have away from William instead of wanting him by my side the moment he is gone, and then detesting that I have to take care of him when he is back in my arms. I should be able to sleep when he's sleeping so I'm not so tired. I should . . ."

"Forgive me for saying so, but in my experience, life doesn't often unfold as it 'should.' Instead, we need to learn to make the best of what it is. Even in the hard times." Ruth smiled reassuringly and Margaret wondered if she could possibly do this. Simply accept herself as she was. It seemed impossible.

The women began walking down the slope and came to yet another spectacular collection of flowers. "Oh, I just love hydrangeas. I carried them in my wedding bouquet." Margaret beamed, suddenly feeling gleeful at the memory of it.

"I'm sure you were a stunning bride."

Margaret blushed.

"Did you know that hydrangeas change color depending on the acidity of the soil they're planted in?" Ruth paused. "I've always loved the idea—that you can change the environment to change the flower itself."

"I never knew that." Margaret shook her head. "It's kind of like me. Like my soil has changed, and now I can't get my old color back."

Ruth looked at her calmly, considering this statement. "Well, if that's true, then I guess you have some options, right?"

"Options?"

"Yes. You can learn to appreciate the new color or, perhaps, you can look for ways to change the soil again."

Change the soil? That was what lobotomy was going to do, Margaret suddenly thought excitedly.

"Hmmm, maybe you're right!" Margaret smiled widely and then looked at her wristwatch. "Oh my, I need to dash off! I wish I had more time, but I promised my mother I'd be home for William's nap. She has the plumber coming. Thank you for today. You have no idea how much better I feel."

"Not at all. I'm just trying to help you see yourself the way I do, to know that you have choices. I'll see you next week then?"

"Yes, next week for sure." Margaret walked briskly toward her car, feeling giddy. Ruth had made her more certain than ever. She had it in her power to make everything right again.

Chapter Thirty-Seven

"Do you have a moment?" Jeremy Mandrake knocked on Ruth's open door. She looked up thankfully from the monthly operating budget she was analyzing.

"Of course. Anything to get me out of these numbers. Although I am pleased to see that we are slightly below projected expenses for the year to date." She smiled. "What can I help you with?"

"Well, you still haven't mentioned what you thought about the lobotomy efficiency study. I noticed you didn't include it in the board briefing. Were you dissatisfied with it?"

Ruth was momentarily ashamed. Several weeks had gone by since she received Jeremy's report. How had she let so much time pass without reading the rest of it? "On the contrary, I was pleased to see your conclusions. But, since it seemed that the information didn't need to be included in this last board meeting, I set the report aside to prepare the rest of the materials. It looks like you did an excellent and thorough job as usual, and I plan to read every word this week. Just as soon as I finish all the follow-up from the meeting that the board requested."

"All right. I am glad you were happy. I was concerned that you might be disappointed by the overall results or take issue with my classifications, but given the population set, it seemed the appropriate way to benchmark." Jeremy looked at her inquisitively; he wanted to engage in further discussion about the report. She wondered why. Was there something controversial in the details she hadn't yet read?

"I am sure I will agree with your methodology. And I really do appreciate what an impressive amount of work you were able to complete in such a short amount of time. I am sorry that I haven't gotten through all of it yet. I assure you that I will." She squirmed a bit in her chair. She needed to read the rest of the report as soon as possible. Alone. "Is there anything else? Unfortunately, I do need to finish this before the end of the day."

"No, I suppose not. Just, do let me know when you have finished it. I want to be sure you are in agreement." Jeremy stood awkwardly and left Ruth feeling uneasy as he exited the room. As soon as he was out of sight, she quietly shut her office door and retrieved his report from under a stack of other files, chastising herself for having let it sit for so long.

She flipped to the detailed section of the binder, beginning with the outcomes classified as "Good." These patients hadn't left the hospital but had improved after lobotomy. As she began reading, her jaw dropped open. The first name was Albert Burdell. Albert Burdell, who was a ghost of the man he had been when he arrived at Emeraldine? Who behaved like a young boy? If he was a typical example of a good result, what was a bad one?

Ruth read on for two solid hours. The report was vastly worse than she had feared. It seemed impossible that Jeremy had concluded lobotomy, overall, had been successful. No wonder he had wanted to talk to her more about the report.

Before she could confer with him, she needed to understand more for herself. She asked her secretary to clear the rest of her day, and then went directly to the continuous care ward.

Ruth returned several hours later disoriented and distraught. Yes, some of the patients she saw this afternoon seemed happy, but so much still disturbed her. Toddler-like behavior in people who had once been quite clever; obesity so extreme as to require more than one bed; epileptic episodes in patients with no prior history of the illness; terrifying, violent outbursts. She couldn't reconcile what she just saw and read with what she had believed for so long. Surely there must be more positive outcomes? She flipped feverishly through the pages of Jeremy's report, looking for some shred of hope. Before she could talk herself out of it, she looked up the number, dialed, and listened to her beating heart and the ringing of the phone. And then she heard it—a sweet, high-pitched voice saying hello. "Estelle? Is that you? This is Ruth Apter."

Chapter Thirty-Eight

Margaret felt oddly nervous as they sat on the bench looking at the sea, waiting for Dr. Apter to open the door. "You'll see, Frank. He's a very reasonable man. Remember from when you first spoke to him?" She grabbed her husband's hand in her own, more to reassure herself.

"Yes, well, at that point, he wasn't proposing sticking an ice pick in your brain. I'll hold my judgment on his reasonableness until I hear what he has to say."

Behind them they heard the door open. "Mr. Baxter, Mrs. Baxter, do come in."

They turned and entered. "So, I finally get a glimpse of the secret sanctum I've been hearing about. And please call me Frank." Frank smiled tightly at the doctor and Margaret gave him a look that begged him to be a little kinder.

"I'm not sure how secret it is," Dr. Apter replied congenially. "Simply reserved as a sanctuary for the people who need the comfort of the space. I'd love to show you around, especially my procedure room, but let's talk a bit first, shall we?" He gestured toward the sofa where Margaret always sat, and she led Frank there to settle in next to her.

"I have been seeing your wife for six months now, and I believe I have come to know her quite well. Her case is of a particular sort that I see quite frequently in my practice, so I'm very familiar with its various iterations and treatment options."

"And what sort of case is that? I'm confused, Doctor. When I spoke to you initially, you said it sounded like Maggie had baby blues. And she seems better, so much better. But now she's telling me that she needs this ice pick thing to fix her?"

Margaret started to feel nervous. Was Frank right? Was she getting better? She looked at the coffee table for something to distract her and started straightening the magazines.

"It's a lobotomy, Mr. Baxter, and I assure you, it's really a very simple procedure. If you'll just let me explain."

"Fine. But know that I'm a salesman and a business owner, and I can smell a bad pitch from a mile away."

Robert cleared his throat. "As I previously explained to your wife, when we see a case of 'baby blues' that doesn't resolve itself within a reasonable time frame, it often means that the pregnancy and its aftermath have revealed underlying tendencies that need to be addressed. Mrs. Baxter is aware that she suffers from something called agitated depression, a condition that, if left untreated psychosurgically, can cause aggressive, even violent behavior."

"Violent?" Frank scoffed. "Maggie can't even kill a spider. She's not going to hurt anyone."

"I agree that your wife is a lovely and gentle person, but I can assure you that she has admitted to urges that are quite worrisome." Dr. Apter looked at Margaret and she felt her stomach begin to churn. She thought those details were private. Now Frank would know what a monster she was. "She has had fantasies of killing young William. Of setting fire to the house."

"Mags?" Frank looked at his wife, anguish twisting his face. "Is this true?"

Margaret didn't remember having these feelings, exactly, but she had felt something like them. He was the doctor, so if that was what he heard her saying, and believed her capable of, it must be the case. She gave a barely discernible nod, flushing with shame.

"You see, Mr. Baxter, a transorbital lobotomy is a quick and easy procedure, easier than a trip to the dentist. And it can make these dangerous feelings go away. Forever."

"But I have read that it can cause brain damage, and should only be used if the patient is in terrible condition with no other options. That's not my wife."

"I assume you're referring to that highly publicized piece in the *Saturday Evening Post*. For every great medical breakthrough, you will find some lesser scientist who wants to argue against the genius. If research is what you require, I can give you multiple pieces that explain in precise detail the nuances of my procedure, and the many benefits of using it as a course of treatment in cases exactly like your wife's. Of course, there are minor risks, as there would be with, say, the extraction of an infected tooth. But the long-term benefits surely outweigh them."

"And what, exactly, are they? The long-term benefits?" Margaret felt uneasy as Frank questioned the doctor, his queries somehow making her, again, less sure of her decision to move forward.

"You see, by severing the connections in the frontal lobe that cause these overblown emotional responses"—he tapped at the front of his head—"I am able to essentially obliterate these negative and dangerous emotional patterns."

"But how do you know you won't obliterate my wife in the process?" Margaret felt as if she might faint. She had never even contemplated that as a possibility. Could that really happen?

"Excellent question." Dr. Apter smiled. "Mrs. Baxter will not be the same when the procedure is done. She will be calmer, happier. More patient with the children. Content with the excellent life you have given her, instead of miserably yearning for some mysterious 'other' that her current mental state is convincing her should exist. She will be freed of the anxious ruminations that prevent her from performing simple household tasks or enjoying an evening out to dinner. She will finally be unencumbered by the crippling illness that currently has her spending her days tied in knots, wishing for a happiness that sits beyond her grasp. She will be free to finally be the best version of herself."

Margaret felt a wave of relief wash over her. To not have to try so hard anymore. To no longer feel afraid. To unconditionally love her children again. To willingly surrender herself to her home and her husband. It was all she wanted. Trying to fight against these other voices in her head was exhausting, and Dr. Apter was going to quiet them once and for all. "Frank, you see? I know you're worried about me, but if I do this . . . we can be like we were before. We can be happy." She looked at her husband, unable to hide the desperation in her face.

"Mags? Is this really how you've been feeling?" Frank gazed back at her, his eyes full of love and compassion, and she turned away, pained. "You know all I want in the world is for you to be happy. And you seem happier. Better. Why, the night you made your mother's roast . . ." Frank smiled at her and her cheeks turned pink.

"Mr. Baxter, I have explained to your wife that it is quite common for a patient to experience a temporary elation simply upon learning about lobotomy as an option. I can assure you that without the procedure this will be temporary."

Yes, the doctor was right. She wasn't really happy; she was struggling. And this would end the struggle. "Frank, I've been fighting so hard to be the wife you deserve. A good mother for John and Maisy and William. And I'm losing. I don't want to lose anymore."

"Mr. Baxter, the area where I perform the lobotomies is just on the other side of that wall. The procedure itself only takes a few minutes. A brief electroshock for anesthetization—no side effects—and Mrs. Baxter will simply sleep through the whole thing. She will be able to walk out of this office within thirty minutes. She'll likely have a headache for a few days and possibly some bruising around the eyes. I usually tell my patients this is a wonderful reason to purchase a new pair of sunglasses." Dr. Apter was so calm, so reassuring. As he spoke, she seemed to forget entirely about the fact that he planned to enter her brain. Her brain. It was unfathomable. But, oh, if it worked . . .

"One other thing I forgot to mention, because Margaret has been a patient of mine for some time now, I will only charge a nominal additional fee for the procedure. So, if cost is a concern, it needn't be."

"I think we still need some time to think about it." Frank looked at Margaret and she smiled at him, reassured. "But if your procedure is really as simple and safe as you say, and it'll help her get back to herself, well, I suppose I have no choice but to give it serious consideration. After all, all I want is for Maggie to feel good again, to be happy."

Chapter Thirty-Nine

The moment Ruth hung up the phone, having very improperly accepted Estelle's invitation to come visit immediately, she realized she had been to Queens only once, during the World's Fair back in '39. But that was with Robert. She had never gone alone in her own car to Queens or any unknown New York neighborhood, for that matter. But her need to see Estelle overshadowed any misgivings. She consulted her atlas, got behind the wheel, and started to drive.

Estelle and her family lived in the modest Ridgewood neighborhood, and as Ruth cruised slowly down the street, scanning the numbers on the small redbrick row houses, she was pleased to see flowers in window boxes and children throwing balls outside. It was a lovely place for Estelle to have settled.

When she found the house, she pulled the car to the curb and took a few deep breaths. She felt nervous, and it suddenly occurred to her that she couldn't remember the last time she had made a house call. She walked with slow and deliberate steps. She needed to calm herself before she saw her former patient. Still, her heart raced when she reached the top of the small set of stairs and rang the bell. "It's Mrs. Apter! It's Mrs. Apter! Quiet, kids. Mommy's old friend is here!" She heard Estelle's unique singsong voice yelling over the noise of children crying on the other side of the door.

"Mrs. Apter! It's you! It's really you!" Estelle grinned at her as she opened the door with a toddler on her hip and another, slightly older, child wrapped around her leg.

"Estelle, after all these years, don't you know to call me Ruth?" She smiled and felt suddenly calm as Estelle took her free hand to wrap Ruth in a sloppy embrace.

"Oh, Estelle, it's wonderful to see you!" How different she seemed from everyone else Ruth had seen today.

"I've been wondering about you, Ruth! Hear from that husband of yours sometimes, but he never tells me anything about you! Would you be all right to sit with me in the kitchen? I have to finish feeding the kids."

"Oh my, I'm so sorry, Estelle. Did I come at an awkward time? I thought you said four thirty was fine?"

"No, no! It's okay. I just like to have 'em fed before Larry gets home. You know, so I can focus on him when he arrives? C'mon, follow me."

"Can I help you?"

"You? You don't need to feed mushy peas and carrots to a two-year-old. Just sit with me so I don't feel like I'm not hosting you right."

Ruth took a seat at the small square table in the center of the kitchen. She was proud of how much progress Estelle had made these past six years. Without her lobotomy, she might not be where she was today: a mother of two children, leading a regular life. Still, as Ruth watched her with the kids, she felt like she was observing a tentative new babysitter instead of the mother of two.

"Are you hungry?" Estelle noticed Ruth watching her carefully. "I can give you some crackers? Soda water? Oh, I am a dolt. Just wasn't expecting company and then you called and . . ."

"No, no, Estelle, you don't need to offer me anything. I'm just so happy to see you and appreciate you inviting me to your home on such short notice. Please, tell me how you've been."

"Oh, me, I'm swell. Just swell. Married, of course!" She laughed as she indicated the children while showing Ruth the thin gold wedding band on her left ring finger. "Met Larry in '48. He was a janitor in the school. Used to hide in the back of the auditorium and listen to me sing during choir. Didn't care that I was a little off, you know?" She touched her head and then put her finger over her lips as if the lobotomy was a secret.

"Estelle, does your husband know about your time with us at Emeraldine?"

"Oh yeah, he knows. Teases me about it sometimes. But I won't let him talk about it . . ." She cupped her hands and dropped her voice to a whisper. "In front of the children."

"I see." Ruth smiled. Estelle definitely seemed a bit simpler than Ruth remembered. Had she been this way at the hospital? Regardless, she seemed capable and happy. Was this all Ruth could hope for? Her spirits lifted. Perhaps she was being too critical. Maybe the prognosis for lobotomy wasn't quite so dire.

The door opened and Ruth heard a man's voice. "Stelle, where you at?"

"In the kitchen, Larry. Just finishing up feeding the boys. Come meet my friend!"

Ruth stood and put out her hand as a large, round man with a receding hairline entered the kitchen. "Ruth Apter, so nice to meet you, Mr.—"

"Simpson, ma'am. Larry Simpson." He had a kind smile and, as he shook Ruth's hand, she liked him immediately.

"Larry, take Ruth to the other room. When I'm done, we three can sit."

"I'm so sorry, I didn't mean to intrude on your evening." Ruth already felt more at ease now that she'd seen Estelle for herself. She could leave them in peace.

"Please, stay," Larry said as he took a beer from the refrigerator and waved her to follow him into the small living room. "You came all this way. Can I get you a beer?"

"Oh no, thank you! Can't risk feeling sleepy on my drive home." She smiled.

As soon as they were settled, Larry leaned toward her and lowered his voice. "I'm glad you came, Mrs. Apter. I've been wanting to talk to someone about Stelle."

"She seems well. And so happy with you and the boys. Is everything all right?"

"Oh yeah, yeah. Things are mostly fine. She's my angel. I tell her every day that I must have done somethin' right for the Lord to have sent me such a beautiful, kind soul for my own. Thing is, though, she has these 'spells.' And I'm not so sure about them. Didn't bother me when it was just the two of us, but now that we have the boys . . . Sometimes I worry about leaving her here alone with 'em, you know?"

Ruth's chest tightened. "What kind of spells?"

"Well, I told the doctor about 'em last time he called to check on Stelle and he said they were normal, no big deal. But I dunno. I don't want Stelle to know that I'm worried about her. She doesn't like to talk about the time she spent in the loony bin." He swirled his finger in circles on the side of his head by his ear.

"Mr. Simpson, Emeraldine is not a loony bin. But I am concerned to hear about Estelle's condition. Did you tell my associate, Mr. Mandrake, when he called you?"

"Not sure I know who you're talking about. He probably just spoke to Stelle if he called durin' the day. And she wouldn't tell anyone about that."

"I see. Well, I would like to help if I can. Can you tell me a little more about what happens during these 'spells' of hers?" Ruth looked anxiously at Estelle's husband as he seemed to consider what to say.

"I don't know. Stelle really doesn't like us to talk about it too much."

"I understand, but I can't help if I don't know what's happening. We can keep it between us."

"All right. Well . . . they're kinda different all the time. In the beginning, she used to take off all her clothes in the middle of a meal or somethin'. Before the boys, I thought she was tryin' to be sexy. Sometimes she just starts screamin'. Like a banshee. Or she'll lock herself in the bathroom with the boys, like she's under attack. Last time she took a knife in there with her. Like I told ya, the doctor said this is all normal after the thingy she had done, but . . . I dunno. Between us, I'm startin' to worry more and more."

Ruth attempted to appear calm, but it was a facade. She was in a panic. She needed to get out of there as soon as possible. "Mr. Simpson." Reaching in her purse, she retrieved a business card. With a pen, she wrote her home phone number on it as well. "I want to reassure you, but I am not sure that I can. Please, keep a close watch on Estelle. If she has another 'spell,' call me immediately. Do you have any friends or family who can stay with her and the boys during the day?"

He shook his head. "Her father passed last year." Suddenly his face lit up. "She does have a cousin in Philly. Maybe I can ask her to stay for a few days?"

"Ask who what?" Estelle came into the room and Ruth started.

"I was just tellin' Ruth about your cousin. You should invite her to visit."

"Mathilda? Oh, sure, I guess so." She shrugged.

Ruth walked to Estelle and gave her a strong embrace. "I'm so happy to see you today, Estelle. I'm going to call you again later this week to say hello and check in with you, does that sound good?"

"Awww, do you really have to go already?" Estelle looked like she might cry.

"I'm afraid that I do. But, I promise, I'll see you again soon. You have a lovely home and such beautiful children. I am just overjoyed for you!"

Ruth drove for three blocks before she pulled to the side and began to sob. It was a disaster. A horrible failure. Their life's work, hers and Robert's, hadn't helped. It had destroyed lives. She had championed lobotomy, promoted and encouraged it, and to what end? Even Estelle, one of the supposedly great triumphs of the procedure, wasn't actually a success at all. What kind of life was it to need constant supervision because you might harm yourself, or your children? How was that better than before?

She had truly believed she was helping patients, but now, how could she possibly justify what they had done? What they were still doing?

When she had cried herself out, she began to drive in a frenzy. She needed to get home. She had to find a way to fix things. To help Estelle and the many others who might be quietly suffering. She had to put a stop to this failed "cure," and she needed Robert's help to make it happen.

Chapter Forty

Ruth paced in the dining room, shifting the silverware and napkins on the formally set table to assuage her anxiety. When had she and Robert fallen out of the habit of eating together? It hadn't happened all at once, but lately, when he wasn't traveling, he spent his evenings writing articles touting the benefits of lobotomy for any medical journal willing to publish them. In the past, she had seen this as his dedication and the critics as uninformed doubters. How could she have been so blind? When Dr. Nolan Lewis, at a psychiatric society symposium in '49, warned that lobotomy was being performed indiscriminately and would "dement too large a segment of the population" or when Jay Hoffman, the head of the Veterans Administration's Neuropsychiatric Services, suggested that the success of lobotomy, in general, shouldn't be measured by whether patients improved over their presurgical condition but by the longer-term outcomes, which were not ideal, she had believed that these men were jealous and conservative members of the old guard. Even recently, when the *Times* reported that members of the World Federation of Mental Health had denounced the procedure as a cruel "violation of the principles of humanity," based on the Russian decision to stop using the procedure, she gave lobotomy the benefit of the doubt. At least Robert's lobotomy.

Now she saw it differently. Perhaps, in extreme cases, lobotomy was still a reasonable treatment for the most severe mental illnesses, as they had believed in the beginning. But she could finally see clearly that lobotomy was not the revolution she had believed it to be. And now, innovators were beginning to look elsewhere for solutions. Why, just a few months ago, she learned of a new type of medication that might have the same benefits. The era of lobotomy needed to come to an end.

"You're in the dining room already? I expected to find you in the library."

Ruth jumped, startled by Robert's sudden arrival. "Yes, well, I was only puttering in here. Not sure why really." She blushed, feeling caught somehow. "Would you like to go have a cocktail before we sit?" Ruth didn't want to drink too much—she needed to keep her wits about her—but she could use something to calm her nerves.

"Whatever suits you, my dear. We can just sit since we're already here." He slid the Chippendale chair out from the large mahogany table. They rarely ate in the dining room. Ruth didn't really like the formality, but tonight, she thought it would help keep her focused.

"Let me tell Liana that we'll eat now. I'll be back momentarily." Ruth gave him a kiss on the top of his head and then took a deep breath as she went down the hall to the kitchen. There sat her husband, the man she loved and admired more than anyone in the world, entirely unaware that she was about to tell him he needed to walk away from their great medical breakthrough. His life's work.

She returned to the dining room to see Robert settled at his seat. He had filled both their glasses and, as she slipped into her chair, raised his in a toast. "How lovely to be having a civilized meal together. Thank you for insisting that we do this, dear."

"It's been a while." Ruth took a sip of her wine and gave a forced smile. "I'm glad you were able to make the time for it this evening." She stopped herself from saying more in spite of the fact that all she wanted to do was say, *Lobotomy is done.*

"How are things at the hospital? It's been forever since I've been there," he asked easily.

"That it has. You're missed, by the staff and the patients."

"Ah, nice to hear. Did I tell you that they have asked me to come to the West Coast?"

"No, you hadn't. When do you plan to go?"

"I leave in a week." He smiled proudly.

A week? She felt like she was jumping in front of a moving train.

"It occurs to me we haven't had any opportunity to enjoy the summer yet," he continued. "How about if we plan for a picnic before I go, out on the island?"

"That would be nice." Ruth looked away from her husband. "But will you really have the time?"

"Well, I'll just have to make the time. It's been too long since we've had any fun."

"All right. Sounds lovely then." Ruth paused as Liana came in with their first course.

"Liana, Mrs. Apter and I would like to take a picnic out to the island this Saturday. Can you prepare something for us?" Robert asked lightly as he cut up his salad.

"Of course, sir."

Ruth gave Liana a smile, letting her know that she could leave. "Robert, there's something I need to discuss with you. It's a bit difficult."

"Difficult? Ruthie, we've never had anything we couldn't say to one another. What's on your mind?"

"I fear you're not going to like it, Robert."

"And have I ever been one to turn away from the unpleasant?"

"I suppose not." She took a deep breath. "I want to talk about lobotomy."

"Lobotomy?" Robert laughed. "We've been talking about lobotomy for decades. Why is this an unpleasant subject?"

In the silence that followed, she watched his jaw set tightly, his eyes harden. "Unless you're starting to be swayed by these damned medical journals? This ridiculousness from the World Mental Health people? These ignorant Russians?"

Ruth's heart pounded as she resisted the urge to retreat. "This isn't about any one article or decree, Robert. It is bigger than that. I conducted a study, at the hospital."

"A study? What kind of study?" His voice had an edge to it that surprised her.

"Well, as you know, since taking over the hospital, I've had very little time to spend with our actual patients. So, I decided to visit with some of them. Do you remember Albert Burdell?"

"Burdell, Burdell?"

"The one who played the piano?"

"Ah yes. The schizophrenic."

"He was not schizophrenic." She gave him a pleading look; she didn't want to engage in this particular argument tonight. "The thing is . . . now, he is nothing. Almost a void of a person. And Rosemary Kennedy, Edward said—"

"You spoke to Edward!" He dropped his fork with a clank. "Good God, Ruth. Have you become that gullible? You know you can't trust anything he says. He has been hell-bent on discrediting me for years!"

"But, Robert, what he said about Rosemary Kennedy, is it true?" she asked evenly, like she was trying to bring a child back from the precipice of a tantrum.

"Is what true? That she was a failure? Yes. Surely you aren't going to pretend you didn't know that at the time. Anyway, that was a prefrontal lobotomy. You know very well that I have long stopped recommending those." The tendons in his neck began to strain.

"I do. It's just . . . he said that you knew she didn't need—" She stopped herself. He was not reacting well already. Could she really push this conversation even more?

"Didn't need what?" he spat.

"My study at the hospital was of four hundred patients who have had mostly transorbital lobotomies. And, frankly, I was stunned by the results."

"Stunned?"

"Robert, do you realize that only twenty percent of the people we've lobotomized have even been able to leave the hospital?" Robert looked momentarily surprised, but he quickly replaced his expression with one of confident conviction.

"Well, leaving isn't the whole of it. The quality of life is improved. Your staff's ability to care for them is vastly easier."

"I know." She took a deep breath. How could she present this in a way that Robert wouldn't find incendiary? "But what was considered a good result among this group was Albert Burdell. And Regina Brooks—do you remember her? The dancer? She became so obsessed with food after her lobotomy that she has become obese. She can hardly move."

"Oh, please, Ruth, you are being hysterical about nothing. Just occasional unfortunate side effects. The point is that they are not a threat to themselves or others anymore. Right?"

Ruth couldn't believe that he wasn't the slightest bit unnerved by what she was saying. "Benny Green? Does that name ring a bell? He was a soldier. Had nightmares, extreme anxiety. Remember him?"

"Vaguely. You do know that at this point I have performed lobotomies on thousands of people, do you not?" *Thousands? Was it really that many?*

"Still, you treated Benny for quite a while so I thought you might remember him. I went to visit with him. Found him in his room, painting the wall with his own excrement." Ruth looked at Robert desperately and watched as he rolled his eyes.

"Good Lord, Ruth, you're being a bit dramatic, don't you think?"

"I don't know, am I?" Her eyes filled with tears. "I went to see Estelle Lennox. Her husband said she locked herself in the bathroom with a knife. A knife, Robert."

"Yes, I've spoken with her husband in the past. Need I remind you that Estelle went from a hallucinatory hysteric to a married woman with children? Thanks to us. We have given so many people such a gift. Can you really not see that?"

"Here is what I see. At *my* hospital, it was the best we had to offer—"

"Is."

"Years ago. But now, I am compelled to cease the use of lobotomy at Emeraldine. And I believe we need to help move the entire medical community away from it as well."

"I see," he said tightly. "Well, I am certain that your college degree has you well equipped to make such an evaluation."

"Then help me understand, Robert. Let's do this together. Have you seen the early work on chlorpromazine? They're saying it is as effective as lobotomy—but clearly less extreme."

"My procedure is not extreme! And it doesn't need to be given repeatedly. It provides permanent improvement all at once, and forever."

"But does it? I know your motivations are good, but it's time to look for new solutions. The tides are shifting in our professional community. And it scares me that you don't seem to be moving with them."

"In the past few years, I have been welcomed as a hero in more than twenty-three states and twice as many hospitals. It seems to me like *you* are the one not seeing the direction of change. Yes, there have been some bad outcomes. Because humans are imperfect beings!"

"All I want is the best for my patients. What am I supposed to do when I see so many failing to thrive after this procedure that was supposed to save them?"

He stood up, pushing his chair back violently. "You are supposed to trust that I, Robert Apter, am a competent enough clinician, an accomplished enough neurologist, to properly treat and diagnose my patients. You are supposed to support me and my procedure, the one I invented that established your hospital and remade the course of treatment across this whole country. You are supposed to believe in me as my wife, stop questioning me about things you can't possibly understand, and know your goddamned role!"

Ruth sat still in her chair, stunned, wounded, scared. She had been bullied like this in the past, but never by Robert. The little girl inside her might have had to take it from her father, but she would not take it from her husband. She stood to face him.

"My role, Robert, is to run my hospital. And in that role, I no longer feel comfortable with lobotomy. Can't we put our heads together and look for new options? I'm sure that we can pioneer something incredible."

"Pioneer something incredible? You really don't get it, do you? I don't need to pioneer anything—I am the inventor of the ten-minute lobotomy, the miracle cure! I am in demand all over the country. I have months-long waiting lists for private patients. Do what you want at Emeraldine; your little hospital is of no consequence to me or my success." Robert turned abruptly and marched out the front door, slamming it behind him.

Ruth sat back down, stupefied. The level of vitriol he had just unleashed on her was well beyond anything she had believed him capable of. She felt suddenly like she had just come back to shore after a long time at sea—her equilibrium was off, and she couldn't discern whether or not the ground beneath her was moving. The entire world she had built was falling down around her. What she had believed was her greatest contribution to mental health was not a cure, but a curse. The man she loved and trusted was lost to his ego, choosing his legacy over the truth. And now, he had to be stopped no matter the consequences, and she was the only one who could do it.

PART 4

RUTH AND MARGARET: JUNE 1953

Chapter Forty-One

Ruth felt like she had whiplash. As she watched the taillights of Robert's car recede into the distance, she had an impulse. Nothing in Jeremy's report made a strong enough case against lobotomy to stop Robert for good. But, perhaps, something in his private files would. Ruth hurriedly made her way to the carriage house. She didn't know how long Robert would be gone, but she hoped she could find something, anything, that would help her expose the truth.

Ruth felt like an intruder. Infringing upon the sanctity of a therapist's treatment room was an utter violation. But the urgency of her mission dwarfed moral code.

She walked directly to the wall of filing cabinets where Robert kept exacting notes on his patients. Surely she'd find something here that would help make her case. She opened several drawers, feeling aimless—what, exactly, was she looking for?—until a bulging packet caught her eye. The name on the label didn't look familiar to her, yet the case filled three complete hanging sleeves. Who might this be?

Ruth removed the first set of files and opened them to reveal a photograph of an average-looking woman, middle-aged, with a serious expression on her face. Ruth could tell from the background that the photo was taken at Emeraldine but didn't recognize the woman at all.

January 21, 1947: Patient D. Rice was temporarily detained at the hospital due to sudden and unprecedented hallucinatory episodes. Performed a transorbital lobotomy and she was able to return home several days later with no further hallucinations . . .

Ruth was relieved to see that she was a short-term, temporary patient. That explained why she didn't recognize her. She read on.

May 8, 1947: Check-in with D. Rice has confirmed success of psychosurgery. She has suffered no further hallucinations and has been able to reengage in her role as a mother and wife . . .

September 16, 1947: D. Rice has returned for further evaluation and treatment. Is presenting with extreme obsessive behavior and bouts of uncontrollable anger. Upon examination, determined that initial cutting had not penetrated deeply enough into her prefrontal white matter (likely out of an abundance of caution due to the relative newness of the procedure). Performed a second transorbital lobotomy, this time with much deeper incisions.

A second lobotomy? Ruth knew Robert performed multiple lobotomies in only the most extreme cases. Each additional procedure incurred greater risk—intracranial bleeding, postsurgical epilepsy. Robert had performed the second lobotomy in his private practice, not the hospital. Appalled, she continued reading.

December 12, 1947: D. Rice seems to have responded well to second lobotomy. Reports that majority of obsessive behaviors and urges have diminished and has had no violent outbursts.

Ruth read pages and pages of Robert's detailed follow-up notes until she finally got to the third set of files. The photo on the first page stunned her. This woman, who had initially appeared perfectly average looking, was now both visibly filthy and obese. At this point she shouldn't have been surprised. Ruth had seen weight gain in some of the lobotomy patients at Emeraldine, but this—the before and after side by side—well, the stark reality of the deterioration made her reach for the trash can fearing that she might retch. She read on.

March 18, 1950: D. Rice returned demanding a third lobotomy. Patient was almost unrecognizable due to extreme weight gain. This seems to be an unpleasant side effect of psychosurgery for some patients. However, obesity is preferable to other psychological conditions that are threatening to society at large.

Patient is requesting further treatment claiming obsessive impulses have returned. Clothing was noticeably soiled, yet she stepped out on six separate occasions to wash her hands. She also had several poorly concealed bald spots and admitted, when asked, that she had been pulling out her hair. She seems marginally untethered from reality. Considering third lobotomy.

April 3, 1950: Several days after third lobotomy D. Rice has suffered postoperative hemorrhage and died. After intermittent success with psychosurgery, she has ultimately succumbed to one of the rarer risks of the procedure.

Ruth gasped. This was worse than she could have imagined and, also, exactly what she had been looking for. Robert had not only performed multiple lobotomies on the same subject outside the hospital, but he had killed someone. She stood for a moment, dizzy from the thought of what she had discovered. This was akin to murder. Suddenly, she heard the sound of tires on gravel. Moving as quickly as she could, and holding tightly to the evidence in her hands, she ran back to the house before Robert found her.

She kept running until she made it up the stairs and into her bedroom, where she locked the door in panic. Peering out the curtain of the bathroom, she saw that she'd been mistaken. Robert's car was not there. *Where was he? Had he gone to the townhouse?* If he went to the city, he could see patients at his office there. She looked at the clock on the bookshelf across the room. It was already 8:00 p.m. Robert would be finished seeing patients today, so even if he was there, it didn't matter now. She had what she needed, and first thing in the morning, she would call the licensing board and have him stopped for good.

Chapter Forty-Two

Ruth didn't even attempt to sleep. Instead, she spent the darkest hours of the night replaying all the mistakes she had made to get her to this point. When had she stopped asking the critical questions that would have shown her that, for most, lobotomy turned out to be a horrible blight? Emeraldine—with her support—had been essential to its broad acceptance. Surely, she could have used that same influence to discredit the procedure? She had let this happen. No, she had *made* this happen. And now the problem was so much bigger than her hospital. Than her.

When daylight finally emerged, the sky turning from black to a purplish blue, similar to the hue under her eyes, she began to get ready. She took a cool shower to shake off the sleepless night, carefully combed her graying hair, and dressed in crisp linen slacks and a tailored blouse. She needed to look as collected as possible since, inside, she was falling to pieces. Glancing out the bathroom window again, she saw that Robert's car was still gone. Her heart started to beat more rapidly. In spite of how he had behaved the night before, she was worried. He had been so upset when he left. What if he had gotten into an accident? She shook off this foolish notion. He had places he could have gone for the night, and for now, it was better that Robert was not there to try to sway her against what she was about to do.

At precisely 9:00 p.m. she sat down at her desk in the study with her third cup of coffee and began. She had met Joe Hunt, the new president of the American Psychological Association, at a luncheon the previous year. She wasn't sure he would remember her, but she was certain he was well aware of Robert and lobotomy. It took a bit of digging but, within fifteen minutes, she had reached him on the other end of the line.

"Hello, Dr. Hunt? This is Ruth Apter from Emeraldine Hospital. We met last year at your introductory luncheon in New York? I really appreciate your taking my call." She was babbling.

"Mrs. Apter, of course. To what do I owe the pleasure of your call today?"

"I have a pressing matter that I need some help with." She hoped her shaky tone was imperceptible. "It is a bit sensitive."

"I see. Well, I'm happy to help if I can. What is it that you need?"

"I need you to suspend a psychiatrist from practicing, immediately. One of my clinicians at Emeraldine." She held her breath as she waited what felt like hours before he responded.

"Mrs. Apter, I'm not sure I understand. The APA doesn't really have that kind of authority. If there is an incident that you would like us to investigate, I can put you in touch with someone who can help, but otherwise . . ."

"Dr. Hunt, you don't understand. It's lobotomy, you see, one of my doctors has killed someone."

"Killed someone? That seems more like a legal matter?"

"Well, yes. It is that as well, certainly, but this doctor needs to be stopped immediately. Can't you suspend him from practicing? Issue a bulletin for all members? He is going on another trip soon. He needs to be stopped . . . now. Today!"

"Mrs. Apter, I can hear that you're upset. But surely you know there are protocols for this kind of thing. I am happy to transfer you to someone who can take a formal complaint from you now. And then, once we receive ample documentation, we can convene an investigation. But, beyond that, there is really nothing I can do to help. Have you notified your own governing board? Perhaps they could enact a suspension."

Ruth sat frozen, the phone poised to slip from her hand. She was a fool. Of course she wouldn't be able to stop Robert through the bureaucratic psychological association. And the board of Emeraldine would be no better; they, too, would need to enact a proper process. Plus, they wouldn't be able to stop him from doing this to his private patients, or even at other hospitals, elsewhere. She needed to do something else, something immediate. Robert needed to be stopped now, today.

Ruth ended her call as quickly and politely as possible, her head a whirl, and then stood to gather the files she had taken from the carriage house the night before. Her hands were unsteady as she placed them into her leather satchel, the only indication of how anxious she felt about what she was about to do. Her husband was a murderer, and if the medical community couldn't stop him, surely the police could.

Fifteen minutes later, Ruth walked through the door of the town's local precinct. She had never been inside of any police station before. As she took in the open room filled with several wooden desks, the smell of stale coffee that had likely been brewing all through the night, and the group of officers gathered in the far corner, she grew uneasy. *How did I end up here?* She stood frozen in the entrance, replaying the words she had rehearsed in her head.

"Can I help you, ma'am?" A young officer approached the front desk. He couldn't have been more than twenty years old.

"Hello. Yes, I would like to speak to the officer in charge, please." She spoke with confidence, in spite of the fact that her heart was thumping in her chest.

"Can I help you with something, ma'am?"

"Thank you, but I need to speak to whomever is in charge. It is quite important." Surely Ruth couldn't explain her case to this child. Robert would knock him over with a single blow.

"All right, ma'am. I'll just go and see if he is available. What can I tell him it's about?"

"I would like to report a murder."

Ruth watched the boy's eyes grow wide as she clutched more tightly to the attaché case in her hands. "Um, okay. Um, just a minute."

Ruth watched as the boy walked to the far end of the room where the uniformed men were talking. They stopped for a moment and looked at her, and then one walked in her direction. He was a solid-looking man; perhaps he had played football in school. He didn't seem old enough to be the captain, but he certainly had more gravitas than the one who had greeted her. She stood up taller.

"Ma'am, I am Officer Johnson, would you like to come sit down?" He ushered her toward a wooden chair next to what seemed to be his desk. "Charlie said you're here about a murder?"

"Indeed." Ruth nodded and began removing the files from her leather case and piling them on the desk. "It happened several years ago now, but I have the proof right here. My husband killed his patient. Not in the hospital, in his office. You see here—it says she died." Ruth pointed to the page in Robert's files. "He did it. He killed her."

"Ma'am, I need you to slow down please. Can we start with you telling me your name?"

She blanched. Of course, this was the next step, but she was suddenly winded by the enormity of what she had to do.

"My name is Ruth Emeraldine Apter."

Even as the words crossed her lips, she felt the respect she had worked for her entire life falling away. The family name that had belonged to captains of industry, who built America and underwrote this town, the hospital, and so many charities, would now forever be associated with barbarism. Failure.

But she had no choice. The lives she would save were more important.

Officer Johnson looked suddenly serious. "Mrs. Emeraldi—Apter. Are you saying that your husband killed someone at Magnolia Bluff?"

"I am."

Ruth spent the next fifteen minutes explaining the nuances of lobotomy to the group of officers now circled around her, most of whom had previously heard about the heiress and the famous doctor who lived at Magnolia Bluff but knew little more. Then she took them through every aspect of Robert's notes on Mrs. Rice in painstaking detail. How there hadn't been one lobotomy, but three. How the woman had hideously deteriorated over the years. Ruth was grateful for the photos and even placed the intake picture next to the final one, where Mrs. Rice looked so obese and unwell, to underscore the extent of the failure.

"So even then, when she was in this state and clearly hadn't been helped by lobotomy, he performed a third one. And this time, he went too far; her brain started to bleed, and she died." Ruth looked up at them, expecting them to share her shock and outrage. To be readying themselves to make an arrest. Instead, they stood calmly, mildly nonplussed.

"Okay, and then?"

"And then what?" she asked impatiently. What more did they need?

"Ma'am." Officer Johnson smiled kindly with an expression that Ruth recognized all too well. She had smiled in the same way at frantic patients at the hospital. "We can see that you are very upset. And this is unfortunate. But—"

"But what? Do you not understand? My husband is not a surgeon. He has no surgical license. Still, he performed surgery multiple times on the same patient, and ultimately killed her. He is a killer!" She stood, pointing again at the final paragraph in the file.

"Mrs. Apter, you seem to be hysterical. I am not sure what you want us to do here."

"Hysterical? How dare you, sir!"

"Okay, okay. Calm down. As I said before, this is all very unfortunate. But I don't see the evidence of any wrongdoing. Unless—is the family looking to press charges?"

Ruth slowly shook her head no. She hadn't spoken to the family but had seen correspondence in the file thanking Robert. She assumed he had found a way to invert the truth for them too.

"People sometimes die in surgery, right? I would think that, since you run a hospital yourself, you would know that a lot better than we do." Officer Johnson stood up and put his arm patronizingly around Ruth's shoulders. "I'm guessing you and your husband had a bad fight, right? And I can see that you're real mad at him. But there is no evidence of any foul play here, ma'am. I'm afraid there isn't anything we can do."

"I see." Ruth stared at the officers in disbelief as her face turned crimson. She hurriedly gathered her papers.

"Do you need an escort home? You do seem upset, ma'am."

"No, thank you. I'm fine." Ruth ducked her head, ashamed, and walked as quickly as possible back to her car. Sitting stiffly behind the wheel, she took slow, deep breaths to steady herself until she got home. She felt humiliated and confused. How was what Robert did not murder? How could the police not care?

She walked aimlessly through the house. There had to be another way, and she wouldn't stop until she found it.

Chapter Forty-Three

Two days later, Ruth rubbed her watering eyes as she looked out her study window to the ocean. She felt as though she had been on the phone since she left the station.

"You know I will do whatever I can to help you, Ruth. But it's been over a decade since I performed a lobotomy with Robert. Any of those patients would be too far in the past to matter."

"I understand, Edward. I didn't really think you would have anyone, but . . . I just don't know where to turn. How can it be that Robert has performed thousands of lobotomies and I can't find a single person willing to file a formal complaint?"

"Well, *I'm* more than happy to file a complaint. And support the allegations you bring to the medical review board. But, unfortunately, I think you'll need more. It'll take some time to build a proper case against him."

"But I don't have time!" she snapped. Estelle's husband, Larry, had refused to come forward. None of the families from Mandrake's report had been willing either. More than one had actually hung up on her. If she didn't find something more, Robert would soon be in California. For all she knew, he had already left.

California. That's it! She had been so busy focusing on his local patients, she hadn't considered what might have happened on the road.

"Edward, I have an idea. I need to go. I need to get back into the carriage house while Robert's still gone."

"Do you know where he is? When he's coming back? Maybe you should wait for me—I can shift my schedule around and be there tomorrow morning."

"No, no. I need to do this now."

"Please, be careful. Call me when you're back in the house, so I know you're safe."

"Of course I'm safe," she scoffed.

"Promise?"

"All right. Speak to you soon." Ruth smiled in spite of herself, glad for his concern.

As she walked outside, Ruth was momentarily blinded by the bright summer sun. For the last few days, she had hardly moved from her desk and, at moments, she felt as if she lived in a dream devolving into a nightmare. How could it be that just a few weeks ago she was a happily married woman with a renowned doctor for a husband, and now, she was desperately trying to stop him as if he were a deranged killer?

She had checked to make sure that his car was still gone before she went outside, but as she walked toward the carriage house, she checked again. She couldn't risk running into him. Not now. She was sweating from nerves as much as the heat as she slipped inside again and began to look around. Her eyes landed on several large piles of newer-looking files, stacked on the floor behind his desk. Could these be from his more recent road trips? He was so meticulous about his files, it would have been unusual for him to leave so many out—but Robert had been away so much, perhaps he hadn't gotten everything properly put away.

Crouching on the floor, she examined the files. There were so many. She wondered, for a moment, if the sheer volume of them might be enough to make a case against him to the board. But she knew better. It hadn't been enough for her. She had accepted his hundreds of lobotomies across the country as the gift to humanity he claimed them to be.

She began to open the files one by one, hoping to discover something, anything, that might help make her case. Most contained just a sheet of paper. Many didn't even have a photo. After nearly an hour of searching, she was near tears of frustration, almost ready to give up, when she came upon something odd. This file contained a picture of a rough-looking man sitting on a bed in a dirty room in what appeared to be some sort of boardinghouse. Decidedly *not* a hospital or clinic or even office. She was about to read the few pages inside when a knock on the door made her breath catch in her chest. She closed the file as quickly as she could and stood. If it was Robert, maybe she could pretend she was tidying up the carriage house as a peace offering for his return? It was absurd, but she was too afraid to think straight.

As she made her way toward the door, she heard a woman's voice.

"Dr. Apter? Hello? Are you in there?"

"Margaret?"

Chapter Forty-Four

Margaret had been waiting for Dr. Apter for more than twenty minutes and he still hadn't come outside to get her. He was always incredibly punctual. She also noticed that the car she usually saw parked in front wasn't there. Had she messed up the time? She started to panic. Could she have gotten the date wrong? No. She couldn't have. She was having her lobotomy tomorrow, and Dr. Apter had asked her to come in today for her preop appointment. Where could he be? Could something have happened to him? What if something happened to him and he wasn't able to perform the lobotomy?

She was *counting* on tomorrow.

Maybe he just got distracted by something, and maybe Ruth had taken his car. Yes, that must be it. She would go and knock on the door.

"Margaret?"

She was surprised to see Ruth standing before her in a wrinkled blouse, untucked from her slacks, her hair a mess, and her eyes red and rimmed with purplish circles. Something awful must have happened to Dr. Apter.

"Ruth. Are you all right? Is the doctor all right?" Ruth looked at her, confused. "I'm sorry—you just look . . . well . . . you don't look yourself. And I was supposed to have an appointment with your husband twenty minutes ago, and he hasn't come out to get me yet and I just—"

"Oh my, Margaret!" Ruth reached to smooth her hair as she stepped outside of the carriage house and shut the door. "I'm sorry, Robert isn't here. Are you sure you had an appointment today? It isn't Tuesday?"

"Yes, I know. It isn't my usual time. I was supposed to see the doctor today because—" Margaret stopped herself. She hadn't told Ruth about her lobotomy. She couldn't bear to hear any more criticism about her decision.

"Yes?"

"Oh, it's nothing really."

"It doesn't seem like nothing. You can tell me. What is it?"

"Well, it's just that your husband is going to fix me tomorrow. Today was my preoperative appointment."

Margaret watched Ruth's eyes grow so wide she feared they might tear at the edges.

"Your preoperative appointment? Maggie, no!" Ruth reached out to the wall to steady herself.

"What is it? You look upset." Margaret was surprised by the intensity of Ruth's reaction. Ruth seemed a little unhinged today. "Is everything okay?"

Ruth looked Margaret in the eyes. "Listen, Robert isn't here and, to be frank, I don't know when he'll be back. But you can't do this."

"What?" Margaret recoiled. "But you told me I could fix this."

"Not this way." Ruth looked around nervously and then waved Margaret toward the house. "Why don't you come inside for a few minutes. We can talk there."

Margaret looked at her hesitantly.

"Really, you'd be doing me a favor," Ruth said, sounding falsely upbeat. "I haven't had much sleep and could use some fresh coffee. Perhaps Robert will return by the time we are finished!" Ruth gave her a smile, putting Margaret a little more at ease.

"All right. I could use some coffee too." Margaret smiled back tentatively and followed her up the path and into the kitchen.

When the women were settled at the table, two steaming mugs in front of them in spite of the heat of the summer day, Ruth made her case.

"Margaret, did you know that I was there when Robert first learned about lobotomy? When he had the idea to do it here in America? I actually helped him develop and popularize lobotomy in this country." Her voice caught.

"No, I hadn't realized. So . . . good. Okay." Margaret smiled. "I feel better already."

Ruth shook her head. "When we began doing lobotomies, it seemed like the only treatment that worked for some of our most difficult patients. And for the very ill, the violent, the psychotics, it was lobotomy or be relegated to a lifetime in restraints, locked up in the secure ward of the hospital. We had a higher standard of care at Emeraldine, but the public hospitals were—are—so overcrowded . . . We thought that Robert was giving people back their lives. And I believed, for many years, that a lobotomy might very well have saved my brother had it been possible at the time."

"Don't you still?"

Ruth hesitated. "No. Not anymore. You see, when Harry was in the hospital, we all just wanted him to get back to normal, to be himself again. And when he died, I spent years wishing I could have done more."

"But look at all that you have created as a result! You are the strongest woman I have ever met. I wish I had just a tiny bit of your force and ability."

"But you do! Don't you see? You know, you are entitled to be frustrated sometimes. To feel angry. It is entirely natural that you will have great days and utterly awful ones. We all do. Now that I've had time to really process my brother's death, I wonder if the best thing I could have done for Harry might have been to tell him it was all right for him to feel what he was feeling. He went through horrible suffering in the war. And we never acknowledged that."

Ruth took a deep breath and looked Margaret in the eye pleadingly.

"Maggie, you can't have a lobotomy. Whatever you do . . . please, *please* don't do that. Whatever my husband says, don't believe him. You can't. You just can't."

Margaret felt her face turn from pink to gray. "What do you mean? The doctor says that I must. And soon. He says the longer I wait, the less chance there is of success. I need help."

"That's ridiculous. Don't you see? You aren't *that* kind of sick. I've been reading more about postpartum conditions. The feelings can linger. I've learned that there have been some cases where, when you're under anesthesia during delivery, the nurses assault the new mothers to keep them more still—it's a horrifying fact, but you can imagine that it could surely cause enduring psychological aftereffects. That might be what's happening for you. You gave up so much of your life for your family, that could also contribute to your ongoing depression. You see? There are many reasons that you may be feeling the way you do, and none of them should be treated with lobotomy."

Suddenly she was standing, gripping Margaret forcefully by the shoulders. "Please, Margaret, please, do not come back here tomorrow. Save yourself."

Margaret stood up too, her eyes wide with fear. "I'm sorry." She walked quickly away from Ruth toward the kitchen door. "I have to go."

The second the door shut behind her, she began to run. Ruth seemed to have lost her mind, and Margaret had to get away, get home, as fast as she could. Nothing Ruth said made any sense. She needed to talk to Frank. He would agree with her. And then she needed to find Dr. Apter so she could fix herself before it was too late.

Chapter Forty-Five

The situation was even more dire than Ruth had comprehended.

Migraine headaches? Lobotomy.

Unruly child? Lobotomy.

Unhappy wife? Lobotomy.

Robert had to be stopped.

Ruth went back to the carriage house and picked up the file she had been looking at before Margaret arrived, desperately hoping that underneath the disquieting photo of the man in the filthy boarding-house room there would be something she could use against Robert. The file contained three pieces of paper. The first was an order from the state of Ohio for a lobotomy to be performed on a Samuel Orenbluth at Midwestern Regional Hospital. The next was a short paragraph of Robert's handwritten notes.

> *Patient failed to appear for court-ordered lobotomy . . . went to Silver Sun boardinghouse . . . subject was agitated . . . applied electroshock for sedation . . . Once patient was unconscious, performed transorbital lobotomy on-site.*

The third piece of paper in the file was a copy of an insurance claim submitted to Blue Cross. Robert had requested reimbursement for the cost of the surgery. Ruth walked to the phone at Robert's desk, her legs unsteady below her. She dialed the exchange for Midwestern Regional.

"Yes, hello, this is Ruth Apter calling from Emeraldine Hospital. I would like to speak to"—she looked down at the form for the name of the administrator—"Mr. Warren, please. If he is available. It's an urgent matter."

Ruth sat anxiously waiting. Could Robert really have been so reckless, so myopic, as to have lobotomized a man in his room with no medical directive to do so? The fact that he was seeking insurance reimbursement meant that the hospital hadn't paid. They were either unaware or did not approve of his performing the procedure. Either could trigger a national medical review and likely cause Robert to lose his license permanently. She realized her hands were shaking.

"Hello, this is Jonathan Warren."

"Mr. Warren, this is Ruth Apter, I'm calling on behalf of Emeraldine Hospital in Manhattan to check in on a patient who I believe was treated by Dr. Apter when he was there in April of last year?"

"Ah yes, Mrs. Apter. We are so grateful to your husband for all that he did for us. And to your incredible hospital for enabling it. Happy to help if I can." He was right. Emeraldine had enabled this to happen. She was momentarily overcome with panic and considered hanging up, but she knew she couldn't. She needed to get to the bottom of this, regardless.

She put on a brave voice. "I appreciate it. I don't usually do patient follow-up, but I was hoping to ascertain some information on one of the lobotomy subjects during the doctor's visit there."

"There were quite a few people that trip. He really is incredible. What is the name? I'll see if I can hunt down the file."

"Orenbluth. Samuel Orenbluth."

"If you don't mind holding on for a few minutes, I'd be happy to look. Lobotomy has really been a godsend to us here. We're finally able to send some of our psychotics home. You must be so proud of your husband."

Ruth's stomach churned. She wanted to shout, *No. Not anymore. Go visit the psychotics and see how they're doing.* But she contained herself. "I am happy to wait while you look for the file. And thank you. I really appreciate your help."

Several minutes later, Mr. Warren returned to the phone. "Mrs. Apter, I've looked through the names of all the files from Dr. Apter's visit, and I'm afraid I don't see a patient by that name."

"I see." *Could this be a dead end?* "Any possibility you might have it elsewhere? It was a court-ordered case."

"Oh, yes then. Those were filed separately from the rest. I'll have a look there and be back." Time seemed to stand still, and Ruth's heart pounded more ferociously. Finally, he returned to the phone. "Mrs. Apter, this is quite odd, actually. I do not see Mr. Orenbluth's file. However, his name is on the list of court-ordered patients. Presumably he didn't show up. I wonder, how do you even have his name?"

Ruth took a girding breath. This was it. If she explained what she believed had happened to Mr. Orenbluth, she would set proceedings in motion that would ruin not just Robert's reputation, but hers as well. Robert's negligence, his butchery, was as much a failure of her oversight as it was his failure of conscience, his complete, pathological surrender to the demands of his ego.

But it didn't matter. Saving lives was more important than her reputation.

"Mr. Warren, that is, in fact, what I am calling about. You see, I have a file here that indicates my husband performed a lobotomy on Mr. Orenbluth at a place called the Silver Sun boardinghouse."

"Well, that is the closest accommodation to our hospital. The court-ordered cases often stay there. But we would never authorize treatment to be performed there. Are you sure?"

"Fairly certain, yes."

"But that's—a complete breach of medical ethics. If that got out, and it was thought that we sanctioned it . . . well, I simply can't believe it."

"I am holding a photograph of Mr. Orenbluth in my hand. Recovering from the procedure. At the Silver Sun."

After a long pause, he said with a heavy voice, "I will be forced to report Dr. Apter immediately."

"I understand. Mr. Warren, may I speak frankly?"

"Of course."

"Some recent information has come to my attention about lobotomy that has caused me to reexamine its efficacy. After much deliberation, I will no longer authorize the use of the procedure at Emeraldine Hospital, and I am recommending that other hospitals follow suit. Much as it pains me, I believe that Dr. Apter has lost his ability to discern when it is an appropriate tool, and I am in the process of recommending that his medical license be revoked." Her voice shook just slightly as she said these words.

"Mrs. Apter. This is your husband. Your hospital."

"I am quite aware, Mr. Warren. But, as I'm sure you can appreciate, the well-being of my patients takes precedence over my personal life." Her eyes filled with tears and she struggled to keep her voice steady and firm. "Mr. Warren, there is paperwork in Mr. Orenbluth's file that Dr. Apter has filed with Blue Cross for reimbursement of the procedure. If they haven't already looked into the matter, they surely will. And both your hospital and mine will be implicated in the process. If I were you, I would do what you need to do to preserve your own reputation."

"But that would mean—"

"Yes. I understand."

"But it wouldn't just be Dr. Apter, it would be you and Emeraldine too."

"I am well aware. This is my mess, and I'm going to clean it up. Thank you for your time, Mr. Warren." Ruth hung up. She tried to inhale, but her chest was so tight she was barely able to take in any breath. She wanted to scream. She wanted to cry. There was only one other moment in her life when she had felt so alone, the day she went to the hospital for her daily visit with Harry and discovered that, just hours before, he had taken his life. She had been the one to tell her parents, weeping in solitude while they comforted one another.

Get ahold of yourself, Ruth. This was not the same. She wasn't alone. She picked up the receiver again, dialing feverishly.

"Dr. Wilkinson's answering service."

Ruth was crestfallen; she was desperate to speak to Edward, to hear the comfort of his calm voice. The reason of his words. She wanted him to give her the strength that she feared she wouldn't have on her own. But he wasn't there. She would have to do this by herself.

"Hello, yes. This is Ruth Apter calling. Will you please tell Ed—Dr. Wilkinson to return my call as soon as possible. It's urgent. Please let him know to call me at my home. Thank you."

It wasn't prudent to linger in Robert's office any longer. She scanned Robert's desk for his calendar and quickly found the names of the hospitals he planned to visit in California. Then she picked up the Orenbluth file, shut out the lights, and went back to the house.

As she sat down at her desk in the study, preparing to call the hospitals in California, she had a flashback to that cold day nearly two decades before. It was here, in this very room, that Robert first had the idea to bring lobotomy to America.

How fitting then that it would also be here where she would finally put an end to his use of it once and for all.

Chapter Forty-Six

Ruth was just finishing a call with the fourth hospital Robert was scheduled to visit in California when the sound of a man's voice made her jump. The sun had set, but in the glow of dusk, she saw Robert's car through the window.

He was back.

She quickly put Robert's files in the desk drawer as he entered.

"Ruth? Ruth? Are you in here?" He looked a mess. His hair was unkempt, and he had a gentleness to his face that Ruth hadn't seen in a long time. Her heart softened. "I'm sorry, am I disturbing you?"

"No, it's all right. I'm surprised to see you. But pleased." She smiled at him awkwardly.

"I apologize for storming off the other night. I've been going over and over it in my head, and I just can't make sense of it all. Can we try to talk again?" He crossed the room to the leather wingback and tentatively sat down.

"I would like that. To talk like we used to. Like two people who love and respect each other and are only motivated by the best interests of our patients." Was it possible that it wasn't too late? Had he seen reason?

"I don't believe I've ever spoken to you any other way."

"Robert. I cannot forget our conversation, if you can call it that, the other night. But I realize that I caught you off guard. You know I wasn't trying to criticize you. I was trying to reconnect with you."

"Well, you certainly have an odd way of reconnecting." His voice quickly sharpened and made her uneasy.

She walked from her desk and sat down next to him, hoping to seem less confrontational. "Please, we've been such wonderful partners for so many years. Can we not be partners like that again?" As she looked at this man, whom she had loved so utterly and completely for so many years, she couldn't help but harbor a flicker of hope.

"Of course we can. As long as you've come to see that you were wrong." Her heart fell. "We've always stood up together for lobotomy— in the beginning when the medical community spouted that ridiculous nonsense about it altering the essence of what made a man a human being; when your father accused me of being medieval in my approach; even when Edward grew so jealous that he made up lies about me and my method. You were always there by my side. That's why I cannot understand what has happened now."

"Robert." She tentatively took his hand, devastated over the loss of all she had believed to be true and, at the same time, sad and sorry for this man who had grown so deluded he couldn't discern fact from his carefully crafted fiction. The winds hadn't simply shifted whimsically away from lobotomy. "I read files while you were gone—Deena Rice, Sam Orenbluth—and what you're doing isn't just failing, it's medical malpractice." She watched his face turn to stone. "I will stand by you and we can find our way through this together, but you must promise to stop, now. Forever."

"Are you mad?" he yelled, snapping his hand away from hers and standing up. "You read my files? My private patient records? Why, I could sue you for that breach."

"Sue me? Robert, don't you see that your career is already over? You're going to lose your license, possibly go to jail. Your reputation, mine, the hospital's—it will be destroyed. All the good we *have* done, obliterated by your recklessness.

"I can't help you undo this, but I can help you move on. We can build a new life, together." She wasn't sure if she would be able to, but she desperately wanted to believe that it was possible. That she could still love him. That they could weather this hideous storm together.

"You manipulative bitch! While I was in the city thinking of the best way to make amends with you, you've been trespassing in my office, reading my files, building a false case against my work."

"It is *not* a false case," she said in a voice steely with determination. "You are ruining lives and preparing to ruin more."

"Ruining lives?"

"And in the end, that's all you'll be known for—" She stood, drawing back her shoulders and lifting her chest to square off with him at her full height. As soon as they locked eyes, she saw her mistake. He was out of control. Beyond reason. Her eyes darted toward the door, hoping to escape, but it was too late.

"Enough!" he bellowed, smacking her across the face with his full force.

She fell hard to the floor.

"Once and for all, shut your goddamned mouth! You're not a doctor, and as soon as I report your breach to the hospital's board, I suspect you'll no longer be an administrator. And, once I retain a lawyer, you'll no longer be my wife."

Robert turned and stormed out of the room. He didn't even turn back to see that his blow had left Ruth knocked out cold.

Chapter Forty-Seven

Frank's foot bounced as he sat on the bench outside the doctor's office. "What's taking him so long? Didn't you have an appointment ten minutes ago?"

"He's usually very punctual. He did call personally last night to confirm this appointment."

Just then Dr. Apter opened the door. "Mr. Baxter, so good to see you. Maggie should be ready to be taken home in an hour."

Margaret was surprised by his appearance. Usually, he was well coiffed and calm, yet today, his hair was wild, his tie was askew, even his eyebrows were a mess—like an absentminded grandpa. She almost giggled at the absurdity of it.

"We want to speak to you together," Frank said as he pushed past Robert and into his office, Margaret trailing behind him. "This won't take long."

"Then please, won't you sit down?"

Margaret gave Frank a confused look as he sat beside her on the sofa. This was not what she had expected. She'd asked him to come along because of the procedure. Because she wouldn't be able to drive herself home.

"Mr. Baxter, tell me, what's on your mind." Dr. Apter tapped his pencil impatiently; he seemed irritated. Margaret didn't entirely blame him.

"I don't think Maggie should have the surgery." Margaret's heart stopped for a moment and her hearing got fuzzy.

"You what?" She turned to look at Frank. All the color had drained from his face.

"Maggie, I don't want you to do this."

"But . . . you brought me here. It's today. We agreed! For the kids, for you, for . . . me."

"Mr. Baxter," the doctor jumped in, "I appreciate that you are anxious about the idea of your wife having any sort of procedure. But I can assure you it is quite safe. She will be just fine."

"Then how come your wife told her not to do it?"

"Frank!" Margaret looked at him sharply. That was supposed to have been between them. She shouldn't have told him about her encounter with Ruth yesterday. It had clouded his judgment. But he hadn't seen Ruth—she was hysterical. Margaret knew better. It wouldn't cloud her judgment.

"No, Mags, I want to hear what he has to say. Your wife told Maggie that she doesn't need a lobotomy. That lobotomy will not help her. She said she doesn't even *believe* in lobotomy anymore. So, Doctor, I want to understand—if *your* wife doesn't believe in it, why should I let you do this to *my* wife?"

"My WIFE?!" Margaret had never seen the doctor angry before and it frightened her.

"Dr. Apter, I met her by chance this spring." Margaret attempted to calm him down. "She was in the garden as I was leaving, and we got to talking after my sessions. I saw her yesterday when you weren't here."

"And what exactly did she say?"

"She said that Maggie shouldn't do this," Frank sputtered angrily.

"I see. And I assume you know that my wife is only an administrator of a hospital? She is not a doctor. She's had no formal training whatsoever. Not a single credential that qualifies her to give you any kind of medical advice or opinion. Why, everything she knows, she learned from me!"

"Dr. Apter." Frank stood protectively. "This is not just about your wife. You haven't been honest with us about the risks of this surgery. We demand to know the truth."

"Mr. Baxter, please. I can see that you are both upset, and I understand. As you know, I do work from my home and, to be honest, my wife and I have had a bad argument. She has a tendency to become a bit hysterical and unhinged when we quarrel. It is really the only explanation for why she would have chosen to speak to Margaret. But I can assure you, Mrs. Apter is not a qualified source of information about what I am proposing here." He took a deep breath and looked sympathetically at Margaret. "I hate to be the one to tell you this, as it seems you have a fondness for my Ruthie, but she is quite ill herself. She lost her brother years ago and has been haunted by it ever since. She has good stretches, excellent ones actually, but when she has these attacks, she cannot be trusted."

"See, Frank. I told you she seemed unhinged yesterday." Margaret looked at Frank, and he shook his head slowly, trying to make sense of what the doctor had just told them. Her heart pumped feverishly.

"Mags, either way, I want you to know that I don't think you should do this." He turned toward her and took her hands in his tenderly. "I don't think you *need* to do this. I think you're getting better." He paused and gently caressed her cheek, looking deeply into her eyes. She was reminded of their wedding day—how earnestly he said his vows. "But I'll stand by whatever you decide. I love you."

Margaret felt like an hourglass that had been flipped over moments before the last grains of sand drained to the bottom. How could Frank say this now? After months of agonizing, the day was finally here.

"Frank, nothing has changed. We made this decision, and we should stick to it. You agree, right, Doctor?" She turned to Dr. Apter, who stood pacing behind his chair.

"Of course I agree," he said curtly. "This is the only way for you to truly heal."

"Frank, go outside." Margaret nudged her husband forcefully, demonstrating more confidence than she felt. "Everything is going to be all right."

The doctor walked toward the door and opened it, standing there until Frank hesitantly walked back through and settled himself on the bench outside.

"As I said before, we should be about an hour. Don't worry. I am an expert at this. I think you will be very pleased with the results."

Chapter Forty-Eight

Ruth awoke on the floor with a throbbing headache. *Where am I?* She struggled to stand, disoriented and groggy. The sun was rising. She didn't remember falling asleep. *What happened?* Steadying herself with the wall, she made her way to the kitchen to get some ice.

"Mrs. Apter, your face!" Liana stared at her aghast, and Ruth caught her reflection in a cabinet. Her lip split and swollen, her cheek purple. "Are you all right, ma'am?"

"Yes, I'm fine. I think it looks worse than it is. I must've taken a fall in the study last night."

"Come, sit down." Liana pulled a steak from the freezer and gently escorted Ruth to the breakfast table. The cold made her wince, but it also seemed to sharpen her mind.

She stood and walked to the back door, peering through the panes toward the carriage house. There sat the green Saratoga, the Baxters' car.

She dropped the steak and ran outside in a panic.

"Frank? Are you Frank Baxter? Is Margaret in there?" She was terrified. Was it possible that Margaret was having the lobotomy right now?

"Are you the doctor's wife?" He backed away from her slightly.

"Yes, sorry. Forgive my appearance. Is Margaret in there, alone?"

He looked as though he wasn't sure what to say.

"Mr. Baxter, please, if your wife is in there for a lobotomy, we must stop her."

"What happened to your face?"

"I think you should go inside now and take your wife home," she said pointedly.

"But she wants this."

"No, she wants to feel better. And this isn't the way."

He looked anguished. Paralyzed.

Suddenly they heard a scream.

"No!" Ruth was overtaken with fear.

"Maggie!" Frank yelled as he went to open the door. The knob didn't turn. It was locked.

Chapter Forty-Nine

"Okay, any final thoughts before we begin?" Dr. Apter shut the office door and sat again in his usual chair. For a moment she forgot that today wouldn't be just another day where they sat and talked. Even though this was what she wanted, a chill ran through her.

"You mean now? You want to do this right now?" Margaret thought there would be more preliminaries before it began. One last chance to make absolutely sure this was the right thing to do. She felt suddenly frantic. Maybe she wasn't ready. "I have been feeling better for longer spells. You know, less down, less angry."

Maybe Frank was right. Was she making a mistake? "But I'm still not myself." Her eyes swept nervously around the room. "It's just, all of a sudden, it seems like everyone around me is telling me not to do the one thing I know will fix me. And . . . I'm so confused. And I am so sick and tired of feeling confused. But I don't want to do the wrong thing either."

"I can see that you are struggling."

"Dr. Apter, are you certain that lobotomy will cure me?" Margaret looked at the doctor expecting a comforting smile, but his eyes darted around the room and his knee bounced up and down impatiently. She shifted in her seat.

"Yes." He looked away from her, toward the room next to the kitchen. The area where, she knew, he performed his procedures. "As

I've told you many times, without lobotomy, your maladies will not simply disappear, Margaret."

"Yes, I know they won't. It's just that . . . I'm scared of making a mistake." She looked sheepishly at the doctor as she played with the strap on her pocketbook, hoping for reassurance. Instead, she saw what she could only interpret as fury. His pinched mouth struggled to contain his disappointment in her; his furrowed brow silently chastised her disobedience.

"So you've said. Frequently. I am not sure how many more times I can tell you that you need this before you believe me. I think you do believe me since you are here." She felt like he was yelling at her. It made her extremely anxious.

"Perhaps you would like to see where the procedure is performed?" His voice and face softened. "Have a look at the instruments. I have a feeling it will help you to see how simple it all really is."

That did seem like a reasonable idea. Maybe if she could visualize what lobotomy would look like, put herself in the moment, she could determine whether it was what she really wanted, what she needed. "All right." She stood. "Why don't I get Frank and he can see too? I think it will set his mind at ease."

"We can show Frank once you make your decision."

Margaret followed Dr. Apter into the small second room. It was a simple space with a reclining chair, a metal tray, and a machine of some sort that Dr. Apter immediately turned on. Margaret started to get more nervous as she heard the humming noise and saw the long metal instruments that would be thrust into her eyes—they really did look like ice picks. Dr. Apter lifted two cuplike pieces attached by flexible cables to the machine now whirring feverishly. She began to step back, toward the door of the room.

"Don't be afraid. This is just a simple electroshock machine. It's what I use instead of anesthesia. It's very gentle, has a calming effect actually. Come, look."

Margaret suddenly felt paralyzed with fear. She wanted to open her mouth and yell, but that would be absurd. This was her doctor. His job was to heal her. Steeling herself, she approached him slowly. As she did, he lunged for her with the electrodes in his hand, and only then did she let out a bloodcurdling scream.

Chapter Fifty

Frank shook the door by the knob but it wouldn't open, so Ruth grabbed a rock and threw it through the glass panel. She reached inside to unlock the door, and the two of them rushed into the room in a frenzy.

"Maggie?" Frank screamed as he tore across the office to the second room.

"Robert?" Ruth was on Frank's heels, panicked about what they might see when they went through that doorway. She braced herself, anticipating that she'd find Margaret in the chair with Robert standing over her, finishing up the lobotomy she never needed. She desperately hoped she was wrong.

"Mags? Mags?" She heard Frank almost whimper and then begin to bawl, and her heart broke. She entered the room to find Margaret on the floor in Frank's arms, sobbing but untouched. "It's okay, Mags, it's okay."

Robert lay next to them seemingly unconscious.

"He . . . he . . . he tried to knock me out. I wasn't ready. I wanted to see the room and then tell you, for sure, that it was going to happen first. But he was like a wild animal coming at me. He had those things in his hands, he was going to shock me, to put me out so he could do it right then. I tried to push him away and he tripped backward on the wire. Hit his head. He fell to the ground . . . he . . ." Margaret started to cry harder. Ruth knelt down next to Robert and checked his pulse, still steady. She checked his head for signs of a cut and there were none.

"I'm sure he will be fine." She stood and went to the kitchen to get Margaret a cool cloth and a glass of water. Ruth approached her tentatively, handing her the glass and giving the rag to Frank.

"What happened to your face?" Margaret looked at Ruth, taking a deep, jagged breath.

"It's nothing." Ruth smiled, though her lip throbbed.

"That bastard hit her, that's what happened."

"He hit you? Are you hurt?" Edward's voice came from the doorway.

"Edward?" She shook her head. "No, I'm fine. But how are you . . . why are you . . . ?"

"I've been worried sick about you. You left an urgent message last night and I called and called, and no one answered. I had a feeling something was terribly wrong. I came as soon as I could."

Ruth felt flooded with gratitude. "Thank you," she said softly, wincing from the pain in her face as she smiled.

"Are you all right? You look terrible."

"I will be." Ruth nodded as she looked behind her to see Robert still unmoving on the floor, Frank and Margaret sitting in stunned silence beside him.

"Frank, Margaret, let's get you out of here. Would you like to go up to the house to collect yourselves? You may stay as long as you need."

"If it's all the same to you"—Margaret pushed herself up to stand, holding tightly to Frank—"I'd just like to go home."

"Let's go." Frank wrapped his arm around her protectively as they walked to the door.

"I am so sorry," Ruth said to them both as she watched them leave. She wasn't sure whether the tears streaming down her face were from guilt about what had almost happened to Margaret or relief that she had been spared. Whatever the cause, she allowed herself to succumb to them and let Edward wrap her in a comforting embrace.

Chapter Fifty-One

Ruth stood momentarily paralyzed, steadying herself against Edward's solid frame. She took in this room, once the place of so much hope and, now, the scene of utter horror. It still made no sense. In the corner of her eye, she noticed a pile of shoeboxes next to Robert's desk; she knew what she'd find inside. Her husband, ever the record keeper, had saved every letter, every Christmas card, every happy family photo from each and every patient he had treated. She knew he liked to take them out to look at them when he needed reassurance. She lifted the top one from the pile and began to read out loud to Edward:

December 22, 1947

Dr. Apter,

We cannot thank you enough for all that you have done to save my father. Before we met you, we thought he was a lost cause. Mother would spend her days crying, counting our pennies to see whether we would be able to eat that week, with Father incapable of working. You saved us all! Father is well again. He was able to return to work—yes, on the factory line instead of at the office—but at least we have enough money now to eat and buy books and clothes for school. And presents! You

*are a miracle, not just for him but for us all. God bless
you and merry Christmas!*
Sincerely,
The Wildman family

Ruth's eyes filled with tears again as she looked to Edward. "This—
this is why he did this. Why we did this. He was helping people! You
both were. So, what happened? How—when did it all go so wrong?"

"Medicine is about progress. About trial and error and a willingness
to always examine what you do with a critical eye. In the beginning,
Robert's quest was to find the best way. The optimal treatment. He was
relentless. It was what we both loved about him. But, once he believed
he had found it, something that he could control—claim as his own—
he lost perspective."

"I should have paid more attention. The things he was doing in
this office, and on the road. It is unconscionable. I had to stop it. To
stop him."

"Stop me how, exactly?"

Ruth gasped, dropping the letter as she and Edward turned to see
Robert staggering into the room. She moved quickly to Edward's side
and, holding tight to his arm, began backing slowly toward the door.
She was no longer certain what Robert was capable of. How far he
would go.

"With him?" Robert motioned dismissively to Edward. "Eddie
here, he can't do anything either. He gave up our crusade, retreated to
his ivory tower. Took the coward's route." Robert teetered on his feet a
bit, still unsteady from the blow. *Serves him right.* Ruth was suddenly
emboldened.

"Enough, Robert. Edward is not a coward! He was just willing to
acknowledge the limitations of your work and move on. How can you
not see that?" She stood a little taller, shored up with Edward by her
side as she inched closer to their escape.

"Trying to run away?" He laughed. "You act as if I am some sort of criminal. Honestly, Ruth. You have become just as blind as he is. Distorting the truth by focusing on the bad outcomes. What about those?" He pointed to the boxes of letters. "How can you argue with those?"

"There is nothing to argue with. You did wonderful things for many people."

"Yet still you question me?"

"Robert, you are not hearing me!" She was startled to hear herself yelling. "I don't question what you did. I am questioning what you kept doing after it was clearly not working. What you are still doing now! Lobotomy is done. How can you not see that?"

"You continue to say that, yet I have a whole country begging for my services."

Ruth looked at Robert. She didn't need to argue with him anymore. She had already taken away everything that mattered to him. The room became claustrophobically quiet. All at once, she was filled with pity, no longer afraid. She took a step in his direction.

"Not anymore. It's over," she said. He propped himself up on the back of his chair, still groggy, and looked blankly at her as she continued. "I told Midwestern Regional all about Sam Orenbluth. Mr. Warren has likely already filed a complaint with the medical review board. I've called all the hospitals in California. They won't have you either. Robert, you've become a danger to society. After what you attempted today, I could have you arrested. But I won't. Because I have made sure that you can never do this again."

Edward looked to her, confused but supportive.

Robert stood and went to his files. He began to pull out the contents and stack them on the ground, opening and slamming drawer after drawer in a frenzy. "I might have expected this from him"—he pointed at Edward, his finger shaking with ire—"but you? Doesn't any of this mean anything to you?" He shook a file in her direction. "All that I did for all these people? I saved them!"

"Robert," she said coldly, "put the files down. It is time for you to go."

"I will go when I am good and ready. These are mine. My life's work. Do you think I am going to hang my head like a dog and walk out of here? You're not just a bitch, you're a fool."

Ruth lunged at her husband and smacked him across the face with all her strength. He stumbled, stunned, and fell backward. She grabbed the file from his hand.

"Get out. Now!" she commanded. Edward moved to her side.

Robert's jaw began to quiver and then went slack. Ruth suddenly noticed the hang of his jowls. He was getting old. His shoulders were slumped down, instead of drawn back in their usual boastful rigidity. He was unshaven, his hair a mess, and his skin had an unpleasant waxy pallor. He was broken. She had broken him. His legs began to buckle, and he slid along the wall to sit on the floor. Ruth felt as if a specter had appeared and, all at once, siphoned every last bit of bravado, of fight, of life from her husband.

"Goodbye, Robert," she said. The pain of seeing him like this was overshadowed by all that had happened in the past twenty-four hours.

He hung his head in defeat. "At least let me take my letters," Robert pleaded as he crumpled before them.

Ruth picked up the shoeboxes at his desk, and handing them over, she looked at him one last time. "I wish it could have ended differently. I hope you find your way."

And then she walked out of the carriage house and back along the stone path, while Edward ensured that Robert left without anything more than the letters Ruth had allowed him.

Inside the house, Ruth collapsed in her study in the first chair she found. She heard the sound of Robert's tires on the gravel, leaving Magnolia Bluff forever. And then Edward came in and sat down beside her.

"Can I get you anything?" he asked, concerned.

Ruth shook her head.

"You are very brave. You know, you might have asked me for help sooner. If I had known . . . I hate that it came to this." He motioned to her face.

"It's nothing. You're here now. Thank you for knowing me so well that you came when I really needed you." She sighed. "The things he was doing, you can't imagine . . . He will never practice medicine again." She looked out the window. "But it's not just him. I did this. I let this happen. My career is over too." She sat stone-faced, overwhelmed by the enormity of what she had done.

Edward grabbed her hand.

"You are a great woman, Ruth Emeraldine. You will find your way. We will find your way."

Chapter Fifty-Two

"Have you been in here all night?" Edward crossed the main room of the carriage house, where Ruth was sitting on the floor collecting and packing files. "You know you don't have to do this yourself, Ruth. I'm sure your staff can pack all this up."

"No. I need to do it. The first step of my penance." Ruth looked at Edward, the sides of her lips curling down slightly in a pained half smile.

"I wish you didn't feel that you needed to do any penance." He put his hand tenderly on her back. "You didn't know what was happening."

"Exactly. I didn't know but I should have. It was *my job* to know. I let the lines between my marriage and my work get much too blurred. I didn't scrutinize Robert as I should have because he was my husband, and because I wanted success so badly myself. My foolish, single-minded desire was a big part of making this happen from the very beginning. And I never opened my eyes. My father would have been disgusted."

"Ruth, stop, you—"

"No. It's the truth. Not like you. You—you saw things for what they were and moved on, moved away from this hideousness."

"I am culpable too. I chose to disappear quietly and let Robert continue on. I could've come to you back then, in '46."

"We both know I wouldn't have listened." Ruth sighed. "How could I have been so taken in by all of this? I was such a fool." All her self-disgust, her pain, her sense of betrayal exploded in a rush of uncontrollable tears. She had never cried this much in her life.

"I did this." She choked on the words as she held up the file she'd been reading—another patient who died from lobotomy. "I . . . let . . . ," she gasped, her face red and soaked with tears, "people . . . die."

"I hate that you feel you need to suffer for this." Edward sat on the floor and took Ruth gently in his arms. "I think you already know that I do not agree. You've only ever wanted the best for your patients. For everyone, really. And you got caught up in something, with someone, who took advantage of that. I did too, for a time. Robert is an uncannily compelling man."

Ruth nodded tentatively. She knew what Edward said was true, but she also knew she should have been stronger. The stakes had been too high. And she had failed.

She stood, wiped her tears, and went to the kitchen, where she poured herself and Edward each a glass of water.

"You have no idea how much it means to me that you came here yesterday. That you are still here."

"I hope you know by now how much I care for you."

Ruth smiled softly. She wasn't sure she deserved to be cared for, but she felt overwhelming gratitude for Edward's steadfast friendship.

"Edward Wilkinson, you are the kindest, most genuine man I have ever known. I am lucky to have you in my life." She squeezed his hand. "If your schedule allows, maybe we can have dinner together tonight, here at Magnolia Bluff?" She felt her face suddenly growing warm. "You know I've always considered that guest room to be yours?"

"I would like that very much." Edward smiled and kissed Ruth, tentative and tender, on the forehead. "I'll just need to call Steven and let him know I won't be home tonight." He blushed and looked away.

"Or invite him along if you like." She smiled back at him. She had been waiting years for him to be forthright with her about his private life. Didn't he know she wouldn't give it a second thought? "Now leave me to finish sorting through and packing this up."

"Are you going to send it back to Robert?"

"I don't think so. At least some of it needs to go to the review board; I want to be sure they have ample evidence to revoke his license. And some to the New York School of Medicine for their archives. Perhaps some research scholar can find a use for it all. And then"—Ruth's face fell again—"I have a contact at the *Times* who would probably be very interested in this story . . . Now go! You're distracting me and I want to get this done."

Edward laughed and walked to the door. "See you for dinner. Although I might come back and bring you some lunch too."

She smiled at Edward in spite of herself. The past few days had been agony, and she knew that the hardest part—the true reckoning—lay ahead. Yet, perhaps, with him by her side, the sting might not be quite as sharp.

Epilogue

One Year Later

"I think they're here." Ruth heard a car on the gravel. "Do you have the paper?"

"Of course I have it." Edward followed Ruth to the front door of the carriage house, a crisp newspaper folded under his arm.

"And you really haven't read it yet? Steven didn't give you a preview?"

"No, he left this morning before I was even up. Had an early consultation. He was sorry not to be able to be here for you today. Anyway, we agreed, didn't we?"

"Yes. And you are nothing if not a man of your word." Ruth smiled appreciatively at him as she stepped out on the front porch of her little home.

The car had barely stopped before the back door burst open and John and Maisy leapt out. "It's so warm today, can we swim in the ocean? Please? Please?"

"Kids! Give Auntie Ruth a moment before you bombard her. We've only just arrived." Margaret laughed as she stepped out of the car and walked around to give Ruth a warm hug. "As you can see, the children have been waiting all spring for a warm day to play on your beach."

"Well, aren't we lucky that the weather has cooperated. As a matter of fact, I had a feeling you might like some time in the sand. Susie and

Meg are already waiting down by the water with a picnic! Shall we head to the beach?"

"Hooray! A picnic! We don't have to use forks!" the children yelled as they ran ahead of the adults.

"Watch for your brother. He's still little," Margaret chided her two eldest. "Did you look yet?" she asked as she pulled a newspaper from her large bag.

"No," Ruth said with some trepidation. "Did you?"

"We waited too." Frank stepped from the car and shook Edward's hand before embracing Ruth warmly.

"All right then, let's get down to the beach and have a look."

The four friends made their way through the property, the smell of blooming flowers washing over them as they walked. It was a fresh summer full of hope and possibility.

The property looked quite different now, what with the patients also out for strolls.

"Albert," Ruth said as she passed Mr. Burdell on the lawn. "I'm so glad to see you getting some fresh air on this beautiful day."

He looked over at Ruth and smiled.

"Are we on for tea later this afternoon?"

"Of course. I always have tea."

Ruth knew that converting Magnolia Bluff into an aftercare facility for lobotomy patients was just a tiny step. So many needed more than what she could provide. But it was something. At least those who had remained at Emeraldine had the specialized care they needed, and a place to call home for the rest of their lives.

She, Edward, Frank, and Margaret ambled down the stone steps.

"Took you long enough!" Susie smiled as she and Meg stood up from their Adirondack chairs to embrace Frank and Margaret. "I've been dying to open this paper for an hour already. If I didn't have Meg to keep me honest, I would have already read it three times over."

They laughed.

"No Steven today?" Meg asked Edward as they settled into the remaining chairs.

"Unfortunately, no. He had to work. But he'll be here tonight for our celebratory dinner. He doesn't miss champagne if he can help it."

They all laughed as they watched the children happily playing in the sand.

"Shall we?" Ruth asked, and they all opened their newspapers and together took in the headline:

FROM MIRACLE TO DISASTER: LOBOTOMY EXPOSED AS HORROR PERPETRATED BY MONSTER DOCTOR ON THOUSANDS

Ruth felt her heart pounding. She had provided all the information for this story, and even after everything that had happened, she still felt guilty for ruining Robert's life. She wished there had been another way.

As if predicting what she was about to say, Edward grabbed her hand. "You did the right thing, Ruth."

"Of course she did!" Susie chimed in.

"We wouldn't be sitting here if it weren't for you." Frank lifted Margaret's hand, and they looked at Ruth with appreciation and love.

"I still can't believe it came to this." Ruth sighed. She felt heartbroken at all that had been lost. Robert had been disgraced and his career was over; she no longer held her post at the hospital. She, at least, had started to move on. She kicked Robert out of their townhouse in the city and put the funds toward the conversion of Magnolia Bluff. She had heard that he purchased an RV and now spent his days visiting old patients. Still trying to justify his "miracle."

She donated the Gramercy mansion, which her mother had given to her years before, to the Manhattan Women's Sanctuary, the organization Susie had founded to help women who had no other options find a home. With Ruth's help, they had expanded their mission beyond aid and shelter, to include medical research on female-specific issues—things the broader medical community had yet to acknowledge as illnesses. One of their first projects was the development of new, humane treatments for postnatal maladies.

She then converted the carriage house into a cozy one-bedroom home where she now lived with Edward. She dedicated her time to caring for lobotomy patients whose lives she had once believed they had saved. It still pained her to remember her hopeful past. To see the horrific reality of all the good she thought she and Robert had done. But she deserved that pain. She wanted to live with it for the rest of her life.

And yet, as Ruth heard shrieks of joy from Frank and Margaret's children, as they ran up to their ankles in and out of the icy-cold water; as she looked at Susie and Meg, still happily in love; and as she held hands with Edward, feeling his unfailing, unconditional support, her heart felt fuller than it had in as long as she could remember.

She thought of all the plans she and Harry had made on that beach. Even if her life hadn't taken the path she expected, somehow, she had still ended up in her favorite place surrounded by people she loved. People she would devote the rest of her life to protecting.

She now understood what she wished she had known decades before, when Harry was alive: for some maladies, there is simply no cure. Sometimes, the best you can do for someone is to stand beside them, appreciate their strength, and acknowledge their pain.

In the end, this was Harry's legacy. She hoped that was enough.

AUTHOR'S NOTE

The first question I was asked by almost every early reader of *The Lobotomist's Wife* was: "How in the world did you come up with this?" The truth is it was an accident. Before I started writing this book, my expertise in mental health treatment was limited to the fact that my mother and stepfather are practicing therapists, and my knowledge of lobotomy started and ended with *One Flew Over the Cuckoo's Nest.*

I am an avid reader of fiction in general and historical fiction in particular, but when I drive, I listen to nonfiction. A few years ago, Audible recommended a book called *Get Well Soon: History's Worst Plagues and the Heroes Who Fought Them* by Jennifer Wright. It was a bit of an oddball choice for me, but I was a history major in college, and it was well reviewed, so I gave it a try. (Side note: great book, funny, smart, and eerily relevant in our postpandemic world.) Anyway, the book is largely about the biggies like the Black Death and leprosy, but Wright also includes a chapter about lobotomy, specifically Walter Freeman II (1895–1972), the doctor who brought the treatment to the US and eventually invented the quickie "ice pick" version. I was stunned to learn that not only did the use of lobotomy peak in the middle of the twentieth century, but also that more than half of those lobotomized were women—Rosemary Kennedy being one of the most notable.

Wright describes Freeman as a charismatic proselytizer who traveled the country lobotomizing thousands. She tells of an incident where, while on the road, he went to a man's motel room to sedate him because the man hadn't shown up for his court-ordered lobotomy, and Freeman decided to perform one on the spot. (I fictionalized this moment into the Sam Orenbluth scene.) This was a man who sounded, to me, one beat shy of a serial killer. I was horrified and fascinated.

At the time, I was working on my first novel, a contemporary fiction about a woman who feels trapped and unhappy in her suburban life. I couldn't get this sick lobotomist out of my head and started to think: What if you were this same woman in the early 1950s, the small window of time when lobotomy was the "miracle cure"? Or, what if you had an actual illness like postpartum depression that wasn't yet considered an illness and were unlucky enough to cross paths with a maniacal lobotomist? From here, *The Lobotomist's Wife* was born.

Initially I intended for this to be Margaret's story. But when a writer friend asked me whether Freeman was married, I became fascinated by the kind of woman who could stand by a man doing this to so many. My research revealed that Freeman's actual wife, Marjorie Franklin, was an economics professor and purportedly an alcoholic. She and Freeman had four children but a strained relationship that included many affairs (on Freeman's part), much time apart, and the tragic loss of a child. This wasn't the story I wanted to tell. So, I invented Ruth Emeraldine, a strong woman singularly devoted to a career in mental health in an era when women often needed men to truly succeed. There were real women who blazed trails in this field, one of the most notable being Dorothea Dix, who made her name as an advocate for the mentally ill a generation before Ruth was born, but Ruth is entirely from my imagination. I did my best to make her lifestyle and the places she frequents historically accurate—for example, the sign she carries at the suffragist march in 1917 is from a photo in the Mount Holyoke archives—but the idea that the lobotomist had a wife who was an American heiress, who worked as his partner and advocate in the popularization of lobotomy, and was ultimately the reason for his downfall, is fiction.

Much of Robert Apter, on the other hand, is based on the real Walter Freeman II as depicted in the rich biography *The Lobotomist* by Jack El-Hai. Some of the details that I took from El-Hai's book are that Freeman dressed to look like a nineteenth-century psychiatrist, including a signature goatee. He was an avid photographer who chronicled his patients in detailed photographs. He worked incessantly and needed very little sleep. He had a strained relationship with his father, an ear, nose, and throat specialist who hated medicine. He most admired his maternal grandfather, William Keen, who was a renowned doctor and surgeon and who encouraged Freeman to pursue medicine, using his connections and influence to help establish Freeman in the field. El-Hai attributes Freeman's drive at least, in part, to a desire to follow in his grandfather's footsteps.

Like Robert, Walter Freeman II was a neurologist and a psychologist but not a neurosurgeon, in spite of the fact that he performed lobotomies. He was a dramatic showman; his medical school lectures were apparently so entertaining that they were a date night activity for his students. He performed stunts to make his lobotomies more interesting for audiences—like using a carpenter's mallet instead of surgical hammers, or driving both ice picks into the patient concurrently, with both of his hands (some say he was ambidextrous).

The development of lobotomy and the people in my book are all real. The Second International Neurological Congress, the place where the seed of the idea for lobotomy was planted, did, in fact, take place in London in the summer of 1935 as described. It was one of the anchor dates for my timeline. The SS *Manhattan* was the official ship of the conference, the Metropole the official hotel, and the topics and presentations are from the official agenda. Freeman was stationed next to Egas Moniz, the Portuguese doctor who invented the original "leucotomy," on the exhibition floor of the congress, and it is purportedly here that they began the professional friendship that would lead Freeman to adapt Moniz's leucotomy in the US. Freeman was also responsible for nominating Moniz for the Nobel Prize in 1949.

The presentation at the Second Neurological Congress by Drs. John Fulton and Carlyle Jacobsen about their pioneering work on the frontal lobes of chimpanzees at the Yale primate lab was real and is said to have influenced Moniz and, subsequently, Freeman. (An interesting aside, Freeman was actually apparently responsible for overseeing the transportation of the chimpanzees used in the presentation.)

To the extent possible, I followed the actual timeline for the development and popularization of lobotomy in America, although I changed places and invented patients. Freeman lived and worked in Washington, DC, was the chairman of the Neurology Department at the George Washington University, and worked at Saint Elizabeths Hospital. I moved the location to New York and modeled Emeraldine Hospital partially on Bellevue. While I made up the specific *New York Times* article touting lobotomy in the book, there were many similar pieces when the treatment was first introduced in 1936.

Robert's surgical partner, Edward Wilkinson, is loosely based on Freeman's collaborator, neurosurgeon Dr. James Watts. Edward's background and personality are fiction, but like Robert and Edward, Watts and Freeman pioneered the American prefrontal lobotomy together, with Freeman as the scientist and Watts as the surgeon. Freeman "invented" the new transorbital ("ice pick") method a decade later to make lobotomy accessible to state mental hospitals across the country, and he supposedly used an actual ice pick in one of his first procedures. Even though this change enabled Freeman to perform lobotomy as an outpatient office procedure, Watts still believed lobotomy should be confined to a hospital setting. Their partnership dissolved in 1950, when Watts found Freeman photographing an in-process transorbital lobotomy in their private office. However, unlike Edward, Watts remained collegial with Freeman, keeping his criticisms of the new form of the procedure to himself.

Over the course of his career, Walter Freeman II lobotomized more than three thousand people and trained doctors responsible for thousands more. Between the late 1940s and mid-1950s, he traveled the country in a station wagon that he supposedly dubbed his "lobotomobile," training hospital staff and lobotomizing patients like they were cars in an assembly line. "Operation Ice Pick" in the book was an actual trip that Freeman took to West Virginia in 1952, where he performed 228 lobotomies.

Other than my invention of Ruth, the most dramatic divergence between the fictional Robert Apter and the real-life Walter Freeman II is the end of his career. In the mid-1950s, lobotomy lost popular support in the medical community, and the antipsychotic drug chlorpromazine (Thorazine) began to replace it as the preferred treatment at hospitals. Freeman, who had already lost his standing at Georgetown and left his post at Saint Elizabeths, moved to California, where he performed lobotomies until 1967, when he finally lost his license after a patient died from a brain hemorrhage following a second lobotomy. Like Robert, Freeman was obsessed with tracking his former patients, and after losing his license, he spent the remainder of his life traveling to visit them. He died of cancer in 1972.

ACKNOWLEDGMENTS

I reach this point in the manuscript (the part most readers skip over) with intense emotion. I feel gratitude to so many for supporting and enabling me to write this book. My very own actual novel!

Since my journey as a novelist began at the Writing Institute at Sarah Lawrence College, I'll start by thanking my first-ever writing teachers: Annabel Monaghan, a terrific writer and all-around superstar who is incredibly hilarious and gives the world's best comments; Ines Rodriguez, who helped me move from a story I was stuck on finishing to one that was secretly inspiring me; Dan Zevin, the master of humor, who taught me how to write about my personal life and make it funny, so that I could write fiction about more serious things; and, especially, Eileen Moskowitz Palma. You galvanized my journey with the simple sentence: "I think this book will get you an agent." You helped me decide when to stop taking your class and just write, and met me with your constant smile to make sure I was doing it. To my first writing group: Candace, Claire, Elise, Lea, Lexy, Mauricio, and Rachelle, you suffered through some uncomfortable sex scenes and a mediocre manuscript before this one, yet you always gave support and feedback with snacks and smiles; and to my subsequent SLC crew: Alexis, Autumn, Susie, and Christine, with whom I attacked my imposter syndrome and began to feel like a "real" writer.

My amazing, levelheaded, supportive agent, Kathy Schneider at JRA, who saw something in this book and took a chance before the first draft was even done. You and Hannah Strouth have been such careful and thoughtful readers and unwavering advocates. And, damn, you write excellent promotional copy. Jodi Warshaw and the whole team at Lake Union, thanks for believing in a first-time novelist with a quirky story and working so hard to bring it out into the world. Tanya Farrell and the team at Wunderkind PR, thank you for shaping my "author brand" and doing your best to make sure anyone and everyone knew about this book.

Nicola Weir, you brought the critical eye that I needed to break open my manuscript and figure out how to properly weave the braid of Ruth, Robert, and Margaret into an actual novel. I am certain that *The Lobotomist's Wife* would not exist without your help.

If this were the Oscars, they'd be playing the "get off the stage" music already. But I'm not done.

One of the unexpected "gifts with purchase" of becoming a novelist is the incredible community of women writers who have supported and welcomed me so warmly. Elise Hooper for my very first blurb, Rochelle Weinstein (my BFF before we have even met in person), Lea Geller and the whole Lake Union family for embracing me as one of your own, and especially Susie Orman Schnall—you named this book at our meet-cute, and you have been so full of support and advice all along the way; I don't think I would have made it through this process without you.

To my besties who held me up and cheered me on: Carrie, Dom, Jessica, Karen, Liz, Melanie, Stephanie, and Shelby (my secret agent, publicist, and number one cheerleader). I feel blessed to have so many incredible women in my orbit.

To my family readers and supporters: Elaine, Patti, Doug, Julia, Amy, Joey, Kelly, Alana, and Mark. You asked great questions, devoured early drafts, and just made me feel good about what I was attempting to accomplish.

Dad and Steven, how did I get lucky enough to have both a dad and a stepdad who are excellent copyeditors? Thank you both for your careful critical reads and honest feedback. And, Dad, I forgive you for sharing the manuscript even when it was "top secret"—I know it just means you are proud of me, and that means the world.

Lila, my sweet, smart, and sassy tween, you have been so curious about my writing from the beginning. I'll never forget listening to you at nine years old tell your friends, "My mom is writing a book about lobotomy." And now it's on your Goodreads list. Alex, my baby boy, thank you for being so excited about every step of my progress. The happy dance you did when I found out I was "going to be a published author!" will be one of the greatest memories of my life.

My mom, a true parent of the '70s who read me *Girls Can Do Anything* at bedtime. You have always been my biggest supporter and sounding board. You jumped into the world of *The Lobotomist's Wife* with two feet, and your thoughtful insights (and clinical expertise) made everything in it richer. Thank you for reminding me that writing this book was my job, even if I wasn't getting paid for it, for being there to help in any way I needed, and, especially, for being such a terrific role model of independence and determination.

And finally, to my husband, Jack, who knew that writing this story would bring me immense joy, possibly before I did. Thank you for pushing me to prioritize my writing and supporting everything I needed to do to make that happen—even during a pandemic, with two school-aged kids at home. I love you.

BOOK CLUB QUESTIONS

1. *The Lobotomist's Wife* is inspired by the real story of a doctor whose passion turns to deadly obsession. Can you think of other similar moments in history when science and medicine have crossed the line of ethics and morality in the name of progress?

2. The novel explores how ego can distort best intentions into horrifying results, with broad-reaching consequences. Do you believe Robert did indeed have the best intentions? Can you pinpoint a scene or series of scenes in the book where his character began to deviate from the initial plan?

3. The book takes place between the 1930s and 1950s in New York at a time when the medical community endorsed lobotomy as a "miracle cure." By the early 1940s, it was in broad use for extreme psychosis. How does the author convey mental health treatment in the era, and does it help explain why lobotomy was embraced by the medical community? Do you have a sense of whether the author remained true to the events and social structures of the time period?

4. Throughout the beginning of this novel, lobotomy is depicted as an innovative and revolutionary solution to

what was believed to be insanity. Compare and contrast this depiction of lobotomy to other titles that also reference it, such as *One Flew Over the Cuckoo's Nest.*

5. Is this a time period you knew a lot about before you read this book? If so, did you learn anything new? If not, did you come away with a greater understanding of what this particular time and place in history, especially for women, was actually like?

6. Ruth mourns her beloved brother, Harry, and his suicide played a significant role in her decision to devote her life to caring for the mentally ill. Do you think Ruth is trying to compensate for not being able to save her brother?

7. Ruth falls for the brash and innovative neurologist Robert and his perceived compassion for his patients. Is she too readily accepting of his self-proclaimed cure for insanity and radical new treatment?

8. How did the blended genre of historical fiction and suspense/thriller impact your reading experience? Did you have a sense of foreboding because of the knowledge we have today of the harmfulness of lobotomy?

9. Ruth is torn between her role as supportive wife and caretaker and administrator of the hospital. Both identities are at war throughout this book. When was the turning point for Ruth to accept that her role as a supportive wife shouldn't be the reason her patients are mistreated? Do you think it should have happened sooner?

10. The novel keenly depicts postpartum depression in the character Margaret Baxter. As a young housewife humiliated by her inability to be a "proper" wife and mother, she's desperate for a cure for her "baby blues." Describe how mental illness awareness has changed over the course of time and how it hasn't.

11. Margaret believes lobotomy will "fix" her. Does this desire to find a quick fix for the woes of being a housewife and mother have any parallels in today's world?

12. Ruth and Margaret are both strong female characters who were held to a specific standard of their time. How did these standards impact their journeys? In what ways are they victims of society's standards of typical loving, supportive wives?

13. Ruth blames herself for Robert harming her patients and others. Do you believe she could have done something different to deter him from acting so recklessly, or was he predetermined to be on this path?

14. The story is told in the close third person from Ruth's and Margaret's perspectives. How does this affect the story and how might it have been different if another character was telling the story?

ABOUT THE AUTHOR

Samantha Greene Woodruff has a BA in history from Wesleyan University and an MBA from the NYU Stern School of Business. She spent most of her career telling stories to executives at MTV Networks as the senior vice president of strategy and business development and, subsequently, audience research for the Nickelodeon Kids & Family Group. After leaving corporate life, she pursued her varied passions, teaching yoga, cooking, and taking classes at the Writing Institute at Sarah Lawrence College. It was here that she combined her multifaceted background with her wild imagination and passion for history, reading, and writing. *The Lobotomist's Wife* is her first historical fiction novel, and she is already at work on her next book. Sam lives in southern Connecticut with her husband, two children, and two dogs.